AF265564

Hel's Heroes 2: Christie & The Pirate

Gerry McCullough

ISBN 13: 978-0 9955404 3 9

ISBN 10: 09955404 3 8

First published **2019**

10a Listooder Road, Crossgar,

Downpatrick, Northern Ireland BT30 9JE

Christie & The Pirate

Gerry McCullough

Thanks to my husband, Raymond, for cover design, editing, proof-reading and general encouragement.

Chapter One

The Present

It was a lovely day in early May, and the sun streamed through the library windows. Christie McCafferty, gazing through the nearest window, shifted a heavy pile of newly returned books from one arm to the other, and wished she could be outside, swinging along the streets of Belfast, heading for the country or the seaside. It was no day to be indoors working.

But, alas, her holiday wasn't due for another month yet, so there was nothing for it but to carry on.

Her colleague Hazel Murphy undulated over, her hips swaying sexily as she moved.

'Did I tell you about my evening last night, Christie? Unbelievable!'

'Oh?' Christie pushed her soft, mousy hair back from her face and opened her grey blue eyes wide. 'So?'

'It was this guy I told you about. He came into the library a few days ago and made a beeline for me as soon as he saw me.'

Christie remembered him well. Tall, dark and handsome, as the cliché went. He had been riveted by Hazel as soon as he saw her. No wonder, Christie reflected moodily, with her bright red hair, voluptuous figure, and fascinating smile. Sex personified, as another customer had told her, a comment which Hazel had had no hesitation in passing on to her colleagues. The fact that Christie had also found him very attractive hadn't seemed to matter.

'He took me for a meal at the restaurant on the Belfast Barge, down by the river,' Hazel continued. 'Really expensive, but he didn't seem to mind. I wore my new slinky silver dress – you know, the one I got in the sale last week. A great success, if I say it myself. Oh, look out! Here comes the Patterson on the warpath.'

She hurried off to stack her own armful of books on the appropriate shelves, leaving Christie to deal with the irritation of Miss Patterson, the Senior Librarian.

'Daydreaming again, Christie?' Miss Patterson asked acidly. She was a thin, grey haired woman of around fifty, who took her job of supervising the junior staff far too seriously for their liking.

'Sorry, Miss Patterson,' Christie muttered hastily. 'Just going to put these returned books on their shelves.'

'Well, do it then!' Miss Patterson snapped, and strode purposefully off, determined to demonstrate how busy she was herself.

Christie sighed and began to wander round the bookshelves, putting a John Grisham in place among the thrillers, and a Jilly Cooper in the romance section, then wondering if Colin Bateman's latest should be under thrillers or Irish. She hadn't been daydreaming before, but now she started to. Might as well commit the crime, since she'd already had the punishment.

Start with an even more handsome man who looked rather like Brad Pitt and who came into the library, paused thunderstruck when he saw her, and came straight over.

'You're the most beautiful woman I've ever seen!' he said in a low, intense voice. 'Your eyes are the colour of a limpid mountain pool at dawn. I can't live without you. My name is Brad. Come with me now and we'll travel the world in my yacht.'

He seized Christie in his arms, kissed her passionately, then swept her out of the building and down to his sports car while Miss Patterson gibbered helplessly behind them. They roared through the streets, the wind blowing Christie's hair out in a stream behind her, and Brad could hardly concentrate on his driving because he had to keep looking at Christie. Then they were at his huge white gleaming yacht with its sails billowing in the breeze, and he lifted Christie in his arms and jumped on board with her.

'Cast off!' he ordered his crew, and next minute they were sailing down the Lagan, down Belfast Lough and out into the Irish Sea. The sun shone, turning his golden hair to a shimmering perfection, and he laughed exultingly as he looked at her. 'Where shall we go first, my darling girl? The Mediterranean? The South Pacific? Or shall I sail you along the Milky Way to the Mountains of the Moon?' Then, with a groan, he seized her in his arms again and began feverishly to kiss her and hold her …

'Christie!'

It was Hazel's voice.

'Now that Super Pest has gone back into her office, I must finish telling you about last night.' And so she must, Christie supposed, unwilling to hurt Hazel by telling her to shut up.

But before Hazel could get well settled in with her story, the library door swung open again and another stranger came in. That tended to happen, of course. Most of the people who came into the library were strangers to Christie, although she was beginning to get to know and recognise some of the regulars. Hazel, who had been there for longer, knew quite a few of them. The branch library where they worked, out a little from the centre of Belfast, got clients mostly from a limited neighbourhood.

This stranger, however, wasn't tall and handsome. On the contrary, he was medium height with hair as mousy as Christie's own, and he looked shy. Eyeing both girls, he must have decided that Hazel looked too intimidating, for he came over to Christie instead.

'I'm looking for books on fly fishing,' he muttered.

'You're not J R Hartley?' Christie asked and was pleased when an attractive grin broke out over his face.

'How did you guess?' he responded. 'No, I'm his son, actually. But surely you aren't old enough to remember that old ad?'

Christie blushed. 'No, but it was a favourite joke of my Dad's. He used to love fly fishing. He used to take me with him, sometimes –' her voice faltered and broke off. The loss of her father was too recent for her to remember it or speak of him without ending up in tears.

The stranger was obviously a perceptive man, for he hurried to change the subject.

'No, to tell you the actual truth my name is Steve Armstrong. I joined this library quite a long time ago, but I don't know if my ticket is still valid.'

'It should be,' Christie mumbled. 'But I'll check if you like.' She sat down at the computer and scrolled through the list of names. 'Armstrong, Steven. Yes, you're still there. So, you'll find books on fly fishing over past the magazines.'

'Thanks. Sorry to have upset you.' Steve Armstrong hesitated. 'I might have known your dad. We fly fishers are a friendly bunch. What was his name?'

'McCafferty. John McCafferty.'

'So you must be Christie McCafferty.' Steve sounded delighted with his newfound knowledge.

Christie looked down at her name badge – first name only – and laughed.

Steve went on quickly. 'I remember him, I think. But I didn't know him well.'

'He died two years ago.'

The conversation dwindled away to nothing.

'Well – over there, past the magazines, you said?'

'Yes.' Christie couldn't think of anything else to say, and clearly Steve Armstrong couldn't either, for he grinned again, and headed off to the Sports and Hobbies section. Christie sighed to herself. This was how it always went for her. A man seldom showed any interest, but if by chance he seemed to, she grew tongue tied almost at once and ran out of conversation. What she needed, she decided, was a man who talked a lot. But then, might he quickly become a bore? It was a hard thing to decide.

'Christie, I want you to go up to the children's library and take the story telling hour today. Moyra McManus has just rung in to say she's sick and can't manage it. Talk about leaving it till the last minute! I don't know why we keep using her. All these retired teachers are the same – claim they'd love to help, that they love children and miss spending time with them, and then they let you down. But you're always so obliging, Christie, so I'm sure you won't mind taking over. You'll get the extra payment, of course.' Miss Patterson smiled ingratiatingly. She knew none of the librarians liked being lumbered with the children's story hour, extra money or no.

Christie smiled at her. 'No problem, Miss Patterson. When should I go?'

'Oh, straightaway, Christie. It's supposed to start in five minutes. Thank you, dear.'

Christie quite enjoyed reading to the children, unlike Hazel, who complained bitterly that the kids never listened to her. 'They scream and pull each other's hair and plaster my clothes with their sticky hands when I try to stop them. I don't know why they come.'

Christie suspected that the kids didn't enjoy Hazel's reading because she didn't put any life into it. They knew that Hazel disliked them, and disliked the books she had to read to them, so they didn't feel inclined to like her reading either.

Christie liked reading to the kids, and never had any trouble with them. But, she thought wistfully, she'd have been happy to swop her success with children for Hazel's success with men, any day.

As she made her way upstairs to the Children's Library, she realised with some slight disappointment that Steve Armstrong would probably have made his selection of books, checked them out with Hazel or Miss Patterson, and be long gone by the time she got back. Ah, well, she thought, no big deal. It's not as if he was drop dead gorgeous or anything.

When she got back to the main library, Hazel told her that her 'fly fishing friend' had gone. Then she told Christie in pitiless detail about her night out. She only stopped when the man in question – his name was Luke, Hazel had said, sounding as if it was the most impressive name in the world – came into the library again. He and Hazel whispered together for a few minutes, with much eyelash fluttering and giggling from Hazel. Then he disappeared again, and Hazel began at once to tell Christie that he was taking her out again that night.

Christie thought wistfully of her own unplanned evening, then brightened up as she remembered that she had downloaded one of Serendipity Fox's books this morning just before rushing out to work. She'd read some of the other ones, such as *Barbara's Lover*, and had been told that this one was even better. It was called simply *The Pirate* and had sold over a million in eBook format, apparently. The friend who had recommended it had told her that Serendipity Fox's real name was Helen McFadden, Hel for short. The evening suddenly took on a glow of promised enjoyment. After all, what man could be better to spend the evening with than one of Serendipity Fox's heroes – Hel's Heroes – especially a pirate?

The working day came to an end at last. Christie left as quickly as possible. She dived into the nearest pub, the Errigle, one where she often ate, and had a bowl of Irish stew and a glass of white wine. Outside again, the bus came almost at once. It was nice not to stand waiting for ages. Then she was home, at the house where she had grown up with her loving parents until first her mother, then her father, had died and left her alone. She grabbed a bottle of wine from the kitchen and a glass, and retreated to her bedroom. She stripped off her working skirt, kicked off her sandals and then stretched out blissfully under the duvet, poured out a glass of wine, picked up her Kindle, and clicked happily on the new book.

In great contentment Christie swallowed a slug of wine, set down the glass, and began to read.

Chapter two

The Pirate

*by **Serendipity Fox***

1794

The wind howled around the ship, making the rigging creak and the masts sway dizzily.

Prudence Rydesdale, wakened from a light, already disturbed, sleep by the loud noises and the increased motion of the ship, the Golden Dawn, sat up suddenly in the bed in her cabin and threw back the covers. What was happening?

She could hear the crew shouting, voices issuing orders, feet running overhead.

It was impossible to sleep any longer. Prudence retied the long strings of her very becoming nightcap more securely beneath her chin, tucking a few stray dark curls firmly underneath it, seized the voluminous dressing gown she had laid aside when she settled down to sleep what seemed like hours ago, and swung both legs out of bed. She had to discover just what was going on.

Climbing over the motionless body of her maidservant, deeply asleep and uttering faint, not unattractive, snores as she lay on the truckle bed which had been set up across the cabin doorway, Prudence pushed open the door and moved carefully along the passageway leading to the ladder that would take her to the upper deck. It was necessary for her to hold onto the walls, while holding up the skirts of her dressing gown with one hand, and when it came to climbing up the ladder, Prudence, finding she needed both hands, was forced to tuck the ends of her gown into the belt corded around her waist.

Until now, Prudence had not been frightened, but as she emerged onto the deck the howls of the wind, the noise it made as it whistled through the rigging, and the creak of the billowing sails, together with the crazy swaying of the ship, brought fear to the surface of her mind.

Pulling herself together, and telling herself that it was out of place for the daughter of a soldier to be afraid of anything, and particularly of inanimate Nature – although inanimate seemed the wrong word for this shrieking, howling monster – Prudence stepped out on the upper deck, immediately releasing her tucked up skirts for decency's sake. She was engulfed straightaway in a crowd of busy crewmen, some giving orders, others obeying, all, it seemed, struggling to control the rolling, threshing vessel which heaved and groaned desperately under their feet.

A faint light from an almost hidden moon peering nervously from behind the huge dark clouds which covered the sky allowed her to see a little, but not very much. Prudence stood for a moment, staring round her, trying to understand what was happening, and clutching firmly to the rail at the top of the ladder to prevent herself being thrown off her feet. Then one of the hurrying men caught a glimpse of her from the corner of his eye and came to a sudden halt.

'Mistress Rydesdale! Why are you out of your cabin? You can do no good here. You will only be a hindrance to the crew while this storm persists. Go down again at once! Do you want the captain to see you? You'd get a real tongue lashing from him if he found you wandering about above decks in this tempest!'

It was young Ensign Peter Willoughby. He was one of the men who had been sent as escort to Prudence on her journey from the Caribbean island of Jamaica to her aunt Rebecca's home in London, after her father's death. There was no sign of Captain Elliot in spite of Willoughby's words. Probably he was up at the wheel.

Willoughby was a good looking, fresh faced youngster with a laughing face and he had until now shown Prudence nothing but the greatest respect. It was a shock to her to hear him speak so roughly, and an even greater one when her took her firmly by both arms, turned her around, and propelled her back down the ladder.

'Stay in your cabin, and don't come out unless you are called', Willoughby said. Then after waiting to be sure that Prudence was obeying him, he turned and hurried back to his job, which seemed to be seeing to it that everything on deck was safely lashed down. Willoughby was not, strictly speaking, one of the crew, but clearly this was an occasion when everyone needed to give what help they could – everyone except women, thought Prudence angrily.

Chapter 2

Prudence's indignation was tempered with the realisation that what he had said was only too true. What help could she be, she who knew so little of the sea and ships, to these men, a seasoned crew who understood what was needed in a dangerous storm like this?

Yet something in Prudence rebelled against being treated as a child, and a useless one at that. She was no child, having passed her nineteenth birthday some months ago, and although she knew little about ships, she could pull a rope as well as the junior midshipmen.

If her father had been an admiral instead of a general, she would have known more, she thought wistfully. But her skills were all those of the land. She could ride a horse as well as the best captain of cavalry under her father's command, handle a pistol and shoot without missing her mark at nearly any distance. But what use were these skills to her now?

Back in the cabin Prudence found that her faithful maid Jane Brigham was awake and sitting up in her truckle bed. Jane had been her maid since they were both in their early teens. She had been more like a friend than a maidservant to Prudence when her weak, sickly mother had finally succumbed to the hot climate of the Caribbean island, Jamaica.

General Rydesdale had been posted there after the loss of Britain's mainland American possessions at the time of the American rebellion, when Prudence was a babe in arms. Prudence found it hard to remember the frail, pretty woman, still in her twenties, who had brought her into the world and left her so soon. Her father, much older than his wife, had been the dominant factor in her life. She had admired him, looked after him, and learnt from him to be more of a son than a daughter.

It had been a lasting grief to the General that he had a daughter rather than a son, and Prudence, aware of this in spite of his evident love for her, had done her best to make it up to him by learning from him all the skills he would have taught his son. Now, on his death, she was travelling to England to live with her father's only sister.

Prudence wondered what her aunt would think of her. She would, she feared, have to learn to be a young lady again – a prospect she found repulsive.

'Oh, oh, Miss Prue, what is it?' Jane gasped out when Prudence came back into the cabin.

'Nothing to worry about, Jane. Only a bit of rough weather. The captain and crew have it under control.' But she wondered, as she tried to reassure Jane, if what she said was true. Was Captain Elliot getting the ship under control? There was no sign that she could see of the motion growing less wild, and the howls and shrieks of the wind grew ever louder, until she and Jane found it next to impossible to hear each other speaking.

Suddenly there was a horrendous crash and the ship rocked violently under the impact of something of major importance. Was it a mast down?

It was no use, Prudence found it impossible to stay in the cabin any longer. There must be something she could do.

'Stay here, Jane,' she ordered abruptly. 'I'm going up to find out what's happening.'

Darting out of the cabin, she took time to tuck up her dressing gown before making for the ladder. It would be easier to do it now than when she had already started to climb.

Up on deck, the moon had disappeared behind thick clouds and Prudence found it hard to see anything. A heaving mass almost at her feet must, she thought, be a sail, or maybe more than one. The sound of groaning from beneath it made it clear that some member of the crew was trapped there. Prudence bent over, trying to haul the heavy canvas aside to at least see him.

After what seemed years, but could only have been a few minutes, her efforts were rewarded in some extent. At least she could see a face, and with a sick horror she recognised it, in spite of the blood streaming down from the cuts in his scalp, as that of young Peter Willoughby.

Prudence knew a little about nursing. She had even, although not much more than a child, on one occasion helped to look after the wounded soldiers after an attack on her father's men. The first thing would be to clean the wounds, the second to bandage them. But there might be other things wrong.

She looked round quickly for something she could use to wash Willoughby's scalp, then stopped as his voice came to her weakly.

Chapter 2

'Mistress Rydesdale? Don't waste your time on me. My back's broken where the mast landed on me. I haven't long for this world. Help someone who you really can do something for, not me.'

The words were hardly out, forced from his lips by a huge effort, when Willoughby gave an enormous groan, blood gushed from his mouth, and it was over. He was gone.

There must have been internal injuries as well, Prudence realised. She choked back her sobs. Such a short time ago, Peter Willoughby had been a bright, lively young man. Now he was gone. It was not the first time Prudence had seen death from injuries, but it never failed to shock and distress her.

He was right, she should look for someone else to help. She stood up and, as the moon appeared again and the available light grew stronger, she saw someone lying not far away. She went over to him.

It was one of the crew whom she knew only vaguely by sight.

'Can I help you?' she asked. 'Do you know where you're hurt?'

'It's my leg,' the man muttered. 'The two masts – one of them caught me. Captain Elliot's gone – knocked senseless, then swept overboard by a huge wave. So many dead.'

Prudence shuddered in horror.

'Hardly anyone left but me. All injured. The ship's going down. Damage to the hull. Save yourself! There's a boat you can take over there. Don't wait or you'll be sucked down with the ship when she goes.'

'But what about you? And the other injured men?' Prudence asked in horror. 'I can't just leave you!'

'You'll have to. I can't get into the boat with this leg. My arm is broken, too, and who knows what else. I can't crawl, and you couldn't carry me,' the sailor pointed out. 'And I don't think anyone is in a better state than me. Go on, girl, stop wasting time.'

'I must get my maid,' Prudence said breathlessly. 'I'll bring you some water.'

'Thanks.' The sailor grinned wryly.

Prudence sped back to the ladder and swarmed down at great speed, calling out to Jane as she ran.

'Jane! Come quickly! You'll have to help me with this boat!' Reaching the cabin, she hurried in past Jane and filled a bottle with drinking water from the wash stand. Then she hustled the scandalised Jane out of the cabin.

'We're never going like this, Miss Prue? We need to dress!'

'No time, Jane. Would you rather be dressed or drowned?'

Pushing Jane ahead of her, she got them both up the ladder onto the deck. But when she reached the sailor who had advised her to take the boat a few minutes ago, it was already too late for him to drink the water she had brought. The staring open eyes and gaping mouth told their own story. Another death.

Prudence knew that there was nothing more she could do. At least she could see to it that Jane survived. She could see the boat the sailor had spoken of, hanging at the edge of the ship by an arrangement of ropes.

The two women scrambled into it, then Prudence stood up to untie the ropes which would lower it into the heaving sea. Jane, holding firmly to the side of the boat, reached out one hand to take a good grasp of Prudence by the skirts of her dressing gown, and it was as well she did, for as the boat came down with a rush, due to Prudence's inexpert handling, Prudence over balanced. If it had not been for Jane's firm grasp she would have been overboard.

'Whew!' she exclaimed. 'Thanks, Jane!'

Then they looked around.

There was nothing to be seen in all directions but the huge waves of the stormy sea.

'Come on, Jane. We need to start rowing, It's important to get as far as possible from the ship before it goes down and sucks us with it.'

'Yes, Miss Prue,' Jane replied gloomily. 'And then, what?'

And, as Prudence realised, that, indeed, was the question.

Chapter Three

The Present

A loud knocking at the front door of her house dragged Christie away suddenly from the stormy seas of adventure and back to the prosaic reality of her own life. With a sigh she switched off her Kindle, dragged on a pair of jeans, and hurried downstairs.

On the doorstep stood her long time friend, Tina. She had known Tina since her first day in Primary School, when their mothers, who knew each other, had met by chance at the school gate, each delivering a new pupil, and had agreed without consulting the girls that it would be lovely for them to be friends. 'You'll have someone you know from the very start, darling!' her mother had said, beaming.

And, indeed, it had been lovely for Christie, a shy, nervous child. Tina, a much more bouncy, self-confident person, with curly red hair tumbling over her shoulders and bright twinkling eyes, might not have cared much one way or the other, but she smilingly accepted Christie as a friend at once, and had happily taken charge of her.

'Just wondered if you'd like to come out with me for a drink or something, Christie?'

It was a while since they had had a night out together, and Christie didn't feel she could turn down the offer without offending Tina – especially as her only reason for doing so would be that she was reading. Tina, not much of a reader herself, wouldn't understand.

'Great!' she said, summoning up some sort of enthusiasm. 'Where do you want to go? The Errigle?'

'Aw, no, let's be more adventurous! We've been there loads of times. How's about somewhere in the city centre?'

'Okay.' Christie successfully concealed her doubts about this idea. They'd probably have to pay for a taxi home, instead of walking as they could have done from somewhere nearer. It looked like adding up to an expensive night out, and she was trying to save up for a holiday later in the year. Still, nice of Tina to invite her. 'Do I need to change?'

'No, jeans are fine. On second thoughts, do you have a more interesting top?'

Christie squinted down at herself. 'This is what I was wearing to work today,' she explained. 'But all my tops are something like this.' In other words, baggy and of a neutral type of colour.

'Time you got a few new ones, then!' Tina said briskly. 'I'll take you shopping on Saturday and we'll see what we can do.'

Christie came outside, pulling the door behind her so that it locked. Tina took her arm and they walked down the road towards the nearest bus stop.

'That would be my Saturday on at the Library,' Christie said as they walked.

'So, is it all day, or do you get out early?'

'Well, yes,' Christie said. 'My shift ends at three. I'd be free then.'

'Okay, I'll come and pick you up at three. Deal?'

'Deal,' Christie agreed reluctantly.

'You'll never get a man if you go round dressed like that!' Tina continued. 'You want a few sparkly tops for evenings, right? And a lot tighter. Like this one I'm wearing. I was wearing one something like this when I met Joe and he had me up dancing straight away, and we've been going out ever since.' Then forestalling Christie's question, 'He's away in England for his work this week, or I'd be out with him tonight.'

Christie didn't feel flattered, either by Tina's criticism of her clothes or by the fact that she was a second best companion for the evening. Still, Tina probably had a point. Maybe if she had more attractive clothes?

They reached the bus stop and joined the queue, which for once was very short.

'Is there anything else you think I should do, Tina?' Christie asked.

'Yes, you should get a decent haircut. Not short, but something with some shape to it. And maybe lighten it a bit. You used to be a lot fairer when we were kids, if I remember.'

Yes, Christie remembered it, too. There was a photo of her when she was around seven or eight which used to sit on Mum's dressing table, and in it her hair was certainly very fair. Perhaps it might be a good idea to have it done?

'Gentlemen prefer blondes, they say,' Tina giggled. 'Not that I've ever had any trouble, as a redhead!'

Just then, the bus pulled up beside them and they got on.

'Let's try a lot of different places, Christie,' Tina suggested. 'We can keep moving on unless we decide to stay somewhere. Let's start with the Sunflower. There's usually a nice crowd there. Don't worry,' she added, seeing the shyness in Christie's face, 'I'll introduce you. You'll like them.'

Christie wasn't so sure, but there didn't seem much she could do except go along with Tina's ideas.

The Sunflower was a bar behind the Central Library, full of character, which had recently survived an attempt to demolish it. Christie had signed the petition to keep it standing. It was crowded with a mass of people talking loudly and drinking. There was a real buzz for a weekday night.

'There should be live music on in a wee while,' Tina told her. 'I wonder who's in tonight? Oh, there's Tommy and Aine over there. Let's see if we can grab a stool at their table.' Propelling Christie in front of her as a type of battering ram, she squirmed and shoved her way across the bar to a corner table where three or four people were laughing together.

'Hi, guys!' Tina said breezily. 'Any room for a little one? Two little ones, actually. This is my friend Christie.'

'Sure, we can squeeze up a bit, Tina,' said one of the men, brightening when he saw her. 'No Joe tonight, then?' He smiled briefly at Christie and shuffled along the bench against the wall, behind the table. There was just about room for one.

'You can sit on my knee, darlin',' he said cheerfully to Tina. 'And your mate can squeeze in beside me, right?'

Christie felt like a squashed lemon, as Tina flopped down happily on her friend's knee, dragging Christie after her onto the bench. 'This animal is Trevor, Christie,' she said. 'And by the way,

Trev, in case you're getting ideas, Joe is over in England right now, working, but he'll be back next week, so watch it!'

There was no attempt made to introduce the rest of the crowd around the table, but Christie gradually picked up most of the names as she listened to the conversation. The big man sitting opposite to them was Tommy, the slim, pretty dark haired girl beside him was Aine, and the other girl was Shirley.

And presently a fifth member of the party returned from the bar bearing drinks, and then, after distributing them round the table, hurried back again to get two more halves of lager for Tina and Christie. Christie didn't like lager, but didn't want to ask for anything more expensive.

Presently the drink purchaser returned, handed over the drinks and was introduced as Colm.

'Someone's nicked my seat,' Colm said, grinning. He looked about for a spare stool, brought one back from a nearby table and settled down. He was now directly opposite Christie, and she caught her breath as she was able to take a good look at him for the first time. Her daydream of that afternoon came flooding back to her.

For here was the tall, blond man with the blue, blue eyes, the carbon copy of Brad Pitt, whom she had imagined sweeping her off to his yacht and kissing her passionately. Could this be a dream coming true?

But, alas, Colm was looking down at his drink. And when, in a few more minutes, the music started, he swivelled his stool round so that his back was to her and concentrated on listening. And, indeed, the noise level in the whole bar had gone dramatically lower as most people switched off their chatter and listened to the guitars and the singer.

'On a Sunday night, they have Irish Traditional music,' Tina whispered to Christie between songs. 'But most nights it varies between right up to date stuff and the sort of songs that are always popular, like these guys. They play mostly Dylan, Beatles, Bruce Springsteen, and that sort.'

Christie tried to relax and enjoy the music as everyone else seemed to be doing, but she was uncomfortably cramped, and embarrassed to be crushed up so close to Trev, who turned to wink at her every now and then.

Presently Tina reached for her wallet and pulled out a twenty pound note. 'Get another round for us, Tommy,' she said. 'You can get out easier than me.'

Christie realised in horror that it would be her turn to pay for a round in a while. She had a twenty pound note, okay, but she hadn't intended to spend so much tonight. A couple of cheap drinks, that had been her plan. At this rate, she would be very broke before the end of the month and might even have to dig into her holiday savings.

However, before her turn came, Tina suddenly sprang to her feet and said, 'Come on, Christie! Time to move on.' And Christie found herself outside on the pavement, and following Tina along Royal Avenue towards High Street and the Victoria Centre.

'I thought we might try the Kitchen,' Tina explained. 'We should catch some music there, too, but it won't be such a squash. Sitting on Trev's knee for half an hour or so is okay, but after that it gets to be a bit of a problem, trying to stop him feeling my leg. He's supposed to be a friend of Joe, but all I can say is, he didn't act like it.'

Christie hadn't noticed. The action must have been on the side away from her.

'Nice enough crowd, aren't they, though?' Tina went on.

'Oh, yes!' Christie sighed, thinking of the Brad Pitt lookalike, Colm.

'Oh ho? You fancied one of them, did you? Don't tell me, let me guess – Colm?'

'Well –' Christie mumbled.

'Oh, I suppose he's drop dead gorgeous, but when you talk to him he's a complete dumbo. I'd forget him, if I were you.'

'Not much point in me doing anything else, is there?' Christie asked glumly. 'I don't suppose I'll ever see him again.'

'Oh, I don't know. If you hang around with me, we'll probably bump into him again before long. Tell you what – let's go out together on Saturday. Joe won't be back until Monday at the earliest. We'll get you some new gear and sort out your hair, and then who knows?'

By this time they had reached the Kitchen, an attractive old bar which wasn't quite so crowded as the last one had been. They were able to get seats at an empty table and to catch the tail end of the music. As before, Tina knew some of the crowd, and was soon chatting with them, introducing Christie (who was getting used to being pretty well ignored by Tina's friends) and clearly enjoying herself.

Christie produced some money to buy Tina and herself a drink, but Tina told her not to bother. 'This evening's on me,' she said cheerfully. 'Keep it for your new gear.'

It was as they were coming out of the Kitchen, much later, that they heard the shouts and panic stricken screams.

'It's a heist!' Tina cried out. 'Come on, Christie, let's get out of the way!'

Grabbing Christie's arm, she dragged her round the nearest corner out of harm's way.

But she had picked the wrong corner. As they flattened themselves against the wall, three men flourishing hand guns came leaping past them, heading for the exit. Two of them were wearing stocking masks. The third had pulled his off to see better where they were going.

Christie caught her breath sharply.

Surely – she stared at the third man, her mouth open. Surely that was Steve Armstrong – the one Hazel had called her 'fly fishing friend'?

Chapter Four

Christie found it hard to relax that night. She arrived home exhausted after the weird evening with Tina and her friends, ready only to collapse into bed. She still wondered if they should have told the police about seeing Steve Armstrong. But Tina had been adamant that they should get offside straightaway, before they got dragged into the business.

'We don't want to be sitting in a police station all night, and having to give evidence in court!' she had insisted, dragging Christie out of the Victoria Centre and towards the nearest taxi stand. Christie, to her shame, had allowed herself to be dragged. She felt guilty and upset. At the same time, she was conscious of a reluctance to give Steve Armstrong away. She knew she would find it hard to get to sleep now. She picked up her Kindle in despair. If she couldn't find something to help her to relax, she would be awake for the rest of the night.

Ah, thank goodness, she thought, as The Pirate flashed up on her carousel. Something worth reading. She turned the page, to the second chapter of the book.

1794

The storm raged around them. Prudence and Jane shivered and shrank down, trying to hide from the cold blasts of wind which hurled freezing gusts at their defenseless bodies. They both wished they taken time to put on warmer clothing. But then, they might have been too late to be saved, to escape into the boat. They might have been trapped on board the Golden Dawn, and might, instead, have gone down into the icy depths. Better to be cold than drowned.

They needed to row hard.

'Keep going, Jane!' shouted Prudence above the icy blasts. 'Keep rowing!'

It was essential that they moved far enough away from the Golden Dawn *to keep themselves from being sucked down into the depths with it as it sank.*

As they forced themselves to row ever harder, they knew that the effort they were making was helping to keep them warm, helping to prevent them from dying from cold.

The night was dark around them. They had moved away from the wrecked ship, far enough to be quite sure that they weren't going to be pulled down with it into the depths. Far enough to feel safe from that danger at least. But what about the other dangers that surrounded them? Would they ever reach a safe haven? Would they starve or die of thirst? Prudence sensibly didn't share her worries with Jane, but it still preyed on her mind. They hadn't brought any provisions with them.

A sudden thought occurred to her. Weren't boats like this provisioned with some basic things at least? She looked around her. There were some cupboard like things in the stern, below the boards where she and Jane were sitting to row.

'Jane,' she said, 'can you keep on rowing if I stop for a minute? I just want to have a look at something.'

'All right, Miss Prue,' Jane gasped obediently. She took over Prudence's oar.

Prudence knelt down to examine the cupboards she had noticed, and wrenched one of them open.

Sure enough, there were dry captain's biscuits, and a flagon of water. Enough to keep them going for a while at least, with the bottle of water Prudence had brought for the dying sailor. Prudence turned to the companion cupboard on the other side. In it she found more water, and a first aid kit, with bandages, ointments, a small flask of brandy. The more essential things that might be needed if someone had been injured before boarding the boat. Prudence gave a sigh of thankfulness. She and Jane should be able to keep going for a few days at least. If only they could meet another ship which would take them aboard.

The sky seemed to be lightening in the east, or in what Prudence assumed must be the east – the direction in which the Golden Dawn *had been sailing, she thought. Towards England, towards her aunt, who now no longer seemed to Prudence like a strict, unpleasant person, but instead like a haven of safety and shelter.*

She had picked up her oar again and was rowing as hard as Jane, but she realised that her maidservant was near to collapsing.

'Jane,' she said, 'I think you need a rest. In fact, we should take it in turns to rest. Ship your oars, and curl up here in the stern, while I take my turn at rowing, Sleep, if you can.'

'But, Miss Prue, you should be the one taking a rest,' protested Jane. 'I'll be all right.'

'No you won't, Jane,' said Prudence firmly. 'Now, do as I say, and rest.'

And Jane thankfully did.

Prudence pulled heartily at the oars. When it seemed about time for Jane to wake up again, she would serve out some water and biscuits. Then she would take her rest and, she was pretty sure, sleep, while Jane rowed.

The time passed slowly. Prudence had no way of telling how long she rowed and Jane slept. After what seemed an eternity, she heard Jane stir, wake and sit up.

'Miss Prue, I'm so sorry. I've slept far too long.'

'Nonsense, Jane. You had a much needed rest. Now, can you open the left hand cupboard and get out the biscuits and the water, and we'll both rest while we eat something? Then I'll take my turn at resting while you row.'

Jane obediently fished in the cupboard and produced the water and the food. Then Prudence carefully shipped the oars – it would be a real disaster if she lost them and could no longer row – and the two girls sat in as relaxed a position as they could and nibbled thankfully ate the dry captain's biscuits and sipped water in turns from the flagon. Prudence was firm about controlling how much they ate and drank.

'Once this is all finished,' she pointed out, 'we'll have no way of getting more. We need to reach either land or another boat before that happens.' Then, seeing Jane's checks pale, she wished she'd been less forthcoming. But there was no use pretending to Jane that things were any better than they were.

'We'd better pray, Jane,' she said. 'For land or a ship, no matter which.'

'You're right, Miss Prue,' Jane agreed. So they did.

When they had finished the meagre allowance of food and water which Prudence had ruled would have to be enough for now, they resumed their journey. Jane rowed this time, while Prudence, every bone in her body aching, did her best to make herself comfortable in the stern of the boat and tried to sleep.

At first it seemed impossible. Then, gradually, she found herself drifting off, and then she was walking through the warm, lush plantations of what had been her home for most of her life, talking to her father who was, it seemed, still with her. Prudence luxuriated in the joy of her experience, and with some part of her brain hoped that she would never have to wake up.

Then, out of the mists of sleep, came Jane's voice.

'Miss Prue! Miss Prue! Wake up!'

'What is it, Jane?' asked Prudence sleepily, trying hard to under-stand that she was adrift in a small boat on the ocean.

'Oh, Miss Prue! Praise the Lord! It's a ship!'

Prudence sat up. Sure enough, a ship loomed over them, not far away. Huge, but such a blessing!

Prudence grasped the oars energetically and cried out, 'Row, Jane! Row for all your worth! We can't let it go without seeing us!'

'Let's call out, Miss Prue,' suggested Jane eagerly.

'Excellent idea, Jane!' Prudence said.

Together, the girls called out, as loudly as they could, 'Ship ahoy! Ship ahoy!'

And to their profound relief, before long they heard the answering cry, 'Ahoy, there!'

The ship loomed nearer. Prudence found herself wondering what country it belonged to. They spoke English, at any rate. The 'Ahoy there!' seemed to make that clear. There was a flag fluttering at the mast head, but so far it was too distant to tell what nationality it displayed.

Chapter 4

With sobs of gratitude for answered prayer, they fell into each other's arms, weeping tears of relief. Then Prudence pulled herself together, and said, 'We must be all set to go aboard her when they're ready for us, Jane. Gather yourself together.'

The two girls sat up, waiting eagerly for the ship to signal to them, ready to obey whatever they needed to do.

Then Prudence's heart sank to her feet with an enormous thud.

'Jane! Look! Do you see the flag?'

Jane looked in the direction of Prudence's pointing finger.

High above the ship, fluttering joyously in the light breeze, they could now see the ship's flag clearly. It was the Jolly Roger.

Hel's Heroes 2: Christie & The Pirate

Chapter Five

The Present

The Kindle fell from Christie's hands, waking her sufficiently to let her switch it off and set it on her bedside table. A moment later, she was asleep.

Nothing much changed in the Library over the next few days. Hazel talked unendingly about Luke. No one interesting came in. Miss Patterson was as bossy as ever. Christie worked extra hard, and found herself dropping straight off to sleep at night without reading a word. When three o'clock came on Saturday afternoon, Christie heaved a sigh of relief and left in high spirits to meet Tina at the nearby coffee place, the Roasting Bean, as they had arranged.

Tina was there, sitting over a cup of Frozen Latte, and looking, for once, rather down.

'Tina! What's wrong?' Christie said at once, sitting down opposite her with her own cappuccino.

Tina brightened up as soon as she saw Christie. 'Och, sure, I'm just missing Joe, I suppose,' she said. 'Come on, get that into you, girl, and then I'm going to take you to a few good places. Maisie's boutique, for one. But first of all, the hair. I've made an appointment for you with my own hairdresser, Hannah – she's really clever and expert, actually – and I've told her just what you want. No need to thank me – I'm not paying! You'll do that yourself when she's finished. Do you need to go to the hole-in-the-wall first?'

'No, I'm okay for cash,' Christie said, hoping this was true. How much would Tina's hairdresser cost?

She just hoped this Hannah knew what she was doing. If she made a mess of Christie's hair, she would just have to live with it, at least until payday at the end of the month.

But Hannah didn't make a mess of it. Christie looked in delight at herself in Hannah's mirror an hour later. She wasn't strikingly, artificially, blonde, just light enough to be interesting. And the new style, not too much shorter but shaped around her face to flatter her little pointy chin and high cheekbones, added an indefinable something to her appearance. Christie was pleased, and said so.

'Now we'll hit the boutiques!' Tina said briskly.

They headed first for Maisie's and after that for Claire's, and Christie tried on top after top, deciding finally on three particularly pretty ones.

'And tighter jeans, Christie,' commanded Tina. 'Go and try these on, with that last top.'

Christie went obediently into the fitting room. She slipped into the jeans, which were certainly tight enough. In fact, slipped was hardly the right word. She had to struggle quite hard to finally zip them up. But the result was worth it. She stared at herself in the fitting room mirror. The new hair flattered her face. The top, a dark blue scattered with sequins and silver flowers, turned her eyes into a startling blue for once. And its close fit combined with the tight jeans gave her, for the first time, a figure to die for.

'Wow!' Tina said when she came shyly out onto the shop floor, 'so that's what you've been hiding under those baggy jeans and T-shirts, girl! Don't you ever dare to go back to them!'

And Christie thought to herself that she never would.

They left the new purchases and Christie's discarded top and jeans at her house, then went to Nando's.

'So, Tina,' Christie asked as they sat presently over chicken fillet burgers before starting on their night out, 'is Aine going with that guy Colm we met with her the other night?' The Brad Pitt lookalike hadn't been far out of Christie's dreams recently.

'Aine would have more sense!' Tina said crisply. 'I told you he was a dumbo – bore you to death in the first ten minutes. No, Aine and Tommy have been together for ages, Colm's a free bird – but take my advice and forget him.'

'Well,' Christie said, and changed the subject. But later, as they caught the bus into the centre, she couldn't help asking, 'So, are we going to meet up with any of the friends you introduced me to last time? Trev, Shirley, Colm?' She hoped she had dropped Colm's name in casually enough, but Tina looked at her sharply and then laughed.

'You won't be told, will you? Och well, you'll just have to find out for yourself what he's like. Come on, sure, we'll get off here at the City Hall, right? We'll walk round to White's Tavern, okay?'

It was all one to Christie. She knew hardly any of the Belfast night spots.

Outside in the courtyard at White's people were sitting at tables, drinking, and listening to music. A few were dancing, but the crowd was such a size that there wasn't much room for that. Tina pushed in, dragging Christie after her, and greeted some old mates – no one Christie had met as yet. Christie was a bit disappointed. She was still hoping to see the gorgeous Colm.

As she stood beside Tina, sipping cautiously at a lager and trying to take part in the conversation over the noise of the band, she realised with pleasure that the guys Tina introduced her to seemed a lot more interested than she was used to. A tall, red haired one, Brian, she thought Tina had called him, was bending over her speaking at the top of his voice, but when he saw that Christie was having difficulty making him out, he shrugged, laughed, and indicated by sign language that he wanted to dance with her. A moment later he had her out on what passed for the floor – a few inches of space between the band and the tables – and was holding her tight.

Christie, who was still holding her glass, wasn't sure what to do for the best. Then Brian, leaning even further down, began to kiss her. Christie decided sharply that enough was enough. Breaking free, she dived back to where Tina was standing laughing at her.

'Want to move on?' Tina shrieked in her ear. Christie nodded. She gulped down the remains of her drink, found a nearby table to set her glass down, and pressed after Tina to the entrance way.

'A bit too much, tonight,' Tina said blithely. 'I like somewhere where you can hear yourself speak. Was Brian annoying you?'

'For sure.'

'Well, that's what you have to expect when you look as good as you do now, Christie pet.'

Christie nodded. She still found it hard to believe. 'Where next?' she asked.

'Let's try the Kitchen again.'

'Just so long as we don't run into any more gunmen.'

Laughing, they headed round to the Victoria Centre.

In the Kitchen they found a less crowded atmosphere, and also Tina's friends Tommy, Aine, and Colm. Christie couldn't help being pleased. She was even more pleased when she noticed that Colm, who had ignored her at the Sunflower, was looking at her now with considerable interest.

Presently he sidled up to her and suggested that they might dance. Christie nodded and took his hand, and he led her out into the small space where a few people were dancing.

He didn't seem to have much to say, but Christie was happy just to look at him. When he came up much closer and drew her into his arms, she sighed with content and when shortly after that he began to kiss her she almost expired with happiness.

'You're beautiful,' he murmured.

Wow! thought Christie. *Is this an example of my dreams coming true?*

But almost at once she began to realise that it was far from being the fulfilment of her dreams. When she pulled back from his kissing, that seemed to be it. No further talk.

Until he finally said, apparently in desperation, 'Do you like foot-ball?'

'Well –' Christie said, reluctant to tell him that she loathed it.

That did it. Colm began to tell her about the match he had been to that afternoon. He told her about every goal, about every bad decision by the ref, about every member of his own team, in enormous detail. Christie couldn't remember having been so bored since school.

Colm, as Tina had told her, hadn't much to offer, only a few standard moves. And he had nothing interesting to say except for the unending flood of information, detail upon detail, about football. They continued to dance, and still Colm talked on. In fact, it was getting too awful to put up with for much longer. Christie found herself flooded with disappointment. Surely someone who looked like this must have more to him?

But it seemed that he hadn't.

'I need to slip out to the Ladies,' Christie muttered, detaching herself from Colm's arms. A moment later she had left him on the dance floor and was finding her way to the washroom.

Surprisingly, there was no queue. The place seemed fairly empty. Christie pushed open the door and went in. At once, she was aware of the sound of weeping coming from one of the cubicles.

Christie hurried into the next cubicle so that she could pretend not to hear. But when she came cautiously out again a few minutes later, she found that she hadn't waited long enough. Aine was standing at the wash hand basin, splashing water over her face and looking very woebegone.

It was too late to pretend not to have noticed anything.

'Aine!' Christie said. 'Are you okay, pet? What's wrong?'

'Oh – the usual sort of thing,' Aine said, trying to smile but not succeeding.

'A man?'

'Yip – that's it.'

'I'm so sorry,' Christie said, suddenly flooded with guilt. 'Is it Colm?'

'Colm? No way!' Aine looked very surprised. 'Sorry if you think differently, but to me Colm is a bit of a wimp.' She laughed, then at once her tears began to flow again. 'It's Tommy,' she sobbed, continuing to splash water on her face and at the same time ruining any effect this might have had in removing the signs of her outburst by continuing to weep.

'Tommy?' Christie remembered that Tina had told her that Aine and Tommy were an item. How stupid of her to have forgotten that. She put her arm round Aine's shoulder.

'So, if you want to tell me about it, go ahead,' she said. 'But not if you don't want to, of course.'

'No, I'd like to. It might help.' She said nothing while Christie waited patiently. Eventually it seemed necessary to do some prompting.

'The usual thing?' Christie inquired. 'He's dumped you?'

Aine laughed. 'No, nothing like that. I was going to say it's much worse, but maybe it isn't. I suppose I have that to be thankful for – Tommy would never dump me – at least, I'm pretty sure he wouldn't. But, Christie – promise you won't tell – not even Tina?'

'Promise,' Christie said, wondering why Aine was willing to confide in a stranger like herself, but didn't want even a good friend like Tina to know. But she had lots of experience before now of people telling her their troubles. They told her she had a kind face, the sort of face you could trust. Christie supposed it must be true, since this sort of thing kept happening. Sometimes she wished her face was a bit more forbidding.

'It's this,' Aine said abruptly. She gulped, and pulled something out of her shoulder bag. It shone and glittered in the harsh overhead light.

'Wow,' commented Christie. 'Looks almost real, doesn't it? Did Tommy give you that?' She looked in some amazement at the necklace dangling from Aine's fingers, a chain of diamonds in a gold setting, the many facets of the stones shining brightly enough to nearly dazzle her.

'Not exactly give,' said Aine. 'And Christie, it *is* real. I know. I tested it by scratching it on some glass. These are genuine diamonds.'

Christie said nothing and waited for more.

'Tommy didn't tell me where he got it. He wants me to pawn it for him – pretend it belonged to my granny or something. I'm afraid he must have stolen it. Otherwise he could just pawn it, or sell it even, himself.'

'I suppose so,' Christie agreed. 'But, Aine, surely you haven't agreed to do such a crazy thing? Have some sense, darlin'!'

'Well – I didn't exactly agree. But Tommy seemed so upset. It was just before we came here. He thought being out and seeing some mates would cheer us both up.'

'And what did he say about it – about how he got hold of it, and stuff like that? Has he been getting involved with a gang or something – people who do break-ins or muggings?'

'I don't really know, Christie. I think it must be something like that. Oh, Christie, I don't know what to do!'

Chapter 5

'Give him the necklace back and tell him you'll have nothing to do with it,' Christie said briskly. 'You don't want to end up inside for a long stretch yourself, do you?'

'No. But I don't want that to happen to Tommy, either.' Aine sniffed and took another tissue from the box on the counter to blow her nose. 'Oh, Christie – ' she brightened up suddenly – 'you wouldn't come with me, would you? It would make it so much easier for me.'

'No, Aine, I wouldn't,' said Christie firmly. 'I like you. I want to help you. But there's no way I'm going to help you dispose of stolen property. Give it back to Tommy, like I said.'

But as they left the cloakroom, Christie remained uneasily convinced that Aine had no intention of taking her advice. So few people ever did take advice. Advice was something they asked for, but used simply to clarify their minds, to show them what they had really intended to do all along.

When they rejoined the others, Tina said almost at once, ' Let's move on somewhere else, guys. How about the Sunflower?'

There was general agreement. They left the bar and gathered on the footpath outside.

'Might as well walk,' Colm said. 'No distance from here.'

They headed off in a chattering bunch, Tina leading the way with Christie and Colm beside her, followed not far behind by Tommy and Aine.

It was as they were standing on the footpath waiting to cross Royal Avenue that it happened. Without any warning Christie was aware of someone staggering out into the road beside her, unable to keep her balance, tripping and landing on her knees almost beneath the wheels of the huge bus roaring towards them.

For the crucial seconds that mattered, Tina, Colm and Tommy stood frozen with shock.

Christie knew she couldn't afford to wait. Leaping forward she seized Aine by the arm and dragged her back just in time as the bus swerved out of the way. Then Tina, recovering, moved forward to help. Between them they got her back onto the pavement.

Aine, it presently appeared, wasn't badly hurt. But she needed to sit down somewhere and recover, drink a cup of coffee probably.

They found an open coffee shop nearby, and sat around a table. The evening was over, as far as Aine was concerned, and Tommy, who was certainly very upset, wanted to take her home as soon as she felt able to go.

Christie also just wanted to get home and to bed, to forget what had happened and to try to banish the thoughts ringing through her mind.

Had Aine done it on purpose? Had the business of the necklace suddenly been too much for her? Aine didn't want to refuse to help Tommy, but she was frightened of going to pawn the necklace. Had there seemed to her no other way out?

'I think I'll call it a day, too, Tina,' she said when the coffee was finished and Tommy and Aine had said their goodbyes. 'I don't feel like going anywhere else tonight.'

'Fair enough,' Tina agreed. 'I'll come with you. An early night won't hurt after a shock like that.'

Christie didn't notice whether Colm headed home as well or went on to the Sunflower. Her interest in Colm seemed to have evaporated since their dance. She and Tina made for the nearest bus, and before long she was safely tucked up in her own bed, Kindle propped against her knees.

A good long read at *The Pirate* seemed a very necessary comfort. She wanted to remove her mind from the present day and the various upsetting events of the night.

She touched the book on her Kindle list and it opened at her place, as she settled down to escape from her worries for a few hours at least.

Chapter Six

1794

The little boat rocked in the swell from the big ship. Prudence didn't feel happy about being picked up by a pirate ship – but surely it had to be better than continuing to drift helplessly about on the wide ocean? So Prudence and Jane, working hard at the oars, did their best to bring their boat as near as they could to the ship, without danger of flooding or overturning.

They could see that there were several men leaning over the rail watching them. As they looked, they saw one of the men push something over the rail to hang down towards them. It was a rope ladder – something which they could use to scramble up to the deck above them and climb aboard.

'You go first, Jane,' Prudence instructed her maid. 'I'll keep the boat level and near enough. Then I'll follow you.'

Jane stood up cautiously and began to climb the ladder. It was difficult enough for her, Prudence could see. And it wasn't made easier by the raucous shouts and cheers of the waiting men. But it was their only chance of escape from the dangerous ocean.

When Jane was halfway up, Prudence stood up in her turn. She took the mooring rope attached to the stern of the boat and fastened it carefully round her waist, to prevent the boat from drifting away. Then she began to climb.

'Pull your skirts up more, sweetheart,' called a rough voice. 'It'll help you climb, and we wouldn't mind it, either!'

Prudence flushed with anger. What way was that for these men to speak to someone in her position, someone just rescued from danger of drowning? Didn't they care about what she and Jane had been through? It appeared not.

Prudence reached the rail of the deck. She climbed over carefully. She didn't want to reveal more of her legs than necessary, but she understood that a certain amount of such exposure was unavoidable. She felt her face flushing and glared around her.

'Thank you for rescuing us,' she said stiffly. 'Where is your captain? I would like to thank him personally.'

'I'm sure you'll be able to think of ways to thank him, lady!' one man guffawed. Prudence looked at him coldly. He was tall and fat, with a red complexion, much weather beaten, and a black patch over one eye. Under Prudence's look he squirmed and went silent.

Another of the men, one who had said nothing, but had grinned at his companions' remarks, came forward. He was a younger looking man, good looking in a fair, quiet way, and reminded Prudence of young Ensign Peter Willoughby who had looked after her so well before he had been killed by the falling mast on board the Golden Dawn. But when he spoke, his speech was nearly as rough as the other man's had been.

'Captain's down below, in his cabin. Reckon he'd like to see you both. I'll take you there. I'm the Mate, Josh Tompkins. This way.'

He headed for the companionway nearby and both Prudence and Jane followed him.

The climb down the ladder bringing them below decks necess-itated another gathering up of skirts, but by this time Prudence was hardened to it, and at least their young guide made no salacious comments. They followed him along a passageway and paused behind him as he stopped and knocked on an oak door, lavishly decorated with knots and roses and crossed swords.

'Come in!' a voice from inside the cabin invited them, and Josh Tompkins pushed open the door and made his way in first, leaving Prudence and Jane to follow him.

'What, Tompkins! What have you here?' the same voice roared out in astonishment. A tall, slim man who had been lying at ease on a comfortable looking bunk swung his legs to the floor and sat up, pushing a lock of dark hair back from his twinkling blue eyes. He stood up and came over to them.

'By the Lord Harry, this is a pretty catch!'

'Shipwrecked, Captain,' Josh Tompkins volunteered by way of explanation. 'In an open boat, looking to be rescued. We hove to and took them on board.'

Chapter 6

'Quite right, Tompkins! Nothing else to be done.'

Prudence looked at the man who now stood facing her, and found herself for a few moments at a loss for words. She never remembered seeing such a striking person before. Not only was he handsome, dark haired and with blue eyes like her own, but there was something about him which made her feel weak at the knees. And she noticed that there was a gleam of something much more than interest in the bright eyes which were fastened on her face. She dragged her own eyes away from him and managed to pull herself together enough to speak.

'We have to thank you and your crew, sir,' Prudence maintained her cold air, endeavouring to infuse sufficient gratitude into her words while maintaining a proper distance. She was determined to make this person, apparently, judging by his ship's flag, a pirate chief, understand that he needed to show her a certain respect. It would not do to allow him to start off with the impression that he could use her or Jane as he might wish. It was hard to display dignity while dressed in a nightgown and dressing robe, but she did her best. 'You will add to your kindness, sir, if you land my maidservant and myself at a suitable port as soon and as conveniently as possible.'

The pirate gave a shout of laughter. 'You don't ask for much, my beautiful lady! Don't you realise that if I put in to any port except my own place, I'd be thrown into prison as soon as they clapped eyes on me! I'm afraid, much as I admire you, I'm not prepared to go to those lengths. I'm sure you would like to go back to America, but it's too dangerous for me. You'll just have to stay on board, and sail home with me eventually to my island. No doubt we can find something for you to do when we get there. Ever wanted to be a female pirate?' He laughed again at the look of horror on Prudence's face.

'Sir, you can't possibly keep me on a remote island. It's no more and no less than kidnapping!'

The pirate continued to laugh. 'Don't worry, sweetheart. We'll work something out when there's time to think about it.' He bowed ceremoniously. 'I should introduce myself. You are speaking to one of the most famous pirate chiefs in the Caribbean – Black Nick Hawkeye.'

Prudence dropped a very slight courtesy. Her manners and up-bringing demanded as much, although it went against the grain to courtesy to a pirate.

'And do you intend to return the compliment, Mistress? Or am I to continue calling you sweetheart?'

Prudence flushed angrily. 'I am Mistress Prudence Rydesdale, sir. And this is my maid, Jane Brigham.' She waved one hand to indicate Jane, who was weeping quietly in the corner of the cabin nearest the door.

'Your servant, Mistress Rydesdale, and yours, Mistress Brigham.'

He swept them another, even more elaborate bow.

'And now, Mistress Rydesdale, Josh will find you some sleeping quarters. Your cabin would be best, Josh. You may share with the second mate for now. I'll bid you a goodnight, ladies. Sleep well!'

Prudence found herself, with Jane and Josh Tompkins, on the further side of the cabin door, which had been swung shut behind them.

'If you'll come this way,' Josh said.

Although he showed no sign of resentment, Prudence couldn't help feeling apologetic that they were turning Josh Tompkins out of his cabin.

'I'm sorry we're taking your sleeping quarters, Mate,' she began to say, but Tompkins brushed her apology aside.

'Captain Hawkeye makes the decisions round here, Mistress,' he said quietly. 'None of us ever question him. Since he says so, you get the cabin. I can share with the second mate, no problem.' He laughed. 'Just hope he doesn't snore.'

He stopped at a cabin just a little further on down the passage-way. 'It's not ready for you yet, Mistress. Just let me go in and tidy it a bit and take my things out of your way. A few minutes, no more.'

He disappeared through the cabin door, leaving Prudence and Jane looking at each other.

'Oh, Miss Prue, what are we going to do?' Jane began to wail straightaway. 'How are we ever going to get away safely?'

'*Jane, you were so brave when we were castaway in an open boat on the face of the ocean. Now we are aboard a safe ship and with the offer of a comfortable place to sleep tonight. Don't start to show fear now. Especially in front of these pirates.*'

'*No, Miss Prue,*' *Jane obediently rubbed her nose, sniffed and did her best to be calm. '*They seem kind enough, Miss Prue. At least, the captain and the mate do. I can't say much for those other ruffians.*'

Prue put a finger to her lips as the cabin door opened again and Josh Tompkins emerged, his arms full of clothes and other objects.

'*Hope you'll find it comfortable enough now, Mistress,*' *he said.*

'*Well, it has to be a lot better than a boat on the open sea!*' *Prue said, laughing. '*Thank you again, Mr Tompkins.*'

'*Call me Josh,*' *the mate grinned. He waved them in and went on his way.*

The cabin, when they went in, seemed pleasant enough. There were two bunks, so that there was no problem as to where Jane would sleep, and each had sufficient bed clothes, although Prue surmised that she was probably using the bedclothes Josh Tompkins had slept in last night and maybe for many nights. However, that was a minor matter. She was only too thankful to have a bed of any sort.

There wasn't much else in the cabin – some rough and ready washing arrangements and a small cupboard with a few hooks above it, for hanging or storing clothes, she supposed.

'*I do think the captain was kind, don't you, Miss Prue?*' *Jane persisted. '*And so good looking.*'

Prue flushed angrily, aware that the last thought had already come to her as soon as she saw him. A spark of some kind had flashed between them, on his side as well as on hers, she was quite confident. What did it mean?

'*I suppose it was too much to expect him to brave certain imprisonment to take us to a safe port,*' *she acknowledged. '*But I saw no reason for his mocking of us for asking. Still, I suppose in his own way he has done his best for us. We must think of a way of getting to safety ourselves.*' *She frowned anxiously.*

Then she saw that Jane was on the verge of tears again, and gave her a swift hug.

'Don't worry, Jane,' she said. 'We'll think of something. But not until the morning. All I want now is a good night's sleep.'

She took off her dressing gown, climbed into her bunk and rolled herself in the blankets. Jane in turn settled herself in the other bunk. Prue realised suddenly how sleepy she was. Before she had time to do more than reflect for a few moments that it was a mystery why someone who seemed to be a gentleman, like Black Nick Hawkeye, should be roaming the high seas as a pirate, instead of living comfortably ashore, she had drifted off into oblivion.

Whether the pirate chief came into her dreams, we should not ask. A girl's dreams are her own business, after all.

Chapter Seven

The Present

Christie went into the library on Monday morning wishing she could go somewhere else for several weeks – the other side of the moon, for instance. Not only was she worried about Aine and Aine's demands on her, and the risk of Aine doing something silly, but also she was hoping not to see her 'fly fishing friend,' Steve Armstrong.

She had liked Steve when they had chatted briefly in the library when he came in to get books on his subject. But since then she had seen Steve in a different light. She knew that it was Steve she had seen, part of a gang of men escaping from a hold up at the Victoria Centre. She had allowed Tina to persuade her not to tell the police that she could identify one of the robbers. But now, she really didn't want to run into him again. If he came to return his books while she was on duty, what could she say to him? She was sure he had seen her at the same time as she had seen him. He must know she had recognised him.

It was midway through the morning that Steve Armstrong walked in.

Christie just managed to repress a gasp of horror. Her imaginings about this man had been so vivid that she almost expected to see him brandish a sub machine gun and begin firing wildly all round the place. It took her a moment to reconcile her wild picture of him with the quiet, harmless looking man who was coming over to her at the desk.

'Christie?' he asked doubtfully. 'It is Christie, isn't it? Yes, of course. Just, you've done something to your hair.'

'Don't you like it?' Christie found herself asking in disappointment – foolishly, she realised a moment later.

'Er – yes, oh yes, it's great.'

Christie waited.

'Listen. I know you saw me the other night. Have you told the police yet?'

'No, as it happens, I haven't, so far.'

'Well, please don't until you've given me a chance to explain. Please!' he added as he saw Christie's expression.

'Why shouldn't I?'

'Look, we can't talk here. You get a lunch break, I suppose? Will you let me buy you lunch somewhere quiet and try to tell you what was happening?'

Christie must still have looked doubtful, for he said 'Please!' even more urgently.

'Okay,' she said after a minute of indecision.

'Great! What time do you get out? I'll wait for you at the door. I know a place quite near where we can get a table in a corner where no one will hear us talk.'

So just after one o'clock, Christie found herself sitting at a corner table at The Purple Cat opposite Steve Armstrong, watching him as he ordered mushroom, chicken and tomato omelettes from the young waitress, with chips for himself and salad, by her own request, for Christie.

The restaurant, although clean and pleasant looking with an interesting décor consisting mainly of pictures of cats and the occasional illustrated poem (*The Owl and the Pussycat*, *Hey Diddle Diddle*, *Three Little Kittens* and others), wasn't exactly busy. There were no occupied tables anywhere near enough to them for their discussion to be overheard.

'Well,' Christie said when the omelettes had arrived and the waitress had gone. 'What did you want to say?'

She noticed again the grin which she had found attractive break out on Steve's face, and felt the anger draining out of her. Surely this guy couldn't be a crook? She thought suddenly of the pirate chief in Serendipity Fox's book. She had been sure, when reading the description of their meeting, that some strong attraction was boiling up between him and Prue. But it was all very well for the heroine of a book to fall for a handsome pirate. In real life, it had to be different. Right and wrong had been ingrained into Christie from her childhood, and they mattered to her. She wasn't going to just abandon all her beliefs because she seemed to be taking a liking to a crook. *He wasn't even an especially handsome crook*, she reflected. *Or, on second thoughts, he was no Brad Pitt, okay, but wasn't there maybe something about him?*

She waited for him to speak.

Steve ran a hand through his mousy coloured hair, and grinned ruefully again. 'It's so hard to know where to begin. There are things I can't tell you. And if I say anything at all, you'll begin to guess a lot more, I know. Well, look, it's my job to keep an eye on those two guys you saw me with. I don't want to say more than that. I was with them for good reasons, that's all. Do you think you can believe me?'

Christie looked at him and found that she was believing him with no difficulty at all. She must catch herself on. She mustn't be such a fool as to swallow everything he said, just like that.

'You mean you're a sort of undercover cop or something?'

'I really can't tell you. I knew you'd start guessing if I said any-thing. Can't we just leave it at what I've already said? I should never have taken my mask off. But I've always hated things over my face – they give me a sort of claustrophobic feeling, And those tights were – well, really tight!'

Christie found herself laughing. 'I know what you mean, Steve. I've always hated things over my face, too. And especially stuff round my neck. It gives me a breathless, shut in feeling.' She stopped suddenly. What was she doing, sympathising with a crook?

He leaned forward and took the hand that was holding her knife.

'I like you a lot, Christie. I liked you as soon as you made that joke about J R Hartley. I was planning to invite you to go fly fishing with me at the weekend, but you disappeared. I'd still like us to do that, maybe next weekend? I really think we could be friends.'

Christie found that she thought so, too.

'Maybe. We'll see,' was what she said, however. She was deter-mined not to be stupid, not to jump into more trouble. 'If you've finished your meal, I need to get back to the library, now.'

Christie arrived home after work that night just as her mobile phone began to ring. She glanced at it quickly to see who was ringing. No name, and a number she didn't recognise. Probably Spam. She opened her front door, and clicked on the phone as she went inside, just in case it wasn't.

It wasn't.

'Christie? It's me, Aine. I got your number from Tina – hope you don't mind. She said not to ring until you finished work. Is this okay?'

'Yeah, fine, darlin'. I have to keep it switched off while I'm in the library. You just caught me stepping through my front door. Hang on a minute.'

Christie went into her kitchen, stripped off her coat, and switched on the kettle. On second thoughts she opened the fridge door and fished out a bottle of wine. Propping the phone under her chin, she got herself a glass from the overhead cupboard, twisted off the bottle cap, and poured. Then she sank into a comfortable chair and prepared to be friendly and if necessary helpful. She just hoped Aine didn't want too much help. But she had seen the girl walk out in front of a bus, possibly on purpose. Christie didn't want to be responsible for Aine doing something similar because she'd been refused help which Christie could give.

'All right, go ahead, Aine. Is everything okay?'

'No, it's awful, Christie. I took the necklace to the pawn-broker today and tried to get the money for Tommy. But the pawnbroker wouldn't take it. He asked me for evidence that it belonged to me, and of course I couldn't give him any. I thought he was going to ring the police, but thank goodness he didn't, and I managed to get out safely. So that was all right. But then a man started to follow me when I came out of the shop, and I'm frightened. He's behind me now. I got on a bus, and he did too. He's sitting four or five seats back, watching me phone you, but I don't think he can hear what I'm saying. Please come and help me!'

Christie, who was tired after her day's work and still shaken by her meeting with Steve Armstrong, and unable to decide what to think about him, found this fresh demand on her nervous energy almost too much. With difficulty she refrained from snapping at Aine.

'You really took that necklace to a pawnbroker after what I said to you about it?' she said.

'I had to, Christie. I talked to Tommy again and he told me a bit more about why he needed me to help him.'

'And are you going to tell me?'

'I don't think he'd be very happy if he knew I did, but I can't help it, Christie, I can't keep it all to myself. Tommy was given the necklace –'

'Given it?' Christie repeated unbelievingly.

'Yes, he was, but I know what you mean, yeah, it was stolen property in the first place. It was one of the guys who stole it who passed it on to Tommy and told him to turn it into cash. He threatened Tommy with all sorts of stuff if he didn't. See, Tommy has a record, and his boss doesn't know about it. He'd get the sack for sure if the boss knew. This guy said he'd not only tell the boss, but he and his mates would beat up Tommy as well if he wouldn't cash in the necklace for them.'

'And it didn't occur to Tommy that he was asking you to do something quite likely to be dangerous?'

'No, it didn't seem particularly dangerous to either of us.'

'So, now you know otherwise, Aine. Listen, do you think this guy who's following you is one of the crooks or a cop? What does he seem like to you?'

'Oh – I didn't think. Well, I suppose I just thought he was a crook. If he was a cop, wouldn't he have just arrested me if he thought I was trying to pawn a stolen necklace? And if he didn't know that, why would he be interested in me at all?'

That made sense.

'So, where exactly are you, Aine? Where is the bus heading?'

'It's heading out the Ormeau Road, towards my flat. I got on it automatically, but now I wish I hadn't. I don't want this guy to know where I live.'

'Well, here's what I think you should do. Get off the bus at the next stop, way before you get home. Make sure there are other people about. If this fella gets off too, you'll know for sure he's after you. As soon as you see him, tell a few people that he's stalking you – get it? Make a big fuss. If that doesn't scare him off, I'll be very surprised. Then go straight home on the next bus and lock yourself in. Ring me again to let me know when you're safely there, okay, pet?'

Aine voice quavered, but she said, 'Okay, Christie, Thanks.' Then she rang off.

Christie finished her wine, wondering if she had given Aine the best advice. But surely the man, whoever he was, wouldn't try anything with a lot of people watching? It was still early enough for the streets to be fairly busy. And it was still light, which was important too, of course.

Christie found she was too worried to pick up her Kindle and get back to the adventures of Prue and her pirate chief. It wasn't often she felt too strung up to read. Pictures chased each other through her head of things that might be happening to Aine at this minute.

When her mobile rang at last, she pounced on it with a huge sigh of relief.

'Aine?'

'I'm home now, Christie, and I've locked the doors and windows, like you said.'

'So, how did it go?'

'Well, I got off the bus and yer man got off too, like I knew he would. But I grabbed a couple, a guy and a girl, who were passing and told them, just like you said, that this fella was stalking me. They were great, Christie. The guy turned on him and shouted at him and told him he was going to ring the police, and you should have seen the fella's face! I could have laughed if I hadn't been really frightened!

So after a moment, he turned tail and bolted for it – I never saw anyone move so fast. So then this couple stayed with me until another bus came, and they were all for coming home with me to see I made it safely, but I said not to. They were just great! So then a bus came, and there was no sign of the guy who'd been following me by then, so I hopped on and here I am. You were great, too, Christie! Amazing idea!'

'No problem.'

'But, Christie, I need to see you. I need you to help me. Can you come round here, maybe?'

'Not tonight, Aine,' Christie said firmly. 'But, tell you what, I have the afternoon off tomorrow. I could call round then, if you like. But I don't think there's much I can do to help you except advise you to go to the police, right?'

'Oh, Christie, I can't! But, hey, you will come?'

Christie sighed. 'Yeah, okay, text me the address.'

When she finally got Aine off the phone, it was getting late. It had been a long day. Christie ate something quick, and was thankful to crawl into bed with her Kindle. In a minute or so she was deep again in *The Pirate*.

Hel's Heroes 2: Christie & The Pirate

Chapter Eight

1794

To her surprise, Prue slept long and deeply.

She woke to a confused noise of shouting overhead. Something was going on on deck. Wondering whether it would or would not be wise to go out of the cabin and find out what was happening, she sat up and saw that Jane was also in the process of wakening.

'Lor', Miss Prue, whatever is all that noise?'

Prudence peered out of the porthole and saw another ship not far off.

'I'm afraid it's our kind pirates attacking another victim, Jane,' she said wryly. 'We would probably be wise to stay where we are until things have settled down. I don't think there's much we can do to help that other ship, alas.'

Jane's mouth fell open. She stared at Prudence aghast, and was at a loss for words.

'Meanwhile,' Prudence said briskly, 'we'd better get ourselves washed and so on, and tidy ourselves. We have nothing to change into, but at least we can do our best to stay as clean as we can in these strange circumstances.'

They had been used for some time to managing these basic things while on board ship on the Golden Dawn, and Josh's cabin seemed quite well equipped with washing things. By the time Prudence had tidied her dark curly hair and they both felt ready to face the world, things had quietened down outside. The other ship had vanished from their sight. Prudence hoped it was merely being towed along at the back of their own ship, rather than sunk beneath the waves. She shivered at the thought, and smiled encouragingly at Jane.

'We had better make the best of things, Jane. There's no point in trying to steal a boat and escape that way. We would just find our-

selves back where we started. Perhaps when we get on shore we may be able to arrange something.'

Someone knocked on the door, and Josh Tompkins called out, 'Are you awake, ladies? I've brought you some breakfast, if you're ready for it.'

'Yes, indeed we are. Come in!' Prudence called back, and the door opened on the sight of the mate carrying a tray with bread, cooked meats, and wine.

It occurred to Prudence to wonder if the door that been fastened on the outside in some way. She hadn't thought to try it when they first were left in the cabin, or at any time since. It would make her very angry if she found that they had been imprisoned.

Josh set the tray down on a handy chest, and said, 'The Captain sends his apologies, Mistress. He knows it's not what you're accustomed to, but it's all we have available on board. When we get safely to port, the island is teeming with variety, and we can guarantee to serve you with more pleasant meals. I hope you can enjoy this rough fare until then.'

'Yes, indeed we can. Thank you Josh,' Prudence said graciously. 'If you had not rescued us, our breakfast would have been water and dry biscuits, and before long, not even that. So we thank you.'

Josh backed out of the cabin, smiling at them in a pleased fashion, and closing the door behind him. Immediately he had gone, Prudence hurried to the door and tried it cautiously. To her relief, she found that she could open it. There was no question, then, of their being locked in.

They sat down to their breakfast with a hearty appetite. It seemed a long time since they had had a proper meal, and if it was rough fare, with no butter for their bread and no chocolate such as Prudence was used to drink in the early morning, at least there was plenty of it. The bread was even fresh, and must have been baked on board.

When they had finished eating, Prudence said briskly, 'Now, Jane, I'm going up on deck to get some air. You may come with me if you wish, but it might be safer for you to stay here.'

'I need fresh air, too, Miss Prue,' Jane protested.

'Very well.' Prudence opened the cabin door and looked cautiously out. There was no one in sight.

They made their way along the passageway and climbed the ladder to the deck.

On deck, there was no shortage of people. Members of the crew were milling around, scrubbing decks, doing something which Prudence didn't understand with ropes, and polishing brass fittings. Prudence looked aft, and saw, with a certain amount of relief, that the ship she had seen under attack from the cabin porthole was attached to the stern of their own vessel, and sailing along after them. She could see figures on board, clearly some of the pirate crew which had been put there to steer the captured ship, whose name, she could see, was Freedom. She wondered for a moment what was the name of the ship she was sailing in.

But her attention was immediately distracted by the sight of a young man, one arm bloody and bandaged, standing in the centre of a bunch of crewmen and obviously waiting for something.

He was tall, broad shouldered, and fair haired, and what she could see of his face seemed attractive.

Was this a man who had been captured from the ship Freedom?

Prudence was sure it was.

It seemed that he was waiting for the captain to come and deal with him, and Prudence, memories of stories she had heard of pirates forcing their captives to walk the plank, stared at him, her heart in her mouth. Surely they weren't going to see such barbarism happening before their eyes? If so, she certainly didn't intend to stay back and allow it to go forward without protest.

But she was aware that no protest or action of hers would be likely to make much actual difference to events.

As she watched, Josh Tompkins came down from the bridge and came towards the crowd.

'Captain will see him now,' he said briefly to the crewman who seemed to be in charge, a small stocky man with sandy hair. Was this the second mate? Prudence wondered.

'Aye aye, sir,' the man said, and gave his captive a push.

'Come on, you, we don't keep Captain Hawkeye waiting on this ship. Get moving!'

Between them he and Josh propelled the young man towards the bridge, and out of Prudence's sight.

'Oh, Miss Prue, what's going on?' Jane whispered.

'We'll find out soon enough,' Prudence said grimly. 'I would guess that that is the captain of the ship Freedom which has been taken over by our pirate friends. I just hope they have no bad intentions towards him.'

Frowning and preoccupied, she stepped forward, closely followed by Jane, and was immediately noticed by the crowd of rough seamen.

'Look, men! What have we here?' one of them cried, and in a moment they were surging round Prudence and Jane, moving in ever closer until Prudence found that she had to exercise all her willpower not to retreat. Instead, she stood stiffly without moving, and stared the ringleader in the eye.

'Let me pass, please!' she said in a haughty voice.

'Not just yet, my pretty,' the man sneered. It was the man who had greeted them as they climbed aboard on the previous night, a hulking brute, ginger haired and burly, with a red face and a patch over one eye, and he towered over the two girls so that he almost seemed to surround them by himself. Prudence, pushed up against the bulkhead, found his huge arms stretched out one on either side of her against the woodwork, trapping and imprisoning her.

The other crewmen crowded in behind them, and Prudence had time to notice that two of them had Jane cornered in a similar fashion. If Jane was frightened, her face showed no sign of it. Instead, her cheeks were red with anger and her eyes sparkled furiously. She was cursing the men for vulgar brutes, using some words unfamiliar to Prudence, although the men seemed to recognise them to judge from their roars of laughter.

But she had little enough time to take this in, for her own captor was swooping down on her. 'Just a little kiss for One Eye Jake!' he leered, grinning unpleasantly. His thick horrible lips, stretched over a mouth full of dirty broken teeth, with breath smelling of *onions and rum, descended on her own in a hateful kiss. Prudence struggled to get free from his embrace, and succeeded in getting her mouth into a position which made it possible for her to bite him viciously on his underlip.*

'Bitch! Vixen!' he roared, pulling back for a moment and clapping one hand to his mouth in pain. For a second Prudence thought she was going to escape, but before she had done more than wriggle from under his other arm, he had seized her again, and hauled her back, his rough grasp on her clothes ripping both dressing gown and night dress from her shoulder.

Prudence was filled with horror at the prospect of his next move, but her mind was clear. She wasn't going to give in. She would fight him off as long as she had breath in her body. There was no more time to worry about Jane, her attention was fully occupied in her own struggle. She wished she was wearing her riding boots or at least outdoor shoes instead of the light slippers she had worn while escaping from the Golden Dawn, but she managed to get in several hard kicks on the man's legs which he seemed to feel.

As he pushed against her, his heavy body impossible to resist, she felt her legs rocking under her, and realised in horror that if she wasn't careful he would soon have pushed her unto the deck. What would follow when he had her helpless beneath him she dreaded to think. But before that could happen, there was a sudden roar from behind him.

The thong of a whip slashed through the air, cutting into the man's back.

One Eye Jake roared with pain. The whip slashed down again. A strong arm came over Jake's shoulder and pulled him away. A moment later, Jake was hurling through the air, to land with a crash against the far side of the deck, where he lay helpless himself now, groaning and wincing. The men who had been cheering him on began to melt away as quickly and unobtrusively as possible.

'Take him to the brig, Josh!' commanded a familiar voice. 'Twenty lashes with the cat-o'-nine-tails. And after that we'll dump him on the nearest island.'

A tall, commanding figure had loomed up out of nowhere. He stood, arms now folded, gazing round with a bright threatening eye at his unruly crew men. As Prue looked at him, her heart bursting with thankfulness, the scowling face was turned towards her, and she felt herself tremble.

It was Captain Nick Hawkeye.

Chapter Nine

The Present

Next morning Christie woke bright and early. The sun was shining through her bedroom curtains. Jumping out of bed, she pulled the curtains apart and stretched luxuriously as she gazed out at her small back garden. The tulips she had planted back in the autumn were coming up nicely, and the blossom on the lilac bush was still there, and beautiful. As she pushed open the casement window she caught a whiff of its sweet scent blown towards her on the gentle eastern breeze. For a moment everything seemed good.

Then, with a sinking feeling, she remembered Aine, and her own promise to go round and see her that afternoon.

'Why do you get into this sort of thing, Christie, you eedjit?' she muttered to herself.

Well, couldn't be helped now. Time she got herself washed, dressed, and fed, if she wanted to get to the library without being late. She found herself wondering, as she drank her coffee and dipped her toast into the yolk of her soft boiled egg, if Steve Armstrong would turn up again. It might be interesting if he did. She still wasn't sure about him. Had he been spinning her a yarn yesterday over lunch? Or rather, hinting at one? Was it just an attempt to pull the wool over her eyes and keep her from going to the police about him?

Come to that, Christie wondered again, why hadn't she done that in the first place, instead of allowing Tina to persuade her not to? She was behaving in a way well out of line with her normal behaviour. She wasn't Mistress Prue Drysdale, falling for a pirate chief in spite of her belief in right and wrong. At least, she had no intention of being like Prue. So far.

She had advised Aine quite firmly to go to the police, but she hadn't applied her own advice to herself. She must be mad!

The clock struck the half hour, and Christie jumped up in a hurry from the breakfast bar, gathered up her cup and plate and began to wash them, along with the cutlery, as quickly as possible. Leaving them to dry in the plate rack, she seized her handbag, took a last quick look in the mirror, and gave her hair a final comb. Then she rushed out to catch the bus.

At the library, everyone was at panic stations. Christie remembered that a well known local author was coming to the library book club that morning. Miss Patterson was hurrying round, arranging chairs in the side area, and flustering the staff by issuing conflicting orders about setting up a book display of the author's books near the entrance.

'We must have more of her work than this!' she was crying in a high, almost hysterical voice. 'Ah, Christie, you're here. Maybe you can help – Hazel doesn't seem to have any helpful suggestions about where we could find the other books. And Maurice doesn't want to leave the computer – apparently several faults have been reported recently, and as he rightly says, his job is first and foremost to sort that out.'

Maurice Thompson was a youngish, strong minded man who for some reason was a prime favourite of Miss Patterson, even though he never paid much attention to her instructions. His job, a part time one two days a week, was trouble shooting the computer system, and he regularly refused to get involved in anything else. Christie saw Hazel shoot him a resentful look. Until Christie's arrival, she had been bearing the brunt of Miss Patterson's fussiness, and she was clearly angry about this.

'Last time I'll come in early, Christie,' she muttered in Christie's ear. 'She caught me as I was going home yesterday and asked me to come half an hour earlier than usual, and since I thought I'd like a bit of time to get myself ready for Luke (he's calling round this morning) I said I would. More fool me!'

Christie, glad Miss Patterson hadn't managed to catch her, moved forward to inspect the display of the visiting author's books. 'Yes, we certainly have more titles than you have here, Miss Patterson,' she said. 'Have you looked in the Irish section?'

'Oh, I didn't think of that!' Miss Patterson confessed, and rushed off to make up for her omission. Shortly afterwards she returned with a beaming smile and an armful of the missing books, which she proceeded, with Christie's help, to arrange suitably.

Chapter 9

Then it was time to open the library doors. The first customers trickled in, and were dealt with by Hazel at the desk, and in due course the members of the book club, armed with tray bakes, bottles and glasses, arrived looking for a table to use in setting them out. It was Christie's job today to help with all this, and to provide a separate table prominently placed for the author's books, which would be available for people to buy – apart from the display arranged in the entrance by Miss Patterson of those kept by the library for borrowing.

The event was to be held in the side area normally used by the book club, but with room for overspill, when something like this was on. Finally the author herself came in, looking shy and pleasant, not someone to cause the amount of upset Miss Patterson had generated on her behalf.

Christie already knew that it was Helen McFadden, otherwise Serendipity Fox, author of the book she was currently reading on Kindle, *The Pirate*. She also knew that Helen had recently got married. She wondered if she'd met one of her heroes in real life. She hoped very much that she would have an opportunity to talk to her after the event.

Presently the book club members, with extra friends who had come along for this special occasion, were sitting round in a half circle, while the author stood at the front.

Christie, looking at her with interest, saw that she was quite young, only a few years older than Christie herself, probably, was very pretty, with blonde hair, and was very smartly dressed.

Helen – or Serendipity – explained that although she had until recently published in eBook format only, she had recently decided to produce paperbacks as well, and had been pleased with the results so far. She then read some snippets from her various books, and a longer excerpt from her latest one. Then came the questions, which went on for so long that Miss Patterson finally had to call a halt, as lunch time crept closer.

'Thank you for giving us such an interesting morning, Serendipity,' she said at last. 'I understand that you are willing to sign books now for those who wish to buy.' Then she led the enthusiastic applause.

It seemed that nearly everyone there wanted to buy at least one of the author's books. It was only by lingering until the very end, instead of leaving on time for her afternoon off, that Christie got a chance to speak to her.

Coming up to help Helen pack up her few remaining books, she said quietly, 'I was wondering, Serendipity – I know you got married recently. I was wondering if you would think it wise for a girl to get involved with somebody like your pirate, Captain Nick Hawkeye? I'm not just asking for fun – it's a serious question.'

'I can see it is,' Helen said thoughtfully, looking at Christie's worried face. 'You think my books have a bad influence on my readers? Oh, and do call me Helen, please, or Hel – Serendipity is only for formal occasions.'

'Helen, then. What do you really think about what I asked you?'

'To be honest, Christie, I think anyone who got involved with some-one like Black Nick Hawkeye in real life would be off their head. Have you read the book?'

'I'm just part of the way through it.'

'Ah, well, wait until you're finished before you make any decisions about him!' Helen laughed. 'But actually, I know one person who was very badly influenced by my books – and that was me. I thought there were men like my heroes floating around in real life, and that I'd be happy if I found one. But now I've found someone who suits me perfectly in every way – and I don't think he's at all like my heroes, to tell you the truth. It's a good idea not to mix up romantic fiction with real life.'

'Thanks for giving me such an honest answer, Helen. I hope you don't think it was too cheeky of me to ask the question?'

'I'm always glad to give an honest answer to an honest ques-tion, Christie,' Helen smiled. Then Miss Patterson came hurrying up, bringing Maurice Thompson to help with the books, and Christie's talk with the author came to an end.

To Christie's surprise, Maurice, who normally ignored her, was smiling, and when he caught her eye, he gave her an enormous wink.

'Don't disappear, Christie,' he whispered, as he hoisted up the heavy box of books. 'I want to talk to you!'

'What on earth about?'

'Tell you when I get back in.' Then he, Miss Patterson, and the author disappeared through the library door, leaving Christie to help the book club members to pack up their own belongings and bustle out. Hazel, who had been on the desk, dealing with other customers during the event, made no move to help with any of this, although no one had come in for some time.

A few moments later Maurice came back. Making no attempt to help clear away the extra chairs and tables, he sidled up to Christie and whispered in her ear, 'Lookin' good, kid!'

Christie just caught herself in time from giggling aloud. Was Maurice planning to flirt with her? If this was the result of Tina's makeover, she thought she might be wise to go back to her previous look. On the other hand, she had always wondered if there was more to Maurice than met the eye. Would it be worth while taking some time to get to know the man beneath the geeky attitude? He wasn't at all bad looking, certainly, she realised, giving him an unobtrusive inspection. He was a good height, not too tall but certainly not small, he had dark, longish hair, and his eyes, when, as he had done now, he removed the glasses which he used at the computer, were a bright, attractive hazel colour.

'How's about joining me for lunch, babe?' was his next murmur.

'Why not?' Christie murmured back.

'Great. Wait for you outside.' And Maurice went off blithely, still without laying a finger on the chairs which Christie was piling up, in preparation for dragging them to the store room.

Miss Patterson came hurrying back, and took one end of the bigger table which Christie was attempting to move herself.

'Thanks, Christie! You've been a real brick this morning. When we've finished moving this, you'd better run along. Hazel can help with the other table this afternoon. See you tomorrow, dear.'

Miss Patterson was thawing out, Christie reflected, out-of-date slang and all!

Outside the Library, Maurice was waiting as promised, and came over to her brimming with confidence.

'I thought we might go to the pub round the corner,' he said. 'We could share a pizza and a pint there – they do a special lunchtime offer.'

Christie noticed that luxury wasn't being offered. Well, Steve hadn't offered luxury either, but at least he hadn't suggested a special offer.

'We can split the bill, if you like,' Maurice went on.

Christie turned her face away to hide the broad grin as they walked along and literally round the corner to the pub of Maurice's choice. Not just a special offer, then, but half a special offer. Maurice certainly wasn't going overboard.

And when they got to the pub and were seated at a corner table with their order given, it was clear that Maurice wanted, and intended, to talk about himself and his ability on the internet, and his glowing future.

Christie, sipping the white wine which wasn't included in the pizza and pint offer, and which, she was certain, she would be expected to pay for herself, listened calmly while Maurice talked about his plan to set up his own business as soon as he had finished the advanced computer qualification he was working on currently.

Contrasting it with the happy time she had spent with Steve Armstrong the previous lunchtime, Christie found herself wishing she could swop Maurice for Steve. Just because he was a more interesting companion, she assured herself. All in all, not a success- ful date. Dates were all very well, but it wasn't enough to be asked out. It had to be by someone you actually liked. She remembered dancing with Colm, and what a letdown that had been. Now, this lunch date with Maurice was proving to be more of the same.

When the bill came, Maurice said, 'Right, I think we should split the price of the special offer, and then you can pay for your wine separately, Christie.'

'Oh, no, how confusing,' Christie said. 'Let's just split the total, as we agreed.' She remained firm, insisting that that made it so much easier, not saying that, after all, Maurice had drunk the pint which was part of the deal and eaten at least two thirds of the pizza, and Maurice felt obliged to agree. Christie, while not mean, felt a degree of satisfaction that she had got the better of him to some extent.

Chapter 9

'Fancy going out on the town some night soon, babe?' Maurice asked as they left the pub.

Christie tried not to shudder in horror too obviously.

'Sorry, Maurice,' she said firmly. 'I'm a bit tied up for the next few weeks. Anyway,' she added maliciously, 'I don't think I could afford it – I'm trying to save for my holidays.'

Maurice looked disappointed but, as she had expected, did not say, 'Oh, I'd be paying!'

'I must run,' Christie added. 'Look, that's my bus coming. Bye – see you at the Library!' And she took to her heels.

Sinking back into her seat on the bus, she felt considerable relief. Later that afternoon she had to go over to Aine's. But for an hour or two before that, as some compensation for a busy morning and a disastrous lunch, she decided, she would reward herself with an hour or two with her Kindle and Serendipity Fox's *The Pirate*.

And as she lay back in her most comfortable armchair not much later, she breathed a sigh of content as she opened the Kindle and plunged once more into the story. She had just reached the point where Captain Hawkeye appeared suddenly to rescue Prue from One Eye Jake.

Hel's Heroes 2: Christie & The Pirate

Chapter Ten

1794

'Mistress Rydesdale!' Captain Hawkeye exclaimed, his voice still harsh. 'What in thunder are you doing out of your cabin? And Mistress Brigham, too! I thought you would have had more sense than to wander the deck of a pirate vessel full of rough sailors!' The scorn in his voice lashed Prue as painfully, she was sure, as his whip had lashed One Eye Jake a moment before. Leaning towards her, he pulled the ripped dressing gown and nightdress back into their normal position over her shoulder with a gesture every bit as rough as that of One Eye Jake when he had torn them down.

She flushed angrily, the deep gratitude she had felt as she saw him deal with One Eye Jake turning to rage that he should speak to her so slightingly.

'So, sir, were we to remain shut away from the fresh air until we suffocated? I thank you for your consideration!' Her voice trembled with irony.

'Better to suffocate than to be raped, Mistress, I think! If you want to walk in the fresh air, you may tell the mate and he will arrange for you to walk in safe company, for your protection.'

'Why, sir, I expected that you would have your men under better control than seems to be the case!' Prue flashed, and saw with satisfaction that she had scored a point.

'Normally that is so,' Captain Hawkeye said grimly. 'But normally we don't carry ruffians like One Eye Jake. The men would never have behaved so if he had not shown them such an example. We took him on at the last minute because we were short of ex-perienced crewmen – a mistake, I freely admit. Nor, I believe,' he added, glaring round him, 'will these men dare to repeat their villainy, having heard and seen my views on it. Anyone who fails to treat these ladies with the utmost courtesy,' he roared suddenly, 'will suffer the same punishment as One Eye Jake. Be warned!'

'*Aye, aye, captain,*' came a subdued murmur from the remaining crewmen.

'*Now, be about your business! Mr Mate, why are these men not working? The goods we took from the enemy ship should be safely stowed by now.*'

Josh, Prue noticed, was still comforting Jane, whose anger had apparently turned to tears when rescue arrived. He had seated her beside himself on a nearby chest and was hovering over her, holding her hand and wiping away the tears from her red cheeks, and brushing back the curly red hair from her eyes with a large red bandana handkerchief. At his captain's words, he sprang hurriedly to his feet, his face as red as his bandana, and began to give orders to the subdued crewmen.

'*Come on, lads, bustle about! These chests must be lowered carefully into the hold. Bring ropes and secure them first.*'

'*I will return to my cabin in a moment, sir,*' *Prue said coldly, giving Captain Hawkeye an icy glance.* '*But first, I would like to know why you have attacked that ship and robbed it? And what you intend to do with the prisoners you have taken?*'

If the truth be told, her concern was mainly with the fair haired young man she had noticed earlier. If Captain Hawkeye meant to make him walk the plank, then Prue intended to do everything she could to prevent it. Not, she thought ruefully, that that would be much. But at the very least, she could make her opinion felt.

'*What I do with my prisoners is my own business,*' *the captain said roughly.* '*As for capturing the ship, I thought you knew that as a pirate chief, that is my business, too? It's what I do for a living.*'

'*Then it ought not to be!*' *Prudence exclaimed.* '*A man of your ability could surely find some better way to spend your life? You should be ashamed of yourself.*'

Captain Hawkeye turned away, his face and his reactions hidden from her. '*That's enough!*' *he said.* '*Go back to your cabin. And stay there until I have time to speak to you again.*'

Prudence gathered her dignity, and the long sweep of her dressing gown, about her. '*Come, Jane,*' *she said. Together the two girls made their way back to the companionway, aware of the captain's eyes fixed on their backs as they went.*

'*Are you all right, Miss Prue?*' *Jane asked anxiously as soon as they were alone and safely shut into their cabin again. 'I'm sure that evil brute hurt you!*'

'*Not as much as Captain Hawkeye hurt him,*' *Prue responded, a grin on her face.*

'*Oh, yes, wasn't he wonderful?*' *sighed Jane, sitting down on the edge of her bunk. 'And the mate, too.*'

'*You seemed to be getting very friendly with Master Josh Tompkins, Jane,*' *Prue remarked teasingly, avoiding any comment on Captain Nick Hawkeye. She preferred not to think about the pirate captain until she had some time to herself to sort out her reactions.*

'*He was very kind, Miss Prue. It was so marvellous to see him and Captain Hawkeye coming, after those other creatures.*'

'*Yes,*' *Prudence had to agree. 'We would both have been in serious trouble if they hadn't turned up.*'

It seemed a long time before Josh Tompkins knocked on the cabin door and brought in another meal for them. Breakfast might have been light years ago, yet this must be dinner rather than lunch, Prue decided.

Josh set his tray down, as before, on the convenient chest, and said, 'Here you are, ladies. Chicken, wine and fruit, with bread. I hope you enjoy it. And I hope you've both recovered from your shock.' He looked at Jane in particular as he said these last words, a worried frown on his pleasant face.

'*Oh, yes, thank you, Mister Mate,*' *Jane beamed. 'We are none the worse, thanks to your timely intervention. You and Captain Hawkeye were both so brave!*'

'*It was nothing, Mistress Jane!*' *Josh said, going red, but looking much relieved at Jane's words.*

'*Josh,*' *Prue asked, as she and Jane seated themselves as conveniently as they could and started on the chicken, 'what can you tell me about Captain Hawkeye? He seems like an unusual pirate chief, surely? How did he get into such a position?*'

Josh propped himself against the door and pondered. 'Well, mistress,' *he said at length, 'I don't rightly know what I can tell you. I've sailed with Captain Hawkeye for two years, now, and I know everything there is to know about his courage and skill. But I don't know much more than when I first joined him about the man himself and his background. And as for what he's doing sailing the seven seas as a pirate – well, I'm as much as a loss about that as you. From something he once let drop, I've an idea that there's something more to him than just being a pirate – that he's got some reason for what he does beyond what appears on the surface. But that's as much as I can tell you, and that's more a guess than anything else.'*

'Oh.' Prue's disappointment at the lack of information showed itself in her voice.

'But it seems that he plans to visit you himself later this evening, Mistress. Maybe he'll tell you more than he's ever told me, if you ask him.'

'Maybe,' agreed Prue doubtfully. 'Well thank you, Josh.'

Josh grinned and went out, leaving the girls to their meal.

The evening dragged slowly for Prue. Neither she nor Jane had anything to occupy them. They had rested sufficiently. They had no needlework, no books. And they were forbidden to walk out in the fresh air.

When at last a knock came on the door, both of them brightened.

'Josh come back to collect the tray!' Jane exclaimed hopefully.

'Or Captain Hawkeye come to pay us his promised visit!' Prue said. She could not he unaware that her voice sounded just as hopeful as Jane's, and told herself sternly that she was pleased only because it gave her an opportunity to ask for some arrangement to be made for them to walk out of the cabin.

It was Prue who turned out to be right. The knock was swiftly followed by the entrance of the Captain, Black Nick Hawkeye.

He had changed from the serge coat he had worn earlier to work among his sailors, and was dressed in fine dark blue satin over a white shirt trimmed with lace, and Prue acknowledged to herself that he looked well.

'Good evening, Mistress Rydesdale, Mistress Brigham,' he said, bowing courteously to them both. 'I trust you enjoyed your meal?'

Chapter 10

'I thank you, sir, we did,' Prue replied, not to be outdone in courtesy.

'Then, ladies, is there anything else you need or desire? If it is within my power, it shall be done.'

'Sir, a little fresh air after the meal and before sleeping would be a great pleasure.'

'As I explained to you earlier, Mistress Rydesdale, it is better for you not to go among the men unattended. However, if you wish to walk out, it will be my great pleasure to accompany you.'

'Thank you, sir.' Prudence bowed her head graciously in acknowledgement.

'If you please, sir,' Jane said, 'I'm feeling rather tired, and would rather remain here.'

Prudence looked at Jane in surprise. Then she smiled, guessing that Jane hoped Josh Tompkins would be coming sometime soon to collect their dishes.

'That's up to you, Jane,' she said. 'I don't intend to be away for very long.'

It had occurred to her that an opportunity to talk to Captain Nick on his own was just what she had been wanting. Surely, now, she would be able to find out more about this man who puzzled her so much?

He bowed her out of the cabin and led her along the passage to the companionway.

'I'll take you to the upper deck,' he said. 'It's quieter there, especially at this time, when the men are mostly at dinner, except for the few on duty. And they don't come to the upper deck unless I send for them there.'

Prudence waited until they had emerged into the fresh air. The evening sky was just beginning to turn to the dark of night, a few pale stars twinkling far above them and a rising moon losing its earlier whiteness and becoming silver. The Captain offered her his arm, and they strolled along together.

How should she begin?

65

'Captain Nick,' she ventured at last, 'it puzzles me to see you in such company. How do you come to be a pirate, sir?'

He frowned at her, then smiled.

'The eternal curiosity of women! But I suppose I should satisfy it. I became a pirate, Mistress Prue, because there seemed to be little else for me to do. A man must eat, after all, and so I signed up with the Betsy Allen as an able seaman. I worked my way up to Mate, and when the captain was killed in a battle, I took over.'

'But was the Betsy Allen a pirate vessel?' Prue couldn't help asking.

'No, indeed. If it had been known as that, it could never have put into the port where I signed up. But after I became captain – why, Mistress Prue, it seemed like a sensible idea.'

'Sensible!' Prue burst out. 'How could you think such a thing, sir?'

She would have gone on to ask more – for he had not told her why there had seemed to be little else for him to do than sign up as an able seaman, when everything about him declared that he had been born a gentleman – but before she could ask the questions still burning in her head, there was an interruption.

'Captain! Captain!'

It was the small, sturdy man with the sandy hair whom Prue had guessed earlier to be the second mate.

He burst out onto the upper deck, out of breath and red in the face.

'Captain, it's the sailor we captured when we took the ship Freedom! *The Captain! He's escaped! We don't know where he is!'*

Chapter Eleven

The Present

Christie returned to earth with a shock. It was high time she had left to go to see Aine. She knew the address – Aine had texted it to her as she had suggested. It was a flat just off the lower Ormeau Road. She slipped her Kindle into her shoulder bag. She might have an opportunity to read some more at some point in the afternoon, before she got home again.

Cutting down one of the connecting streets to the Ormeau Road, she caught the next bus by the skin of her teeth. Soon she was walking along the road where Aine lived, looking out for the number of the house. This must be it, the tall, rather shabby building with a number of bells lined up beside the door, and names on each.

She rang the bell with Aine's name beside it, and then texted her to say, 'It's me!'

A moment later there was the sound of feet as someone came downstairs at top speed, and then the door was flung open.

'Great to see you, Christie!' Aine said. 'Sorry about the locked door – we all reckon it's safer that way. The people in the various flats, I mean.'

'Well, I think you're wise,' Christie remarked as she followed Aine up the three flights of stairs until they reached another locked door, this time the door to Aine's flat.

Inside everything was clean and neat, like the tiny dark haired Aine herself, with pretty cushions scattered on the chairs and the sofa, and flower pictures on the walls.

'I've put the kettle on,' Aine said. 'It'll boil up again in a second. Do you want tea or coffee or what?'

The kettle, Christie noticed, was in an alcove at one side of the room where there was a microwave as well, a sink, a short work-top and two cupboards. The sofa, she realised as she sat down on it, was one which turned into a bed at night. The door leading off to the rear must be the bathroom, probably toilet, washbasin and shower. She was so lucky herself to have inherited her parents' house. She would have hated to live in such a small space as this. But maybe Aine liked it.

'Tea would be great,' she answered Aine's question. 'Weak, please! Milk and no sugar.'

In a short time they were both sitting facing each other, drinking tea and talking.

'So, Aine,' Christie said presently, when she judged there had been enough small talk, 'what do you mean to do about this diamond necklace?'

Aine pushed her pretty dark hair back from her face, a habit she had, Christie had noticed, when she was worried about something.

'I don't know, Christie! I daren't go to another pawn shop, after that man following me yesterday. And I don't want to give it back to Tommy and tell him I'm not going to help him.'

'What you should actually do it take it to the police. You don't need to bring Tommy into it. Pretend you found it somewhere. Or else, even, post it anonymously to the nearest police station.'

'I can't do that, either,' Aine said forlornly. Her lower lip quivered, then she stuck her chin out obstinately. 'Tommy would get beaten up if he had to tell those guys that he didn't have the necklace any more, or the money he should have raised with it. I can't let that happen to him.'

'Aine, Tommy got himself into this mess, and he should be the one worrying about how to get out of it. He's a big boy now! If you absolutely refuse to go to the police, then give him the necklace back and let him either try to pawn it himself or give it back to the crooks who gave him it, and tell them he couldn't get a pawn shop to take it.'

Tears began to trickle down Aine's face. Christie, while hating to see her friend weep, couldn't think of any other options to suggest.

'I haven't any other ideas for you, Aine,' she said finally. 'If you tell Tommy about the man who followed you, I should think, if he cares about you at all, that he'll be only too glad to take the necklace back and leave you out of it. And if he doesn't care about you, then you'd be better off without him.'

This hard statement of fact only succeeded in producing a cry of despair and an increasing flow of tears. Christie was getting annoyed.

'Come on, Aine, dry your eyes,' she said briskly. 'If you like I'll come round to Tommy's place with you, and explain what you've been through.'

Aine raised her reddened eyes. 'Oh, would you, Christie?' she asked dolefully. 'I just can't face telling him myself that I can't help him.'

Christie, although wondering yet again why she let herself in for these things, had to agree. It would be so much easier to pass by on the other side. But, like the good Samaritan, it wasn't something she could do.

'Shall we go now, Aine?' she asked instead.

Aine sat up and blew her nose. 'I'd better text him and see if he's in, first,' she suggested.

But Tommy wasn't in. He would be back, he texted, by six.

'Okay, let's go into town and get something to eat while we're putting in the time,' suggested Christie, and Aine agreed.

Two relaxing hours later, they took a bus to Tommy's flat.

Christie, as well as relaxing, had been doing a bit of thinking. It seemed to her firstly, that whoever had stolen the diamond necklace could not have been much of a professional thief. A pro would have already known a fence, and would have had no need to rope in Tommy, and threaten him, to get the necklace taken to random pawnbrokers, who would mostly, like the one Aine had tried, have been suspicious, and reluctant to take possibly stolen goods.

Secondly, the thief wouldn't have stolen only one necklace, if he had been part of a gang robbing jeweller's shops. This looked more like a one-off snatch of someone's necklace from a private house, or from a party or event where the owner had been wearing the necklace more or less in public. In which case, the threats to Tommy became less serious. He wasn't up against a dangerous gang, only against an individual thief.

True, the individual thief might still be a serious threat, just not so much of one. If this was the case, the problem was to find out who it might be. Who would have known that Tommy had a criminal record? And how had the threats come to him? Face to face, or by phone? How had the necklace been passed to him? And did he know who was responsible?

Christie decided that the first thing to do was to ask Tommy these questions. Then, she would see.

Tommy was at home by the time they got there. They stood in the street outside the door the house where he had a rented room, and Aine rang him.

'Hi,' she said when he answered. 'Open the door, it's me.'

It was only a short time later that Tommy, looking much more dishevelled that Christie remembered him, but just as big and strong, opened the door cautiously and peered round it. Seeing Christie there as well as Aine was a shock to him. He almost closed the door again, but Aine's voice stopped him in time.

'Hi, honey. You remember my friend Christie, she has some great ideas that will help us. Move over, you big slob, let us in.'

Tommy obediently moved over. It was a revelation to Christie, who had thought that Tommy was the ruling person in this relationship. It now appeared that Aine had a lot more clout than had been obvious. Tommy, Christie thought, got his own way by appealing to Aine's sympathy and love, as a needy guy who loved her and depended on her help, in spite of his size.

Tommy led the way up the uncarpeted stairs to the door of his room. 'Room' was the operative word. There was a gas ring to one side, cupboards above it, no sign of a fridge or microwave oven, a curtained off alcove with, at a guess, a lavatory and washbasin, and the rest a not especially big room with a table and chairs, and a sofa bed.

'Have a seat,' Tommy said. 'Can I get you some coffee or something?'

Christie, although not really wanting anything more, agreed to some coffee. It might, she thought, help to relax Tommy a bit.

When they were all three sitting round the table sipping cautiously at rather hot coffee without milk, she began her questions.

Chapter 11

'So, Tommy. Aine tells me you've been threatened?'

Tommy nodded unhappily.

'Was this face to face or by phone or something? I mean, did you see the guy who threatened you?'

'Yeah, I saw him. He came to my work.' Tommy shuddered at the memory. 'See, I work at loading the forklift trucks, at Wilson and Cromarty's. It's a good job, steady work and pay and the bosses are okay. He came up behind me, hidden by the fork lift, sort of. I don't know how he got in, but I reckon it wouldn't be too hard to walk in by the pedestrian gate – not often anyone would try to stop you. He said he could tell the boss things about me. I had to get him out of there before anyone noticed him, so I gave him this address and told him to come round that evening.'

He paused, and gulped. 'He came, right. He said he knew all about my record, and I'd be out on my ear if the bosses knew. So then he brought out this necklace and told me I had to pawn it for him and bring him the dosh, like. Or else – d'ye get it? I didn't see what else I could do. But I reckoned, if I went to pawn it my-self, the guy might know I had a record – well, maybe they might have. So I was like, stuck.' He looked up appealingly, big brown eyes as pathetic as a dog longing for a walk.

'And what about the threats to beat you up?" Christie asked, refusing to be moved by the pathos. This guy, she remembered, has sent his girlfriend into the danger he himself had wanted to dodge.

'Oh, yeah. I forgot to say. He told me he was only one of the gang. If I didn't get them the money they needed for the necklace, he said the tough guys in the gang would be calling round to see me, and, okay, he spelt it out what they'd do.' He quivered at the memory. 'You may think I look tough, but nobody could deal with half a dozen hard men trained like he said they were, ready to beat me up with extreme stuff – I don't even want to talk about what he said.'

Tommy collapsed with his head in his arms on the table, and Aine rushed forward, pushing back her chair, to cuddle him in her arms.

'There, there, pet. There, there,' she whispered in his ear, stroking his hair. Christie felt a little less sympathetic, but could understand Aine's feelings.

'So, Tommy,' Christie said when things seemed to have calmed down again, 'how do you think this guy knew you had a record? And by the way, if you don't mind me asking, is it a prison record? Or just probation?'

'Prison,' muttered Tommy sulkily.

'So how come your bosses don't already know about it?'

'Oh!'

Tommy was thunderstruck. It clearly hadn't occurred to him that his record might have already been known to his bosses. And yet, surely, Christie thought, it was common knowledge that prospective employers would always be told of a man's record if they inquired, as surely they mostly would, and that regularly many of them would be willing to give someone a second chance.

'I think they probably do, Tommy,' she said. 'So there's actually nothing for you to worry about, no threat. Unless you do something criminal again, like trying to pawn that necklace – or getting someone else to do it for you, right?'

'But what about the hard men coming to beat him up?' Aine asked, her voice quivering as Tommy's had done at the thought.

'My guess is that there aren't any hard men,' Christie said robustly. 'This sounds like a one man show to me. If it's a gang, why don't they already have a fence to go to?'

Aine and Tommy were thunderstruck. Then they came out of the shock and Tommy said, 'Right! I never thought of that.'

'So we've been worrying about nothing!' Aine said jubilantly.

'Well, not quite nothing,' Christie said judiciously. "What's this guy like – the one who gave you the necklace, and threatened you? Is he a danger, himself?'

'Naw, no way,' Tommy said happily. 'I could throw him into the Lagan with one hand tied behind my back. A real wimp, see?'

'Great!' Christie said with relief. 'So, all you need to do now is to hand over the necklace to the cops and tell them what's been happening. I wouldn't mention that you tried to pawn it through, Aine, by the way. What they don't know won't hurt them. Just you be the virtuous reformed jailbird who wants to go straight now, okay, Tommy?'

'Right,' Tommy grinned. 'Nothing to worry about, now.'

It was just at that moment that there was a thunderous knocking on the door of the room. Someone must have got through the locked outer door downstairs. And they heard a harsh voice shouting, 'Open up, there, Tommy! We've come to sort you out!'

Hel's Heroes 2: Christie & The Pirate

Chapter Twelve

Tommy let out a hollow groan, but Aine was made of more resilient stuff.

'Quick, guys!' she hissed. 'Out the back door!'

As she spoke, she seized Tommy by one arm and hustled him through the kitchen to the back door which opened onto a fire escape. Christie followed. She would have liked to find out who was at Tommy's door, but she understood the sense of Aine's suggestion.

A few moments later they were scrambling down the fire escape, dropping from the lowest rung, and breathing the fresh air with considerable relief.

'We should have locked the back door after us,' Tommy moaned. 'They'll find where we've gone and follow us.'

'I did,' Aine said briskly. 'C'mon, we gotta get out of here fast!'

She shepherded Tommy, Christie following, down the back alleyway and into the nearest street. Then after several twists and turns, they came out unto the main road.

'Okay, Tommy and I can get a bus from here to my flat,' Aine said. 'Christie, will you be okay?'

'Sure, I can cut up this next street and I'll be nearly home, pet,' Christie said cheerfully. 'Thanks for your rescue operation!'

Aine laughed. 'We'll be in touch, won't we?' she asked with a shade of anxiety. It seemed she was still holding on to Christie as a lifeline.

'No problem,' Christie assured her. Still, she was very glad to reach her own house and be free of Aine's problems, to say nothing of Tommy's for the time being at least.

A glass of wine, a quick sandwich – she had some cooked chicken in the fridge – and then, relaxation.

Ten minutes later, she had sunk into her most comfortable armchair, and was opening her Kindle to read the next chapter of *The Pirate*.

1794

All Prue's sympathies were with the escaped prisoner. She remembered him well, the young fair-haired man with the bloody and bandaged arm, the captain, she had now learnt, of the ship Freedom *which Captain Nick Hawkeye had taken and was towing behind him.*

The name Freedom *seemed to speak to her deepest feelings. She was glad the young man was free – she hoped with all her heart that he would stay free, and escape.*

'Mistress Prue,' Captain Nick said quickly and pleasantly, 'I'm afraid I must ask you to return to your cabin now. As you will understand, I have serious duties to perform here.'

He bowed ceremoniously, and escorted Prue, politely but firmly, to the ladder she had climbed such a short time before to walk with him on the upper deck. Then, seeing her started on her downward journey, he strode off into the darkness which by now had come with a rush, calling out orders to his crewmen as he went.

Prue climbed down a few steps cautiously, until he was out of reach. Then she stopped.

It was against her nature to retire to her cabin and leave that poor young man to the mercy of Captain Nick and his rough crewmen. If it was humanly possible, she meant to do everything she could to help him.

Slowly, carefully, she climbed back up the ladder. Peeping over the rim at the top, she looked all around. There was no sight of anyone. She scrambled quickly up the remaining steps, came cautiously out unto the deck, and scurried over to the nearest shelter, a cannon placed ready to fire at the edge of the rails, alongside a number of others. Slipping quietly along between them, Prue reached the end of the line, and looked all around.

The shadows cast by the bridge high above made it possible for her to make her way forward. She wasn't sure what she could do next, but as she peered through the gloom, a stray shaft of moonlight shot through the gap between the cannons, and Prue thought she saw movement.

It might only be her imagination, or a rope dislodged from one of the cannons by the movement of the sea, but it was something she wanted to look into.

Slipping along cautiously, Prue moved from her current shelter into the gap between the two cannons where she believed she had seen movement.

As she did so, a hand shot out to grab her, another hand was thrust over her mouth, and a voice, so low as to be almost inaudible, murmured in her ear, 'Be quiet if you value your life.'

Prue froze. The hands dragged her further in between the cannons and the moonlight shone fleetingly on a handsome young face, full of a grim determination. She recognised him at once as the escaped prisoner she had intended to help. 'So much for that idea', she thought in wry amusement. 'I'm the one who needs help instead.'

Her normal reaction in a situation like this would have been to struggle, to bite or kick, but since in spite of his actions she still didn't want the young sailor to be caught she stayed obediently quiet, hoping for a chance to speak and let him know she was on his side.

'If I take my hand away from your mouth,' he said in the same very quiet voice, 'will you swear not to scream? Nod if you will.'

Prue nodded, with some difficulty, and was relieved when his hand moved sufficiently to allow her to breathe more easily.

'I want to help you,' she began to say, but in a flash his hand was over her mouth again, and his voice, harsh in spite of its muted tone, said, 'I told you to be quiet!'

Prue waited, hoping that what she said might have got through to him, and, sure enough, after a few moments, he spoke again. 'Did you mean that?'

Prue nodded vigorously.

'But what could you possibly do?'

He must have realised that he would have to remove his hand again if she was to be allowed to answer, for he said, 'As few words as possible, and very quietly.'

When he had moved his hand, Prue shook her head to attempt to get rid of the ringing in her ears, then said very softly, 'I could smuggle you down to my cabin and keep you there until the hunt has died down.'

She could see him frowning as he considered her offer. Then he nodded briefly and pushed her ahead of him to the edge of the gap where it was possible to see around. Prue peered cautiously out. There was no sign of anyone. She trod silently across the deck towards the companionway she had come up. After a moment he followed.

At the head of the companionway, Prue gestured to him to go first. The sooner he was off the deck the better. He must have understood the wisdom of this himself, for he went past her and was swiftly at the foot of the ladder. Prue, her skirts tucked carefully round her again, followed as quickly as she could.

She pointed out the way, still keeping silent, and they hurried along the passageway to the cabin. It occurred to Prue briefly that Josh Tompkins might well be there, but then she thought how unlikely that was. Josh, like everyone else who could be spared from the active duty of keeping the ship on course, would be searching for the escaped prisoner.

When they reached the cabin, Prue spoke softly again.

'My maid will be here. Don't worry – she won't give you away. But I think I should go in first and warn her.'

The young man nodded. Prue knocked on the cabin door, called in a low voice, 'Jane! Let me in, please.'

In a moment they heard the scratch of the key turning in the lock, and Jane, throwing open the door, drew Prue inside.

'Oh, Mistress Prue, thank goodness you're here at last. I've been right worried about you!' Then she looked sharply over Prue's shoulder, seeing the young man behind her. 'Who's this?'

'I don't know his name,' Prue realised.

'Myles Whiteside,' the young man replied, bowing. 'Captain of the ship Freedom.'

'Well, then, Captain Whiteside,' Prue said tartly, 'don't you think we should all go into the cabin out of sight of the crewmen who are no doubt still searching for you?' And she bundled him into the cabin, pushing Jane gently back at the same time to allow them all room.

'Captain Whiteside was taken prisoner when his ship was captured,' she explained to Jane. 'We saw him on the deck that time, you remember? So now he's managed to escape, and he needs somewhere to hide until we can decide what he should do next.'

'But suppose someone wants to come in?' Jane asked faintly.

'No one is likely to come tonight,' Prue said. 'They'll expect us to be sleeping by now. We'll lock the door, of course.'

'Well...' Jane muttered, 'I don't know. Mr Tompkins said he'd call back to let me know he was safe when they'd finished searching.'

Prue looked at her sharply. She'd already suspected that there was something growing between Jane and the mate, but it couldn't be helped right now.

'You'll just have to pretend to be asleep if he knocks, Jane,' she said firmly.

Jane looked mutinous. 'He'll think I'm so rude!' she said. Then her face brightened. 'I know, Mistress Prue,' she said. 'I'll just open the door wide enough to slip out and speak to him, and pull it shut after me. I'll tell him he can't go in because you're asleep and I don't want you woken up.'

Prue looked, and felt, doubtful.

'Please, Miss Prue!' Jane urged. 'That way, he won't be so suspicious. I told him I wouldn't go to sleep until I heard he was all right. If he finds me supposed to be sleeping, he'll start wondering why.'

'I think Mistress Jane is right,' Captain Whiteside interposed firmly. 'It cuts down the risk. And you could ask your friend, Mistress, to find out if the search is over and the crewmen gone back to their bunks. Then, much later, when we're sure all is quiet, I'll slip out again and go over the side.'

'But you'll drown!' Prue said faintly.

'Not me!' Myles Whiteside said cheerfully. 'My plan is to swim back to the Freedom, *retake her when I've released my men who are prisoners aboard her, and sail her to safety.'*

It seemed so simple when he put it like that, but Prue wondered. There were clearly a lot of possible, even likely, hitches in the simple proposal. Nevertheless.

'In that case, Captain Whiteside,' she said coolly, 'in return for the help we're giving you, you must take Jane and me with you.'

Captain Whiteside looked nonplussed. 'Indeed, Mistress, I would be glad to help you in return in any way possible, but you must see that your idea is impossible. Three of us going over the side are much more likely to be noticed. And can you swim?'

'Certainly I can swim,' Prue retorted angrily. 'And so can Jane, equally well.'

'Better!' Jane said softly, with a wicked grin.

'We're still more likely to be noticed,' said Captain Whiteside obstinately. 'And – er – it would be necessary, as I plan to do myself, to strip off most of my clothes and carry them in a bundle tied on my head. You ladies could hardly do that!'

'If it's a choice,' Prue said soberly, ' between taking off some clothes and remaining captive on this ship, I'll strip as much as necessary. Jane, too, I imagine.'

'Yes, indeed, Mistress Prue,' Jane agreed.

'You're captives?' Captain Myles asked in amazement. 'I didn't realise that!'

'You might say that we were rescued,' Prue told him fairly. 'We were in an open boat. Our ship had been wrecked in the storm. Captain Nick picked us up. But since he can't safely put us ashore at any normal port, he proposes to take us with him to his island, and, I suppose, keep us there. But I won't have it! I intend, like you, to escape!'

'Well said, Mistress Prue!' exclaimed Myles. 'I'll help you as much as I can.'

'So you'll take us with you to the Freedom? *' pressed Prue.*

'Well – yes, all right, I suppose I can't very well leave you behind, now that I know your circumstances,' admitted Myles. 'But we won't attempt to leave for some time yet. We need to be sure the ship has settled down.'

'And that's where I can help!' Jane put in. 'Josh Tompkins will tell me all about it when he comes.'

'You're right, Jane,' Prue agreed. 'So I suggest we rest quietly until then. We don't want him to hear voices from the cabin, when I'm supposed to be asleep, and you aren't even supposed to be here, Myles!' She smiled mischievously at the young Captain, who grinned in return.

They sat quietly, almost dozing, for some time. And were woken by a tapping on the door.

'Mistress Jane!' whispered a voice. 'Are you there?'

'It's Josh!' Jane whispered unnecessarily. She moved softly over to the door, opened it a crack, and slipped through, pulling it shut behind her. Prue could hear a scuffling noise outside, Jane giggling, muffled voices, and then the unmistakable sound of a kiss. It was some time before the cabin door opened again, just widely enough for Jane to slip through. Her soft, dreamy eyes and her blushing cheeks told their own story, even without the evidence of the sounds Prue had heard.

'Josh says the hunt's over for tonight, Mistress Prue,' Jane said. 'They think Captain Whiteside's already gone overboard, since they've searched everywhere possible and haven't found him. They didn't think of your cabin, Mistress Prue!'

'You didn't say that to your friend?' the young Captain asked sharply.

'No, of course not!' Jane was highly indignant. 'What, and give Miss Prue away? As if I would!'

'No, I know you wouldn't, dear Jane,' Prue said soothingly. 'Captain Whiteside doesn't know you as well as I do.'

'But, Mistress Prue, are you really planning to go overboard and swim back to the Freedom?' Jane asked. 'There'll be guards there, you know – Josh was talking about it just now. He said Captain Whiteside won't have nowhere to go, if he's gone overboard, *because they'll be looking out for him on the* Freedom *and they'll just capture him again if he tried to get on board there.'*

'They may try,' Captain Myles said grimly. 'That's not to say they'll succeed.'

'Jane, would you rather stay here?' Prue asked suddenly. 'You'll be safe enough, I know. And maybe you'd rather not leave Mr Tompkins?'

Jane's face crumpled. 'Oh, Mistress Prue, I don't want to leave him, you're right – but I won't let you go off without me to look after you. How could you think I would? I'll see Josh Tompkins again when this is all over. I've been talking to him about giving up this business of being a pirate, and settling down to a decent job on shore, and he's thinking about it, he says.'

Prue didn't know what to say. Instead, she hugged Jane warmly. 'Thank you, dear Jane,' she said. 'I'm sure it will all work out right.'

It occurred to her, as she thought about Jane's reluctance to leave the pirate mate, that she herself had a strong reluctance to leave the pirate captain. Even to go with Myles Whiteside to help him escape, and to escape herself.

'Well, if that's settled, then,' Myles said briskly, 'I suggest that we give your Mr Tompkins time to settle down and sleep, and then get moving.'

Chapter Thirteen

Something jerked Christie back to the present, and with annoyance she realised that it was her mobile ringing. Not Aine again, she sincerely hoped, setting down her Kindle and reaching across to where the phone was charging.

But when she glanced at the caller I D, she realised with unexpected pleasure that it was Steve Armstrong. She remembered that they had ex-changed phone numbers before parting after their lunch together at the Purple Cat.

'Hi, Steve,' she said.

'Christie, have you eaten yet?'

'Just a snack some time ago,' Christie said casually. It had been quite a substantial sandwich, actually, but so what?

'Well then, do you fancy coming out for a meal with me? I wanted to ring you earlier, but I didn't know for sure I could get tonight off.'

'That'd be nice, Steve,' Christie said, trying to sound pleased with-out seemed wildly excited and enthusiastic. 'But will we get in anywhere on a Saturday night.'

She heard Steve laugh. 'Don't worry about that. I booked a table a couple of days ago, before I knew I'd be working today, and I didn't cancel it, just on the off chance. So you'll come, then? Great! I'll pick you up in ten minutes or so.' He had rung off before Christie had time to protest.

Ten minutes? Steve clearly didn't know much about women. How could she possibly be ready in time?

Nevertheless, by dint of rushing frantically, ready she was, and when he rang the bell maybe twelve minutes later she had brushed her hair so that it fell easily into the new style Hannah's cut had given her, repaired her makeup sufficiently, and slipped into the more attractive of the new tops she'd bought with Tina last week. She though she looked okay, and from Steve's expression he obviously thought so, too.

Steve had parked his car, a downbeat dark blue Fiesta, just outside Christie's house. In her quiet cul-de-sac there were no parking restrictions.

He clicked to unlock, then held the front passenger door open for her, and she hopped in.

'I booked for a nice Mexican restaurant in the Victoria Centre,' Steve said, as he started the engine. 'I think you'll like it. If you absolutely hate Mexican food, there are some milder options on the menu. And it means we can park in the centre's underground car park and not have to drive round for ages trying to find a space somewhere – pretty hard on a Saturday night.'

'Wow, you think of everything, Steve,' Christie said teasingly.

'Superman, that's me.' Steve grinned at her, then turned his attention back to the car as they pulled out onto the main road.

They hadn't much difficulty finding a space in the huge underground car park beneath Victoria Square, which had been built not many years ago right in the middle of Belfast, off Victoria Street and Ann Street. Zooming up in the lift they walked over a bridge and along a mall crowded with every variety of eating place, and were presently seated at a pleasant table in one corner of the Mexican restaurant, with enough space around them for some degree of privacy.

A waiter offered them menus, and asked if they would like something to drink.

'Christie?' Steve asked. 'White wine? Or would you like to try something different? They do an amazing range of cocktails.'

Glancing down the cocktail list, Christie was interested to see one which, it seemed, included Turkish Delight among its ingredients.

'I'd love to try that one!' she exclaimed, pointing it out on the menu.

'And a Guinness for me,' Steve added.

While they waited for their drinks they read the food menu, and Christie seeing that they had chicken enchiladas, made a quick decision in their favour.

'I'll go for the beef nachos,' Steve said.

The cocktail arrived. 'I'll bring you your Guinness as soon as it's settled, sir,' the waiter told Steve, who nodded, unsurprised.

'Don't wait for me,' he said to Christie. 'Try yours and see what you think of it.'

The cocktail was all that Christie had hoped for. Attractively presented in the right shape of cocktail glass, its gleaming ruby colour absorbing the light from the candle on their table, it tasted as good as it looked, with a distinct flavour of Turkish Delight which charmed Christie. She sipped enthusiastically, and found, to her surprise, that her head was beginning to swim a little. Used to white wine, which had little effect on her unless she went above her usual one or two glasses, she hadn't allowed for the cocktail's strength.

However, it was quite a special occasion, and she was enjoying it too much to dream of stopping. The effect seemed to be to make her a lot more talkative than usual. Presently, to her further surprise, she found that she had started to tell Steve Armstrong about Aine and Tommy's problems. True, she'd considered the possibility, but hadn't been convinced that it was a good idea. After all, Steve might be some sort of undercover policeman. She didn't want to give Tommy away to the police. Possibly Steve would see it as his duty to give Tommy grief.

She stopped in mid flow.

'I probably shouldn't be telling you all this,' she said.

'I won't pass it on,' Steve promised, drinking the first mouthful from his Guinness, which had just arrived, beautifully settled now with its creamy head smooth and its dark depths free from haze. 'But maybe this isn't the most private setting for something which sounds confidential.'

The arrival of the waiter with their food just then, reinforcing his words, made Christie giggle. 'I'd like another of those,' she said recklessly. 'That first one was lovely.'

'Well, if you're sure,' said Steve doubtfully.

'Yes, please.'

She began on the first enchilada, and Steve dug into the beef nachos.

'You'd better tell me the rest of your story afterwards,' he said. 'I hope you're enjoying the meal? It'll soak up some of the alcohol, and just as well, too, girl!'

Christie, for a moment, wondered if she should feel indignant, but she was too relaxed to bother. And maybe there was something in what he said. She sipped her second cocktail, which had just arrived, rather more cautiously than the first, eating industriously between sips, but found herself getting still more giggly and relaxed.

Steve seemed amused. 'I see I shouldn't have encouraged you to try that first one,' he said. 'Still, never mind, I'll look after you.'

'So, what happened to the fly fishing expedition?' Christie suddenly remembered.

'Oh, I found out I'd be working today, which put the blinkers on it. I only found out I was free tonight at the last moment, like I said.'

'I wonder how you can stick a job where you have so little free time?' Christie said.

'Oh, it's interesting – exciting, even. I enjoy it, most days. Better than a bank counter or an office desk from nine to five. I don't think I could stand that.'

'Yes, I'd hate that, too,' Christie agreed. 'I love the library – working with books. But isn't your job dangerous?'

'It can be,' Steve agreed. 'Just sometimes.' He smiled at her.

'Steve Armstrong, daredevil!' Christie said. 'Do you have to change in a telephone box? Bit difficult, now there are so few around.'

'Yes, that's actually a major problem,' Steve agreed solemnly. Then they both burst into giggles, not just Christie. She finished her last enchilada, and found that she was enjoying herself more than she had done for a long time. Steve was so much better as a companion than, for instance, Maurice, or any of Tina's friends – or even Tina herself. She lifted her glass, sipped, and noticed with surprise that that was the last of it.

'Don't say you'd like another one, because you aren't having it,' Steve told her. 'Now, how about a pudding and some coffee?'

Christie, running her eye down the dessert menu produced by the waiter when he had removed their plates, decided enthusiastically to have an Eton Mess, and Steve put in the order, with profiteroles with salted caramel for himself.

They sat back to wait for them. It was just at the moment when they arrived on the table that Steve's phone went.

He hesitated for only a few seconds, then pressed the green button and said, 'Yes.'

Christie, automatically eating her Eton Mess, and finding it hard to enjoy it as much as she had expected, watched as his face grew grim. Finally he finished the call, folded the phone shut and looked at her.

'I can't tell you how sorry I am, Christie,' he said. 'But that was an urgent call from my work. I'll have to go.'

'Oh.' Christie had nothing to say.

'Look, finish your dessert. Then I'll drop you home.'

Christie picked up her spoon. Then she set it down again. 'I'm not really hungry now. I mustn't keep you. Clearly your call was urgent.'

'Well, it was.' Steve hesitated. Then he stood up, went to the bar, and asked for the bill. When he had paid he turned to go back to the table, but found Christie waiting just behind him.

'Come on,' she said. They walked silently back to the lift, then over to the car. The evening had fallen in ruins about them.

At Christie's house, Steve got out with her and waited politely until she had unlocked the door.

'I'll ring you as soon as I'm free,' he muttered. 'That is – if you want me to? Maybe you never want to hear from me again, now you know what my life can be like?'

Christie unexpectedly laughed. 'Yes, please do ring me,' she said. 'And don't worry. Okay, I'm disappointed – but you did tell me what your job was like.' She leaned over and kissed his check. Not how she'd expected the evening to end, but maybe just as well, considering the effect the two strong cocktails had had on her.

'Thanks,' said Steve briefly. Then, when Christie had gone into the house, he hurried back to his car, and as she pulled the door shut behind her she saw him dive in and drive off hurriedly.

Oh, well, she said philosophically to herself, *at least I can get back now to The Pirate.*

She made her way up to bed and presently was settled back comfortably against the pillows, her Kindle propped against her knees, ready to start reading.

Chapter Fourteen

1794

*They waited in silence for what **seemed** a long time. Eventually Myles said, 'Mistress Prudence, if you and Mistress Jane are determined on this course of action, you should take off what clothes you wish, make bundles of them, and find a means of binding them to your heads. I will do the same, but, out of courtesy, I'll go outside into the passageway and allow you some privacy.'*

'But, Myles,' Prue exclaimed, 'suppose someone comes along!'

'Do you think I can't deal with one person, Mistress?'

'Well, it might be more than one.'

'Unlikely, Mistress Prue. This is a reasonably private area of the ship, only used by the people who sleep in these cabins and by crew serving them, I would suppose.'

'Yes – I suppose you're right.' Prue paused. 'Why don't you call me by my name, Myles? I'm using yours.'

'If you don't object, then I'd be very happy to do that, Prue,' the young captain smiled. Prue found herself smiling back. There was no doubt that Myles Whiteside was a very attractive man, and a brave one, which appealed to Prue even more.

'So, I'll see you outside as soon as you are both ready.' He pushed open the cabin door and slipped out.

'Mistress Prue, I don't think you should encourage him to call you by your name,' Jane said as soon as the door had closed behind him.

'Why ever not, Jane?'

'Well, it might give him ideas – especially as he's going to see you in your altogethers – your chemise and pantaloons!' Jane burst out.

'He's going to see you, too, Jane,' Prue said coolly. 'And he already calls you by name.' She was stripping off her dressing gown as she spoke.

'That's different, Mistress Prue,' Jane objected, following her mistress's example. 'You know it is. I'm a servant.'

'Jane, you're the best friend I have – much more than a servant. I don't want to hear you talk like that again.'

'But you don't invite me to call you by name, Mistress Prue,' Jane said shrewdly. 'So you do recognise the difference'.

Prue hesitated as she lifted her nightgown over her head. 'Jane, that's only because we've known each other so long and I'm so used to you calling me Mistress that I didn't even think of it. But I've been foolish. Do, please, just call me Prue from now on.'

'Mistress Prue!' Jane exclaimed in horror. 'I couldn't even think of it!'

Prue shrugged as she folded dressing gown and night dress into a neat bundle. 'That's your choice, Jane. But remember that I'd like it if you did.'

They stood up, facing each other in their pretty but concealing underclothes. 'Now, what can we use to tie these bundles to our heads?'

Jane looked round. It was hard to find something that would work. Neither girl had any personal belongings other than the nightclothes and underclothes they had been wearing at the time of their escape from the Golden Dawn.

Finally they found some cord which had held back the curtains round the bunks where they had slept, and Prue pulled it down with a ruthless hand.

'This should do,' she said with some satisfaction. 'I think it would be best if we each tied on the bundle for the other. We would see what we were doing more easily, that way.'

They were just about ready when a light knock on the cabin door was followed by Captain Whiteside's voice. 'Are you ready yet, ladies?'

'Yes,' whispered Prue, equally softly, as she finished the last knot securing Jane's bundle.

Chapter 14

They opened the cabin door and slipped quietly out.

Myles Whiteside, standing in his underlinen with a bundle strapped to his head by his belt, turned at once and began to lead them along the passage towards the companionway which would take them to the upper deck. Prue was pleased that he had refrained from looking at them for more than the moment it took him to be sure they were ready.

They tiptoed silently and cautiously along the gangway. They were almost at the ladder to the upper deck when they heard the sound of footsteps, still high up, carefully descending it. Myles Whiteside swung round and hissed, 'Stop! Someone's coming! Go back, right now!'

Instinctively, Prue turned, grabbed Jane, following just behind her, by the arm, and hustled her back along the way that led to their cabin. She glanced round over her shoulder only for a second to check if Myles was coming behind them, and saw with relief that he was. It took a very short time to reach the cabin, swing open the door, and dive inside. Prue, expecting Myles immediately afterwards, was horrified to realise that the scuffling noise further back along the gangway was Myles and the man they had heard descending the ladder. Myles must have been caught before he could reach the cabin's shelter.

She pulled the door almost shut. It would not help Myles if whoever it was discovered that they had been with him. But she left it open enough to be able to hear what was going on.

The initial grunts and gasps turned in a short while into words.

'You villain!'

'Let me go!'

'Never! Not now I've got you again!'

It was the second voice, Prue realised, that belonged to Myles Whiteside. The other voice, she knew, was familiar enough to be recognisable. She should know it.

'You're coming along with me,' that other voice said. 'Clearly, the cabin I gave you, since you are a captain, hasn't been secure enough to hold you. This time, it'll be the brig. I don't think you'll

get out of it so easily. I'm taking you to my island headquarters, my fine fellow, so be reconciled to that.'

Prue knew, as she felt she should have known all along, that the voice belonged to Captain Nick Hawkeye.

She could hear the retreating figures. What hope had Myles Whiteside, or indeed she or Jane, of escaping now? With a sigh of despair, she pulled the door shut. There was no point in keeping it open in the hope that Myles might yet escape into the cabin.

'Well, Jane,' she said, 'so much for our hope of escape. We might as well get back into our nightdresses.'

'Don't you think we could swim back to the Freedom *ourselves, Mistress Prue?' Jane suggested hopefully, but Prue shook her head.*

'No, I don't, Jane,' she said. 'I daresay we could get there, but what then? We were relying on Captain Whiteside to deal with the men on guard. I don't think you or I could do that.'

And Jane reluctantly agreed with her.

They untied each other's bundles, unfolded the neat parcels, and got back into their nightdresses as Prue had suggested. As they were climbing into their bunks, they heard a light tapping on the cabin door.

Prue put a finger to her lips, instructing caution to Jane.

The tapping stopped.

'Mistress Prue?'

It was Captain Nick Hawkeye. Prue knew his voice at once, this time.

She bent close to Jane's ear, and very quietly gave her in-structions.

'Yes?' Jane said in a voice which she managed to make sound half asleep.

'Mistress Prue?'

'No. It's Jane Brigham. Who are you? What do you want?'

'It's Captain Hawkeye. I just wanted to be sure that you and Mistress Prue were safe. The escaped prisoner has been captured not far from your cabin.'

Chapter 14

'We're safe. Mistress Prue is asleep, has been for some time. I don't want her woken up, do you understand?'

There came a soft laugh. 'You look after your mistress admirably, Mistress Brigham. Well, I don't want to wake her either, if she's safely sleeping. Tell her I'll call with her tomorrow.'

Then they heard the sound of footsteps quietly moving away.

Suddenly Prue changed her mind. Springing out of the bunk, she seized the dressing gown she had discarded, pulled it on, and threw open the cabin door, to Jane's horror.

'Captain Nick!' she called to his retreating back. 'Did you want to see me?'

'Mistress Prue!' he exclaimed, turning at the first sound of her voice. 'I didn't mean to wake you.'

'That's all right,' Prue assured him. For some reason, she felt, all at once, a great happiness flooding through her. He had sounded so upset when Jane had told him she was sleeping. And it was so kind of him to want to make sure she was safe. It didn't seem right to turn him away so abruptly.

'We were interrupted in our talk on the upper deck earlier, Mistress Prue,' Captain Nick said, smiling into Prue's eyes. 'I had hoped you might like to resume it – but if you'd rather sleep –'

'By no means, sir,' Prue answered, laughing up at him. 'I would love to resume our walk and talk.'

'Then, Mistress Prue,' the captain said, bowing courteously and offering her his arm, 'may I have the pleasure of escorting you?'

'Certainly you may, sir,' Prue said demurely. She took his arm, ignoring Jane's distressed gasps, and he led her along the passage to the companionway.

All was quiet now. No crewmen rushing about, no voices calling. Above, the moon shone brightly down, not quite full yet but almost there. The stars were dimmed by her beauty.

'A waxing gibbous moon,' said Captain Nick thoughtfully, when they had reached the top of the ladder. 'In a few more days, it will be full. I think that's the most exciting time, when the promise is not quite fulfilled, but we can see it coming.'

Prue kept her eyes cast downwards. She knew the captain meant something more by his words than simply a comment on the beauty of nature.

'Mistress Prue,' he said presently, taking her hand and leading her over to the ship's rail, where they stood, side by side, watching the repeated shock of the waves against the sides. 'Mistress Prue, there is so much I need to say to you – to tell you, to explain. And yet I can't, until – will you trust me?' he broke off abruptly, turning towards her and drawing her round to face him.

Something in Prue told her that trusting him would be safe. That he was speaking the truth, and that if she could bring herself to wait, he would be able to set all her doubts at rest.

But something else told her to beware. This man was a pirate – a cruel, wicked man, and yet one whose personal charm must have made him attractive to a score of women, whom, no doubt, he abandoned when he no longer wanted them. Was she to be one more on his list? No, a thousand times no!

Prue closed her heart to him, and said coldly, 'I know of no reason why I should trust you, Captain Hawkeye, when I have seen you with my own eyes capture a free ship and take its captain and crew prisoner. What further cruelty do you intend to inflict on that harmless young sailor?'

'Harmless!' Captain Hawkeye said sharply. 'Why should you think him harmless? Believe me, Mistress Prue, I had good reason to capture that ship!'

'No doubt it was well laden with gold!' Prue answered scornfully.

'Gold. Yes, it carries a full load of gold, Mistress. And you believe I captured that ship purely in order to take the gold for my own personal gain? To steal it, in fact?'

'Why, captain, what else am I to believe?'

'Not that, Mistress Prue – not that.' Captain Hawkeye sounded devastated. He turned away, his head bowed, and Prue suddenly felt that it was she who was cruel, that she had judged him unfairly and in doing so had wounded him to the heart. She heard him murmur to himself, 'Surely I can at least explain that to her? But no – it's all of a piece, all part of the same story. If I start to tell her some, where can I stop? And I've sworn, given my word –'

Prue could barely hear his words, but was sure she had picked them up correctly.

What did he mean? What explanation could there be?

None.

It was only a moment before Captain Hawkeye pulled himself together. Standing straight again, he turned back towards her and said, 'Come, Mistress Prue. This discussion is going nowhere. You must be tired and longing to sleep. I will take you back to your cabin.'

Prue agreed meekly. It seemed a very short time until the captain, bowing in his ceremonious way, left her at her open cabin door and went away, leaving her to field Jane's anxious questions and to tumble swiftly into bed.

But not into sleep. Sleep was a long time coming to Prue that night. Her thoughts ran through a maze, and came to no clear way of escape. She was lost and troubled. What was Nick keeping secret? Should she have trusted him or not? And what of Myles Whiteside?

Sleep came at last, but Prue had still not found either the centre of the maze or the way out.

Hel's Heroes 2: Christie & The Pirate

Chapter Fifteen

The Present

Christie's Kindle slipped from her hand, and she woke up just enough to set it over and to lie down comfortably. Then she was asleep again.

When she woke next morning, the sun was beaming cheerfully at her through the curtains, and she sat up happily. True, last night hadn't worked out quite as she'd hoped it would, but still, she'd had a really nice time with Steve Armstrong. She just hoped she was right to trust him. But she had no real doubts about that.

It was Sunday morning, and Christie decided that she would go to church. She didn't always go, but today she felt she had a lot to be grateful for and it would be good to go along and express her gratitude.

She'd been taken along to the nearest church, St Peter's, as a child, and since her parents' deaths she had continued to go, even if less regularly. There was something about the peaceful atmosphere of the old building that soothed and comforted her, and she was fond of many of the old people, mostly friends of her parents, who made up a lot of the congregation. She also liked the new young minister, who'd come visiting a few times. Niall McBride – 'Call me Niall' – was bright and enthusiastic, full of plans for bringing in the younger generation, and had already made quite a difference to the average age of the members.

She pulled on her new tight jeans, knowing that Niall wouldn't mind, and that her parents' friends would be only too glad to see her there whatever she was wearing.

She slipped into a pew halfway down beside Mrs Kilpatrick, a plump grey-haired woman, who offered her a peppermint to suck and smiled conspiratorially at Christie as she did so. Christie took it politely.

'Keep it for the sermon,' whispered Mrs Kilpatrick. 'You don't want a sweetie in your mouth when you're trying to sing the hymns, do you?'

Niall's sermon was short and interesting that morning, as, Christie pondered, it usually was. It was about honesty and trust. As she listened, Christie knew that it was exactly what she needed to hear.

'"Be wise as serpents and harmless as doves,"' quoted Niall. 'In other words, don't trust without reason. But if you know someone really well, then it's right to trust them. However, if you realise you can't trust someone, you can still show them the love we as Christians are meant to offer to everyone. "Love your neighbour as yourselves" – many people ignore this, nowadays. But it still matters.'

She had decided to trust Steve for no real reason, Christie knew, except that he had a disarming grin. But then, a con man would be charming, wouldn't he? She'd seen him with two other armed men, armed himself, running from the scene of a crime. Why had she decided to trust his story – no, not even a story, just a sort of hint, that he was an undercover cop? He hadn't even shown her any ID, explaining that he couldn't, that he was sworn to secrecy. What sort of story was that to believe?

Then there was Helen's – or Serendipity's – warning, not to get involved with someone like her hero Captain Nick Hawkeye. Christie shuddered as she remembered the passage she'd read last night, about Prue's growing involvement with the pirate captain, in spite of what she'd seen him do. Prue didn't know whether to trust him or not, and Serendipity had hinted that it wouldn't have been wise of her to do so in real life.

The service drew to a close, and Niall McBride led the congregation in prayer. Christie found herself praying her own private prayer. 'Oh, Lord, give me wisdom. Help me to know if I can trust this man or not.'

It was too beautiful a spring day to go home. Christie wandered down to the river Lagan and leaned over the Ormeau Bridge, peering into its depths. A flight of swallows flew erratically under the bridge, trying to catch the flies which swarmed around them, their normal food. Although one swallow doesn't make a summer, there were enough of them here to make twenty summers, Christie reckoned. A swift flew under the bridge after them, his navy blue chest gleaming in the sun, darting erratically back and forth.

Christie felt relaxed, still happy. Then a thought struck her. She had talked to Steve Armstrong last night about Aine and Tommy and their problems. How much had she told him? Had she added to their danger?

She knew she had stopped herself early in the story, remembering that Steve was an undercover cop. (Maybe! If he wasn't just a plain crook!) She just hoped everything was okay.

Her mobile rang. Steve? No. It was Aine.

'Christie?'

'Yes.'

'Look, Christie, I'm really sorry to land on you again, but I need your advice. I thought Tommy was safe enough here, because even if anyone knew he was my boyfriend, they didn't know where I lived. Thanks to you, helping me shake that guy who followed me from the pawnshop. But Tommy says they probably found out all about him, and that would include me and where I live, before they gave him the necklace.

'I told him what you said about them being amateurs or they would have known where to fence their stuff within dragging him in and sending him to pawnbrokers, but he just said he knew they were the real thing, no doubt about it, and maybe they just wanted to get him involved, so's they'd have more of a stick to threaten him with and then they could use him for other stuff.'

Aine paused, breathless, and Christie replied slowly, 'Right, he could have a point. He knows more about these guys than we do. They sounded serious enough, real thugs, when they were at the door of Tommy's flat.'

'Well, he believes it, anyway. And, Christie, I don't know what to do – he's gone walkabout! Had his breakfast, then grabbed the necklace and rushed out. I've no idea where he is or where he's going!' Christie could hear her breaking down into sobs at the other end of the phone.

There was nothing else Christie could do.

'Okay, Aine, don't panic. I'll be there as soon as it takes, right?'

She clicked the phone off, folded it, and stuck it in her jeans pocket.

Then she moved quickly to the nearest bus stop, rode the bus until she was near to Aine's flat, got off, and walked down the side street, until she could see the building where Aine lived. Pulling out her phone, she rang Aine again and said, 'I'm here. Let me in.'

As she reached the door the buzzer sounded, and she pushed it and found that the door opened, as she had hoped it would.

Christie mounted the stairs, and found Aine on the landing at the door to her flat, hands outstretched and words flowing out of her mouth.

'Oh, Christie, what'll I do? I'm so frightened! They may have grabbed him by now. How am I to know? He doesn't answer his phone, it seems to be switched off, and I don't know where he is or what he's doing!'

'Whoa, whoa, calm down, sweetheart! Let's go in and sit down and think about it, okay?'

Christie put her arm round Aine's shoulders and led the trembling girl through her open door. She could feel the fear cascading through Aine's body, the belief that her Tommy was in such serious trouble that she might never see him again.

'Aine, stop worrying. We'll sort this out, okay? First of all, what time did Tommy leave?'

'About a quarter past one, I think,' Aine said.

'Good. Not too long ago.' Christie glanced at her watch and saw that it was only a few minutes past two o'clock.

'So, he can't have got into too much trouble in that time,' Christie said coolly. 'Was there anything he said that would give you any sort of clue as to where he was heading?'

'Well –'

'Yes?'

'He did say he was going to have a chat with Reddy, see if he could help.'

'So, who's Reddy, then?'

'Well, he's just a guy – Tommy said he was a mate. I met him one time when we were hanging out at White's Tavern. I don't know much about him.'

'Aine, you know more about him than you're telling me. Do you know where he lives, for instance?'

'Yeah, we went there for a drink one time, after we left the bar. On up the Ormeau Road a bit – I don't know the address, but I could take you to it.'

'Great. If Tommy was looking for him, wouldn't that be the first place he'd go to? Especially early on a Sunday afternoon? Let's head!'

Aine, whether she was really happy about the idea or not, wasn't given much chance to resist. Christie whirled her energetically out of the door and down the stairs, and a few minutes later they were sitting together on a bus which would take them up the Ormeau Road.

'Make sure you tell me where we need to get off,' Christie said, and it wasn't long after that Aine plucked at her sleeve and said, 'Next stop, Christie.'

Reddy's flat wasn't far. Aine seemed clear about the way, and Christie allowed her to lead. But she was wondering a little about the wisdom of plunging straight in, as Aine obviously intended to do. Time to ask more questions. They reached the old house and Aine pressed the bell.

'Aine,' Christie asked, putting one hand on Aine's arm, 'do you think this guy Reddy is one of the thugs or a victim like Tommy?'

'Oh, Christie, I don't know. But he didn't seem like a thug when I met him. A bit helpless and pathetic. I wondered what Tommy saw in him, as a matter of fact.'

'Okay.' Christie was relieved. 'So, we'll go up – if he lets us, that is.' For there had been no response to Aine's ring, so far.

'Try again,' Christie suggested, and Aine rang again, but there was no answer.

'Right, try one of the other flats,' Christie said, and as Aine gave her a look full of reluctance, she took matters into her own hands and pressed the bell for the flat below Reddy's.

'Yes?' A woman's voice answered them.

'Sorry, but we're looking for Reddy. Do you know if he's in? Or where he is?'

'Reddy went out an hour ago. Probably to White's Tavern.' The voice clicked off again at once.

Christie wasn't surprised. She herself wouldn't have chatted to strangers ringing her bell, especially if, as seemed likely in this woman's case, she was at home alone.

'So, Aine, it looks like White's Tavern. I suppose it would be open on Sunday afternoon?'

'Oh, yeah.' Aine sounded confident. 'They do Sunday lunches and then stay open after that. Music in the evening.'

'And would Tommy know that? Would he be likely to meet Reddy there?'

'Well, it was Sunday afternoon when he took me there and introduced me to Reddy.'

'Fair enough. Let's head.'

Another bus ride as far as the City Hall, then a short walk down Donegall Avenue and off to the right, and they were approaching White's Tavern.

'Christie, supposing he's not here?' Aine said. 'What do we do then?'

'We think of somewhere else to try,' Christie said determinedly. 'Sure, he must be somewhere.'

'I suppose.'

They walked on through the not quite empty streets. There were people around, but not so many that it was hard to make progress. Suddenly Aine stopped dead and grabbed Christie by the sleeve.

'Christie!'

Christie, almost tripping from the abrupt halt and feeling annoyed because of it, said sharply, 'What?'

'Look!' Aine, quivering with fear, was pointing at someone almost hidden by a small crowd of people just in front of them.

'What at?'

'That man!'

Christie wasn't sure which man she meant. 'Who, Aine?'

'The man behind the ginger guy! Don't you see him? It's the one who followed me from the pawnbroker's – the one you helped me get rid of on the bus! He must be looking for Tommy, too!'

Christie stared at Aine, then looked in the direction she was pointing, and tried to see the man she meant.

Then Christie in turn stopped dead and found herself shaking with something like fear.

The man Aine was pointing at was Steve Armstrong.

Hel's Heroes 2: Christie & The Pirate

Chapter Sixteen

It took Christie only a minute to recover, externally at least.

'Okay, Aine, the last thing you want to do is lead him to Tommy. Let's start walking.' They turned back and Christie steered them towards the buses at the City Hall. 'Do you want to try him on his phone again, in case he's switched it back on? Then at least you could warn him to get out.'

'Right.' Aine took out her phone, but her attempts to ring Tommy as they walked back along Donegall Place were a dismal failure.

'So, the best thing for us to do is to get offside, keep right away from Tommy right now,' Christie said. 'I'm going home, Aine, and I think you should, too. If you go back to your apartment, then Tommy'll be able to find you easily. If I were you I'd keep trying his phone in case he switches it back on, right?'

'Sure, he might do.' Aine brightened.

'Let me know of any developments,' Christie said. They separated and Christie went to her bus stop.

Arriving home, what seemed like another lifetime since she had left it, she opened a tin of lentil and carrot soup, poured it into a bowl, and stuck it into the microwave.

While it heated, she went upstairs to fetch her Kindle.

Then she sat at the kitchen table, propped the Kindle on the table in front of her, and ate her soup, while thankfully relaxing into the next chapter of *The Pirate*. Aine would probably ring sooner or later. She hoped it would be later.

1794

The morning came at last. Prue, still tired, feeling she had hardly slept at all, was still in bed when Josh Tompkins knocked on the cabin door, bringing their breakfast.

'Just a moment, Mister Tompkins,' Jane called, before turning to her mistress and seeing that her eyes were open.

'You'd better get up, Miss Prue,' Jane warned her. 'Josh isn't to know how little sleep we've had.'

And Jane didn't know, Prue thought, that she'd had even less than the other girl expected. In spite of all her tossing and turning, she'd managed not to wake Jane, as the gentle snores from the other bunk had borne witness.

Hurrying out of bed, she pulled on her dressing gown and quickly rinsed her hands and face. Further washing could come later. 'All right, Jane, let him in,' was all she said.

Josh's smiling morning face followed the tray into the cabin as he pushed open the door in response to Jane's invitation. Prue was surprised to see him so happy after the escape of the prisoner last night. But after all, Captain Whiteside had been recaptured, so perhaps Josh felt was all was well that ended well.

Then she realised, seeing his eyes on Jane's face, and remembering their conversation, if it could be called that, outside the cabin on the previous evening, that his pleasure had another cause.

'Good morning, ladies,' he beamed at them. 'Won't you sit down, and I'll set out your breakfast?'

'You seem very happy this morning, Mister Tompkins,' Prue remarked, seating herself beside Jane at the low table, and taking a slice of bread.

Josh blushed, then recovered himself.

'And who wouldn't be, on such a bright, sunny morning?' Josh Tompkins asked swiftly. 'What's more, mistress, we've all got another reason to rejoice today. There's land in sight – our own island, not too far ahead. We should reach it in a few more hours if the wind keeps fresh enough.'

Prue's heart sank. She feared that once they reached the island, their chances of escape would be much slighter than on the open sea.

'You should both come up on deck and have a look,' Josh went on. Then, noticing that Prue was showing no interest, he added persuasively, 'Or, at least, you might like to come, Mistress Brigham, if you, Mistress Prue, prefer to wait until the ship is closer to land?'

Prue could see that this arrangement would suit both Josh and also Jane perfectly.

'That sounds very interesting, Mister Tompkins,' Jane said demurely. 'I'd love to come.'

'I'll come back for the breakfast tray when you've had time to finish, then,' Josh said. 'And, Mistress Prue, Captain Hawkeye asked me to tell you that he would be happy to escort you to the best viewpoint a little later, when he has organised the crew for the rest of the day. What shall I tell him?'

Prue felt her face blushing. In spite of her doubts of the previous evening and, indeed, during the night, she knew very well that she would love to go on deck again with the captain.

'You may tell him I'd be grateful for his escort, Mister Tompkins,' she said coolly. 'But you must allow me time to get myself ready for the day, first. I've only just woken up, as it happens.'

'I'll tell the captain to make it a little later, then,' Josh beamed. 'And now I'll leave you ladies to your breakfast.' With a wink at Jane, he went back out.

'Oh, Mistress Prue, isn't it exciting!' Jane exclaimed 'A real pirate island! I suppose it will have parrots and coconut trees and chests of jewels and – oh, I don't know. Aren't you interested in seeing it?'

'I'm more interested in how on earth we can escape from it, Jane,' Prue snapped. 'No doubt you're reluctant to leave Josh, but unless you're happy to set up as a pirate's moll, you'll want to escape, too, I suppose?'

Jane's face fell, and she said in a forlorn voice, 'I didn't think of that, Mistress Prue. You're right, I've let myself get too fond of Josh Tompkins. He doesn't seem like a pirate, somehow. But I know I can't spend my life with him unless he changes his ways. Oh, Miss Prue!' And to Prue's horror, Jane burst into tears.

Prue leant across the table and put her arms round the weeping girl. 'Jane, we'll work it out somehow. Don't cry, dear, don't cry.'

Jane wept in Prue's arms for a little longer, while Prue stroked her hair soothingly. Then she sat up with a determined air, sniffed, and said, 'I'm making a fool of myself. You're right, Miss Prue, we'll work it out somehow. Perhaps' – she brightened at the thought – 'perhaps Josh will escape with us and stop being a pirate.'

Breakfast finished, Jane went over to the fresh basin of water Josh had brought and washed away her tears. Then she straightened her hair, pulled her dressing gown more tidily round her, and prepared to go on deck with Josh when he came back.

Prue waited until they had gone to complete her own washing and tidying, not wanting to be found in the middle of this by Josh when he returned. Then she stripped, washed thoroughly, put her nightdress and dressing gown back on – longing as she did so for something else to change into. Well, it couldn't be helped. It was better to have only her night things to wear than to have been drowned.

She pulled off her nightcap and fussed with her dark hair for a while, then gave up. There again, it would be nice to have the proper implements to improve it – comb, brush, curling tongs, ribbons – but it couldn't be helped.

It seemed no time at all before a knock came on the cabin door, and she heard the familiar voice.

'Mistress Prudence. It's Captain Hawkeye. Mister Tompkins tells me that you are willing to accompany me on a stroll on deck, to see the approach of my island home?'

Prue stood up, gave a last pat to her hair, and pulled her dressing gown straight. Then she opened the door and smiled at Captain Hawkeye.

'Good morning, Captain. Yes, I'd be interested to see this island of yours, even at a distance.'

'I hope you'll see it from much closer quarters soon, Mistress Prue – and love it, as I do.'

'You must tell me all about it, Captain,' Prue said as she followed him along the gangway and up the ladder to the deck.

To her surprise, the captain took her hand and led her to a further companionway, to where the ship's wheel was positioned high above the rest of the ship.

'This is my own particular place, Mistress Prue,' he told her. 'Whether I'm steering or not – and there are many times when I choose to steer, to make sure all goes well – I like to be here, up high, where I can look out and see everything ahead. The only better place is the crow's nest, high above the rigging, and I've been known to climb up there too when it seems necessary – although not as often. Come over here and I'll point out some things to you.'

Gazing out over the blue ocean, calm today, with only the fresh breeze, which was still moving the ship busily along, ruffling its surface with small waves, Prue was amazed to see how close the island was already. The sun poured down healing rays upon her and she luxuriated in its heat as she tried to take in the view of the approaching island coming nearer and nearer to her. It was still too distant for her to make out more than a mass of green, gold and the dark of what must be rocky cliffs.

'Here, Mistress Prue, if you care to look through this you'll be able to see more.' Captain Hawkeye was offering her his telescope, and Prue accepted it with thanks. Suddenly everything loomed so much larger and, it seemed, closer.

She could clearly see golden beaches, high rocky coastlines alongside them, the waving branches of what she knew must be coconut palms. The beauty of it all silenced her for a few minutes as she eagerly turned the telescope right and left, trying to see more.

As she looked, an idea swam into her head. Surely it would be possible to swim to one of those accessible looking beaches, get ashore, and hide until dark? Then – Prue didn't know what came next, but she was still determined to escape in whatever way was possible. If she timed it right, waiting until everyone was busy in the bustle of bringing the ship to land, and if she and Jane managed to slip quietly overboard without attracting attention –? Surely it could be done.

Hope surged in her breast. It was worth trying, at any rate. And once on the island, and free, they might be able to take a suitable boat and row to the nearest land. It couldn't be too far away. These seas were full of islands, she knew.

They might even be able to find Myles Whiteside and carry out the original plan of recapturing the ship Freedom. *That would be a much more realistic way of escaping, Prue admitted to herself.*

Reluctantly she handed the spyglass back to Captain Hawkeye and said politely, 'Thank you for letting me see your beautiful island, Captain. It certainly seems to live up to everything you've said about it. It seems so close, through the spyglass.'

'Don't be misled, Mistress Prue. It's still at least three hours sailing away, most likely four. But soon you will see it for yourself, Mistress Prudence.'

Prue smiled. 'And now, Captain, I think I must go and lie down for a while. The heat of the sun is becoming too much for me.'

The captain showed concern, and at once escorted her back down to the lower deck and to the passageway which led to her cabin.

'Too much hot sun can be dangerous, ma'am,' he said. 'You should certainly rest for a while. Is there anything I can send you?'

'No, no, there's water in the cabin,' Prue assured him. 'A few mouthfuls of that will be all I'll need.' In fact, the lie she had just told Captain Hawkeye was turning out to be true. She was definitely feeling the effects of the sun and would be glad of some water and a short rest.

Taking leave of the captain, she opened the cabin door and went inside. To her relief Jane was there.

Prue collapsed onto the lower bunk. Jane eyed her in concern.

'Are you all right, Mistress Prue?'

'Yes, I'm fine. I'd welcome some water if you would be kind enough to bring me some, Jane.'

She sat sipping the water for a moment or two without speaking. Then she looked up at the anxiously hovering Jane, and a smile crept over her face.

'Jane,' she said, 'listen. I have a plan. We're going swimming after all!'

Chapter Seventeen

The Present

The phone dragged Christie abruptly back to the present day and life in Belfast.

As she had expected, it was Aine.

'Christie? Still no sign of him. And I can't get him on his mobile either. Christie, I can't wait here by myself any longer. Couldn't we go and look for him again? That guy must have gone by now.'

Christie thought about it. Then she said, 'Okay, Aine. Meet me at the Errigle in about twenty minutes, okay?'

'Okay. See you.'

She hadn't told Aine that she knew 'that guy'– that in fact she knew him quite well. Somehow she was reluctant to do so. She still had no idea what the truth was about Steve. The only thing she knew was that every time she started to distrust him, an instinctive confidence that he was honest overcame her doubts.

She had suggested the Errigle as a suitable place between her own house and Aine's flat, which both of them could reach fairly quickly. When she reached the pub Aine was already there, but hadn't, she said, been there more than a few minutes.

'Let's go in and sit down,' Christie said. 'Have you eaten yet?'

'I had a sandwich when I got home, I think,' Aine said vaguely.

'Then you need something more, now,' Christie said firmly. 'You'll feel better when you've eaten something.'

They found a table towards the back. The place wasn't too crowded yet. Later on it would probably be packed. Christie got two menus, and suggested Irish Stew.

'Whatever,' Aine muttered.

'And something to drink. What do you like? I'll have white wine.'

'Okay, cider.'

Christie suddenly wondered if Aine could afford to eat out – she didn't think the girl had a regular job.

'And I'm paying, of course, since it was my idea,' she added firmly, and saw Aine's face brighten up.

'Do you have a job, Aine?' she asked when they had ordered.

'No, I worked at the checkout at Tesco's for a while but Tommy didn't like it when I was out so much, so now I don't.'

'But if you chucked it in, you won't get dole?'

'No. Tommy said he'd take care of the money side.'

'Oh.'

Christie said nothing more, for the drinks had arrived, but she found that Aine's words had put a new idea into her head.

She let Aine take a few mouthfuls of stew before she spoke again.

'Aine, do you think Tommy told you the truth about how he got that necklace?'

Aine's face went red. 'I don't know, Christie. He doesn't always.' She lowered her eyes for a moment, then looked up again at Christie. 'But that doesn't mean I'm not going to help him,' she burst out furiously. 'I love him, okay?'

Christie smiled. 'Of course, pet. I understand that.' She ate industriously at her own stew, and drank her wine, waiting for Aine to recover confidence in her.

'He can't help lying, Christie,' Aine said, eventually. She had almost finished her stew, and the cider was almost gone, by the time she felt ready to speak. 'He was brought up in a Children's Home and never really knew what a family was or what good relationships between people were about.

'Oh, yes, he had a couple of good friends from then, like Reddy, but that was it, and he's seen very little of either of them since he was chucked out of the Home to get a job at sixteen. He never learnt about trusting people or about telling the truth to the people you cared about. I understand that. I can help him, I know. But not by letting him down just when he needs my help most.'

Chapter 17

She glared at Christie, who said soothingly, 'I know, Aine. Don't worry, I'm not asking you to let Tommy down.' She took the last mouthful of her stew, set the spoon down, and finished her drink. Aine was also at the end of her meal.

The waiter reappeared smoothly to ask if they had finished, and if they wanted to order anything more, desserts or coffee or another drink. Christie, checking with a raised eyebrow with Aine, told him that they had had everything they wanted, and asked for the bill. A few minutes later, they were out in the street.

'I think we need to find Tommy, now,' Christie said. 'We didn't want to lead anyone to him earlier, but your guy must have gone long ago. Let's try White's Tavern in case Tommy's still there. If he isn't, we can think of other places. Ring him again, first, right? If you can get him, it would save a lot of trouble.'

But Tommy's phone was still not answering.

Back just outside White's Tavern, they looked carefully around for Steve Armstrong, whom Aine still only knew as 'the guy who followed me from the pawnbroker's.' There was no sign of him, or anyone else suspicious that they knew of. Christie led the way in.

The Sunday night crowd was already building up. It wasn't as noisy yet as the Saturday night when Christie had gone there with Tina, but it was far from quiet. Glancing round, at first they saw no one they knew, but as they pushed their way into the back of the downstairs bar, they were relieved to see Tommy sitting at a table with two strangers, scowling into his beer glass.

The strangers, a middle aged couple, the woman plump but still attractive, the man lean and harsh featured, seemed to be sitting with Tommy solely because they had found no other seats. As Christie and Aine approached, the man plucked the woman's sleeve and nodded towards a wall booth where the customers were leaving. They both stood up, and went to hover round the booth, until they were able to seize it in the face of any other contenders.

Christie and Aine thankfully grabbed their vacant chairs.

'Tommy!' Aine burst out. 'I've been trying to reach you all day! Why aren't you answering your phone?'

Tommy looked shamefaced. 'Aw, Aine, sorry, darlin' – I just needed some space, see? Need to think out what to do.'

'But, Tommy, Christie and I can help you with that! I really want to help you, Tommy! And Christie's great – she's already helped me so much.'

Tommy's face developed a fearsome scowl, much more threatening than the one he'd been wearing when they first spotted him.

'What have you been telling this bitch, Aine? I didn't think you'd shop me!'

'Nothing, Tommy! And you mustn't call her a bitch – she's my friend. She helped me get away when that guy followed me from the pawnbroker, like I told you. She'll help us now, if you don't put her off entirely.'

Tommy pushed his dark hair back from his forehead where it was drooping over his eyes.

'Okay, if you say she's okay, darlin' I'll take it she is. But I don't see what she can do for me.'

'Maybe nothing, Tommy,' Christie said quietly. 'Nothing, unless you trust me with the truth.'

'What? I can't hear you.' The band outside had started up, its loud drumbeat and guitars drowning out all attempts at conversation within a wide radius.

Tommy stood up abruptly, pushing his chair back noisily. He seized his beer glass and gulped down the last few mouthfuls. 'Let's get out of here!'

They followed his plunging figure as he headed out of the bar, across the courtyard, and into the narrow entry which led to the High Street.

'Let's go somewhere where we can talk,' Tommy said. 'There are too many people after me to hang around here.'

'Okay.' Christie didn't want to argue.

Tommy led the way at a brisk pace along the entry, onto High Street, across to Bridge Street and along until they reached, with several twists and turns, the entrance to the Mac.

'I have a mate, Reddy, works in the restaurant here,' he said abruptly. 'He'll let us come in and get out of sight in the staff only quarters.'

Christie and Aine followed him without asking further questions.

Tommy's mate was a small, ginger haired guy with a snub nose, wearing the usual chef get up.

'Reddy, can we use your cloakroom to talk for a bit?'

'Sure, Tommy, whatever suits.'

Reddy took them along a passage to a room with pegs holding outdoor clothes for several people and a cupboard which, Christie guessed, might have spare chef's outfits and similar things hanging inside it.

'Okay, Tommy, let me know when you're finished.'

'You're a pal, Reddy.'

'Anything for the guy what gave it to big Baldy. I'll never forget the punch you threw at him – had him flat on his back! '

'Reddy's been a mate of mine since the Children's Home,' explained Tommy, more to Aine than to Christie, when Reddy had gone.

'And who was big Baldy?' Aine asked. Christie was glad she'd asked. She'd been wondering herself.

'Oh, just one of the staff in the Home. Awful guy. I punched him out the day I left. He well deserved it, for a heap of reasons. Don't ask.'

Aine didn't.

'Tommy,' she said instead, 'what's going on? Tell me.'

'Och, sure, Aine love, I've told you already! This guy threatened to tell the boss about my record if I didn't pawn the necklace for him.'

'Tommy, that's tripe,' Christie said. 'You're not just up against one guy – it's a whole gang – the people who nearly caught us in your flat yesterday. That wasn't just one guy, right?'

'Right,' admitted Tommy miserably. He scowled at Christie, hating her.

'And if they are a gang, how come they don't have a fence or two lined up to use? Why should they want to drag you in – a guy who knows nothing about fencing stuff, not even which pawnbrokers might take dodgy goods?'

Tommy said nothing, but his scowl deepened.

'Tommy, I want to help you,' Aine said urgently, taking hold of his arm with both hands. 'And so does Christie. But you've got to trust us and tell us the truth.'

'I think I could make a good guess, Tommy,' Christie said quietly. 'You were part of the set up, weren't you? You were part of the gang that pinched not just one necklace but a clatter of jewels – maybe from a shop? And you ripped them off by holding on to that necklace yourself, instead of leaving it as part of the loot. Probably the gang had plans for disposing of the whole lot, and you were meant to get your cut from that, but you wanted more – you thought you could get a bigger cut by swiping the necklace and pawning it yourself. Then you got cold feet and put it on to Aine instead to go to the pawnshops.'

Tommy's mouth dropped open.

'How do you know?' he gasped.

'It didn't take a genius to work out that something like that had to be the way it was.'

'It was for us, darlin' – I wanted the money so's I could give us a good start in life, instead of scraping along like we have to right now,' Tommy said, turning to Aine and opening his big brown eyes appealingly. 'I didn't mean to get you into any trouble.'

'Oh, Tommy!' Aine threw herself into his arms, and kissed him passionately. Tommy held tightly to her, kissing her back. Then abruptly he stopped, and took the necklace from his pocket. 'Hide this for me, babe,' he said to Aine, his eyes pleading. 'If they find me they'll search me for sure. You should go now, go home and stay there safely. I don't want to get you into trouble.'

Aine took the necklace and slipped it inside her jeans, down the front of her pants.

'That's all very well, mister,' Christie interrupted. 'But whether you meant to get Aine in trouble or not, you've done it. These guys know now that Aine's your girlfriend, and they know she had the necklace day before yesterday. So they'll be after her now, as well as you, see?'

'I can deal with them!' Tommy said.

'Oh, yeah? So that's why you're hiding here, and that's why we ran when they came to your flat?'

Tommy said nothing. Aine glared at Christie.

'You're being too hard on him, Christie!'

'I don't think so.' Christie glared back. She was about to walk out, out of that room and out of the problem and out of Aine's and Tommy's lives, when something happened to stop her.

The door was pushed open, and someone who wasn't Tommy's chef friend Reddy, came in, followed by three other men. None of them looked like employees of the Mac's restaurant.

Tommy's mouth fell open again.

'So this is where you're lurking, Tommy,' said the first man. He was tall and thickset, with a heavy jaw line covered in dark stubble, a huge belly, sharp grey eyes, and a receding grayish hair-line.

'Butch!' Tommy said feebly. 'I'm not hiding, mate.'

Butch produced a gun from his pocket.

'Kid! Doc! Sundance! Grab him!'

The other men took hold of Tommy, not in any gentle way.

'And one of these babes is your girl friend, Tommy? Which one?'

'I'm not telling you!' Tommy said fiercely. The Kid, a small wiry man, quite young but clearly very tough, twisted his right arm painfully up his back, and Tommy let out a howl, but otherwise kept his mouth tightly shut.

'No need, then. We'll take them both. Unless you feel like handing over that necklace now, instead?'

'I can't – I haven't got it – it was pinched from me this after-noon.' Tommy jerked the words out painfully as the pressure on his arm was increased.

'That's too bad, Tommy. But do you know, I really think you've got that wrong. Kid, Doc, frisk him.'

The other men seized Tommy again and began to search him. But before very long, it had become obvious to them and to everyone else there that Tommy didn't have the necklace on him.

'Okay, so you don't have it on you,' Butch said at last. 'But that just means you've hidden it somewhere. Where is it Tommy, boy?'

'I haven't got it, Butch – someone pinched it from me, like I told you,' Tommy said miserably.

Butch glared at him ferociously. 'So, you might need something to bring back your memory of where you've put it. We'll need to go somewhere a bit more private, somewhere where we can go into that with you, see? Okay, then. Get moving, all three of you. And don't forget I've got a gun here, you chicks. It'll be pointed straight at Tommy from inside my pocket, but I can take either or both of you out just as easily, you'd better believe it. Outside!'

They moved off in a miserable procession, along a dark narrow passage to the staff exit. No one seemed to be around, or Christie would have risked shouting for help.

Outside the service door a white van was parked. Doc swung the back doors open and the girls were thrust inside. Tommy followed in a sprawling heap. The doors were slammed and bolted. They heard the sound of the front doors opening, the three men climbing inside, and the engine starting.

'Wow!' said Christie. 'Now what do we do?'

The answer seemed to be, 'Nothing.'

'Who are these guys, Tommy?' Christie asked.

'They call themselves the Wild West Gang or variations on that,' Tommy answered gloomily. Butch Cassidy and the Sundance Kid, see? And Doc Halliday and Billy the Kid. And I guess there are a few others with silly nicknames as well. Sounds funny, but it isn't really. They're hard men – bad news.'

They sat gloomily in the hot, uncomfortable van until it came to a jolting halt, the doors were flung open, and they were bustled out through them, along an alley, into a yard emerging from it, and into a dismal looking building. They were too close to get an overall picture of it, but it was shabby and grimy with peeling paintwork – a dismal prospect if they were to stay there for long.

Chapter 17

They were pushed by all three of the men along a twisty corridor and up some rickety stairs, and were thrust with little care into a long, almost empty room which Christie guessed might be the loft over an old, out of use warehouse. The door was banged shut on them. They could hear a key turning in the lock, and what sounded like bolts being shot home.

Aine threw herself into Tommy's willing arms. 'Oh, Tommy,' she wailed, 'what are we going to do?'

Tommy didn't seem to have any bright suggestions, but he began comforting Aine in a much more practical way by holding her tightly and kissing her. They cuddled down together at one end of the loft.

Christie, seeing that this was going to go on for some time, switched off her attention. She was very glad that she had stuck her Kindle into her bag before coming out earlier.

Sitting in as comfortable a position as she could, and as far away from the lovers as possible, with her back to them, she pulled the Kindle from her bag and began to read the next chapter of *The Pirate*.

Hel's Heroes 2: Christie & The Pirate

Chapter Eighteen

Jane gazed in disbelief at her mistress.

'We're going swimming? Mistress Prue, what do you mean?'

'Just what I say,' Prue told her, smiling mischievously. 'In all the bustle of arrival at the island, we should be able, if we choose our moment carefully, to slip over the side and swim to shore without being noticed. Then we'll be free to plan our further escape.'

'But suppose they see us!' Jane burst out. 'When we planned to go before, it was dark – we had a real chance of not being seen. Now, it's broad daylight – they'll see us for sure. And they'll row ashore and be waiting for us!'

'No, Jane,' Prue said, 'because by the time the ship moors, it will be much later. Darkness comes quickly in these tropical islands, as you well know. I expect it to be fairly dark by the time we leave the ship. And even darker, quite quickly, by the time we've swum even a short way.'

'Perhaps, Mistress Prue,' agreed Jane doubtfully. 'It might be worth risking. But what do we do after we come ashore?'

'We find out where Captain Myles Whiteside is imprisoned, rescue him, help him to recapture the ship Freedom, *and sail off in her, as we hoped to do before,' Prue told her briskly. 'We may not be able to do all that straight away, but it shouldn't take too long. Meanwhile, there is food on the island – bananas, coconuts, things like that. And running water – I saw several little streams through Captain Hawkeye's spyglass, which he kindly lent me.'*

'Oh, Mistress Prue!' Jane suddenly wailed. 'They've been so kind to us – the captain especially to you, and Mister Tompkins, to me. How can we just leave them?'

Prue bit her lip. 'Yes, I know, Jane. It seems a hard thing to do. And yet, Jane, these men are pirates – criminals. How can we stay with them, and allow them to think that we are happy about what they are, what they do? Remember that other poor young captain, injured, robbed of his ship, imprisoned – oh, no, Jane, we can't just let all that go, as if it didn't matter.'

'You're right, Mistress Prue,' Jane agreed, bowing her head sadly. 'So, how soon do you think we should try to go overboard?'

'Not for several hours, yet,' Prue said. 'Captain Hawkeye told me that the island was still three or four hours away, although the spyglass brought it so close – and, in truth, it seemed very far away with the naked eye. I think we should both rest now, and eat well when they bring us our meal in a while.'

They lay down on their bunks and tried to sleep, but for both, sleep had never seemed so far away.

Prue closed her eyes, but Captain Hawkeye's face still floated before her inward vision. Surely he wasn't all bad? He had started to tell her something, to explain. But then he had stopped, saying only that he had given his word, and that he could say no more.

Prue found herself again longing to trust him, and it was only by telling herself sternly that his actions revealed his nature more surely than his words that she was able to resist the urge to call off the whole escape attempt and stay, to try to understand this strange man.

The girls both seemed to have been trying to sleep for many hours before a rap on the cabin door told them that Josh Tompkins was there with the food. Struggling to rise, Prue called to Jane, 'Wake up, Jane! Someone's at the door.'

'I'm not asleep, Mistress Prue. I haven't been able to sleep. I'll answer the door now.' She moved over to open it.

'May I come in Mistress Jane? I've brought your supper.'

Sure enough, it was Josh, and Jane's face lit up as she saw him, while he in return beamed happily at her.

'Good news, ladies,' he said. 'We'll be landing at the island in not much more than an hour, and then we'll be disembarking. I think you'll love the place and be very happy there.'

'Doesn't it have a name, this island of yours?' asked Prue curiously.

Chapter 18

'Why, yes, mistress. No official name, I think, as far as the maps are concerned, but we ourselves call it the Happy Isle.'

'Oh, it sounds so lovely!' Jane burst out, then blushed, remembering that she had agreed with Prue that she wouldn't be landing there with Josh to live there.

'We have a parson there, so we're not complete savages, I should tell you,' Josh Tompkins went on. His eyes twinkled at Jane. 'So those of us who would wish to marry can do so.'

Jane dropped her eyes, unable to meet Josh's smiling ones.

'Come, Jane,' Prue said hastily, seeing her maid's embarrassment and wishing to save her from distress. 'Let's sit down and eat, before we need prepare to land. Thank you, Mister Tompkins. We needn't keep you from your duties.'

With one last smile, particularly at Jane, Josh Tompkins left, and the two girls sat at table and ate heartily of the chicken and bread, and drank the wine.

'We won't need to swim for another hour or so, from what Josh says,' Prue remarked. 'Just as well, after this meal. But we should probably begin to get ourselves ready well before that.'

They had no way of telling the time, so were left with guesswork.

When Prue finally judged that the hour was nearly up, she said, 'Jane, set the tray and the remains of our meal outside the cabin door. If Josh or anyone else comes for it, we don't want to have to let him in. It's time we got ready for our swim.'

Once again, they stripped off their outer garments and stood up in their underclothes. Then they carefully folded nightdresses and dressing gowns, and fastened them into two neat bundles.

'I think we should carry them until we're about to go over the side,' Prue said softly. 'Then we can tie them to the tops of each other's head, as we did before.'

They stood up, ready to go.

'This is where we need a generous amount of caution, Jane,' said Prue. 'I'll look out first. If no one is in sight, I'll let you know, and we'll slip out, one after the other. Very quietly, of course, and as quickly as we may.'

There was no one in the passageway when Prue opened the cabin door a chink.

'Follow me, Jane,' she whispered, turning briefly to her maid-servant. Then she opened the door just wide enough to slip through, and Jane, following her, pulled the cabin door shut behind her.

Darkness had descended in the sudden, abrupt way customary in the islands. It was hard to see in the unlit passage below decks. Prue moved forward cautiously, with Jane so close behind that when Prue stopped too suddenly Jane almost fell over her.

'Sorry,' Prue murmured. 'I thought I heard someone.' They stood in silence for a moment, then Prue shook her head. 'I must have imagined it.'

She moved on again.

Presently they came to the companionway leading to the deck. Once they had climbed it, Prue was well aware, they would be in the greatest danger of being seen. If they could manage to slip round towards the stern of the ship, they would be away from most of the activity going on as the crewmen prepared to land. Peering cautiously over the rim of the ladder where her eyes were just at deck level, Prue saw with satisfaction that stores were being raised to the deck from the hold opening in the centre of the deck, its large trapdoor now flung open and lying backwards across the planking.

Already goods were piled high in front of the two girls, and what seemed like a good proportion of the crew were working at hauling the goods up from the hold, piling them up, and securing them with bindings. The others, Prue guessed, would be further forwards, dealing with ropes, anchors and longboats in preparation for landing and tying up. She and Jane had clearly picked the best of times to make their escape.

At more of a distance, she suddenly noticed the young prisoner, Myles Whiteside. He was standing, with chains on his arms and legs, well in sight of the man in charge of the workers. For a moment, Prue was tempted to signal to him, to make swimming motions, and to try to encourage him to break away and join them in their escape.

But a second's thought showed her that this would be madness. Myles would have no hope of swimming, burdened as he was by those heavy chains. Moreover, his guard was keeping such a close eye on him that it would be impossible for him to break free. All she could do by trying to attract his attention would be to give herself and Jane away before they had even reached the stern and gone overboard.

Her original plan, of discovering where he was held once they had reached the island safely and rescuing him then, was, after all, much the best.

Regretfully she climbed onto the deck, followed immediately by Jane, and slipped behind the nearest bundle of stores. Then, choosing her moment carefully, she led her companion along the deck towards the stern railings, forming a silent prayer as she did so that they might remain unseen.

The railings were sharply silhouetted against the night sky, faintly lit by the many pinpricks of light which were the bright shining stars of that ocean. It was time to tie their bundles of clothes to their heads again, and they did so as swiftly and carefully as they could.

Prue put both hands on the rail.

'Now, Jane,' she breathed, 'we don't want to make a splash which someone might hear. Let's try to get over the rail and lower ourselves down as quietly and carefully as possible. We can probably climb down the side of the ship if we take hold of any protruding bits, and so be able to get within touch and reach of the sea and slide gently in, rather than dropping from above and making some considerable noise with our splash. I'll go first, if you like.'

'No, Mistress Prue,' Jane said firmly. 'We'll go side by side. Remember, I'm a better swimmer than you – I can help you along if you need it.'

Prue laughed and acknowledged the truth of Jane's remarks. 'Fair enough, Jane,' she agreed. ' First, check that your bundle of clothes is still securely fastened. It is? So is mine. Let's get going, then.'

Together they climbed over the stern railing and turned to face the ship, feeling their way carefully down the ship's side, holding on until they were sure of a lower foothold or handhold before relinquishing each one.

In a remarkably short time they could feel the water lapping round their feet, then their legs, coming up as far as their waists.

'Time to start swimming, Jane, don't you think?' Prue asked, and Jane agreed. Surrendering themselves to the friendly ocean, the girls struck out.

'Let's swim well away from the ship to start with, Jane,' Prue gasped, spitting out a mouthful of water from an approaching wave. 'Not further away from land – just sideways, so that we won't be swimming close to the action up near the prow.'

'Yes, Mistress Prue,' Jane agreed. 'But stop trying to talk. Concentrate on swimming.'

And Prue meekly agreed.

In a surprisingly short time they were well away from the ship, and looking back at it found that it had been nearer to the shore than they had realised. Turning in that direction they could see the waving silhouettes of the palm trees, swaying in the gentle Caribbean breeze, and could almost distinguish the individual waves as they poured with a gentle but steady motion onto the soft beach. It wasn't easy to see very clearly as yet. The moon had not risen, much to Prue's relief, and they were dependant upon starlight for what they could make out. But then, so were the eyes of anyone on the ship who might be looking their way.

Prue was hopeful that the crewmen, busy at their work of unloading the cargo, would have no time to cast their gaze over the ocean, and that Captain Hawkeye and others working with him would be equally concentrated, for a while at least, in bringing the ship safely near to shore and mooring her.

The two girls swam on, finding that they were moving more quickly, and covering more distance, than they could have expected. It crossed Prue's mind that they might be swimming with the aid of a current. And while that was all very well as long as the current was content to carry them in the right direction, what would happen if it changed its course and began to take them along beside the shore, never reaching land, or, worse still back out into the boundless ocean?

But the current, if there was one, didn't let them down. Instead, it delivered them both safely onto the grateful softness of the beach and its gentle sand.

Chapter 18

Prue stood up and accepted Jane's hand thankfully as she tried to keep a steady footing.

'Well, Mistress Prue, we're safely here!' Jane said. 'Who would have believed it?'

'Yes, but this is just the start, Jane,' Prue told her. 'Now we have to get under cover as quickly as possible, find somewhere where we can hide for the rest of the night, and then, tomorrow, plan what to do next –'

She was interrupted by a distant shout. Spinning round she could see gesticulating figures springing down into the water from the longboat which had just come ashore a lot further along the beach with the first of the pirates – among them, no doubt, Captain Hawkeye. They had been spotted!

'Quick, Jane!' cried Prue. 'Run! Head for the trees!'

Stumbling through the clinging sand, the two girls raced at the top of whatever speed they could muster, across the beach and into the thick ridge of palm trees which edged it, and at once disappeared from sight.

Hel's Heroes 2: Christie & The Pirate

Chapter Nineteen

The Present

Christie was interrupted by the sound of the key turning in the lock, the bolts being shot back, and the door opening. They all three sat up abruptly and looked round. The tall, fat man who had been in charge earlier – Butch, Tommy had called him – came in, flourishing his gun importantly.

'Now, Tommy,' he said smoothly, 'I have time to deal with you. And I mean business. I want that necklace.'

'I'd give it to you if I could, Butch,' Tommy replied desperately, 'but I haven't got it – I told you!'

'Oh, yeah?' Butch sneered. 'Think again, Tommy. So you don't have it on you – we know that, from when we frisked you this afternoon. But you know where you put it, right? And now you're going to tell us.'

He moved forward towards Tommy, waving his gun in a menacing way.

Tommy scrambled to his feet. 'No, Butch!' he yelled. 'I'm telling you the truth. Someone pinched it. It could be anywhere.'

'Well, strangely enough, I don't believe you, Tommy. And now I'm going to find out, okay?'

Christie, in the far corner, was out of range of Butch's gun. She supposed he hadn't thought she was worth bothering about – only a girl, right? She felt quite nervous, but there was no way she was going to sit back and let Butch beat up Tommy.

She edged quietly round behind him, trying to make no noise. Then as Butch came closer to Tommy, she stood up suddenly and launched herself at his back, kicking out at his legs.

Butch jumped abruptly, finding it hard to believe what was happening. His finger jerked on the trigger and the gun went off. Luckily the shot went towards the ceiling and tore a rent in the plaster, which fell in clouds of dust around them all. Tommy gathered his wits together and leapt for Butch's gun hand before he could fire another shot.

Suddenly the tables were turned. Instead of Butch, Tommy had the gun and the control. But for how long?

Christie wasn't sure Tommy knew much more about the practical side of using a gun than she did herself. She didn't like the way the gun seemed to be wobbling in his grasp.

'Let's get out of here while we can!' she gasped breathlessly. 'Remember those other three might come in any moment.'

'Right,' said Aine briskly. 'Come on, Tommy. Keep the gun on him, you eedjit! Back away from him.'

Tommy, who had begun to turn away from Butch, managed to get his eyes, and the gun, back on the gangster before Butch could take any action.

'Okay. As soon as we're out, we'll shut the door on him and lock him in. Then we'll see if we can get past the others, okay?' Christie said.

She and Aine got themselves out of the room. Then as soon as Tommy had backed out after them, the gun still covering Butch, she hauled him out of the way, slammed the door, and turned the key, which was still in the lock from when Butch had opened the door a few minutes ago. The three of them wasted no time in getting downstairs.

As they passed the door at the foot of the steps, they heard sounds of three people talking in the room off to the right. The door was not quite shut. Christie signalled to the other two to keep quiet, and crept over to listen to what was being said, pushing the door open further. Nothing they were saying seemed very important.

Doc, the tall, thin one, she thought it was, was telling the Kid and Sundance, 'I wish we hadn't got into this kidnapping lark. Can't see the point. Where's it going to get us?'

'Well,' the Kid drawled, 'it's the sort of thing the Wild West Gang ought to do, right? We can't let that Tommy guy cheat us out of one of the necklaces.'

'Why not?' retorted Doc. 'We have plenty without it. We're just getting ourselves into more trouble, if you ask me.'

Chapter 19

'Don't be so soft, Doc. Suppose word got round that the Wild Westerners let themselves be cheated? Everyone would be trying it on after that, right? We gotta stop this guy right at the start, see?' That was Sundance, the tall, lanky, balding one.

'Oh, yeah? And how are we going to do that? Beat him up, right? But we'll have to let him go in a while, and suppose one of those girls goes to the cops about us? They'll be able to identify us, won't they? And if you're going to suggest that we bump them off, don't, because I won't wear it, and I wouldn't have thought you would either, Kid or you, Sundance. Don't know about Butch, mind you.'

'Hey, Butch wouldn't do a thing like that!' protested the Kid.

Christie couldn't help feeling relieved, even though they were on their way out and hadn't succeeded in fully escaping yet. Her ideas had been moving in the same direction as Doc's, as a matter of fact. He seemed a bit brighter than the rest of the gang.

Just then they heard noises from above, a faint hammering on the door – Butch must have thought of using his shoe – and the Kid interrupted himself to exclaim, 'Hey! What's that?'

Time to move, Christie reckoned. Ducking away from the door, she seized Tommy and Aine by an arm each and bustled them along the corridor before the Kid, Doc or Sundance could emerge from the downstairs room.

The corridor was long and twisty. They were almost at the door before it became clear that the three men had rushed upstairs and unlocked the door, and were now, with Butch, pelting noisily down the uncarpeted stairs and about to start along the corridor after them.

'Quick!' Christie panted. She reached the outer door first, a huge double door secured by bolts. A moment's effort shot back the bolts, they all joined in pushing open the doors, and a second later they were in the open air.

But there was no way to secure the doors from the outside. They shoved them closed, but had no means of fastening them. Taking to their heels, they tore along the yard towards the alley, aware of the sound behind them of the four gangsters coming nearer.

They burst out into the alleyway.

There, before them was a car, its doors welcomingly open.

'Quick!' said a familiar voice. 'Get in! Don't waste time!'

It was Steve Armstrong.

They tumbled into the car and slammed the doors after them without a second thought. Steve released the clutch, pressed the accelerator, and shot off down the alleyway towards the main road. Just as he reached the turn off, the four men erupted from the warehouse door. Too late.

The van which had brought Christie, Tommy and Aine to the warehouse was there, but it was pointing in the wrong direction. By the time the gang had scrambled in, turned the van around, with the tall, lanky Sundance driving, and started off after Steve, the car had reached the main road and was swallowed up in the traffic.

'Whew!' Christie breathed. 'Hey, thanks, Steve!'

'No problem,' Steve said nonchalantly.

'Well, okay, but there is a problem!' Aine said angrily. 'This is the guy who followed me from the pawnbroker's and scared me stupid. What are we doing jumping into his car? Are we daft? Christie, why did you encourage us to do it? He's just working in with those other guys, right?'

'No, no, Aine! I'm sure he isn't! He's rescuing us! Steve, for goodness sake explain yourself, at least a bit!'

Steve laughed wryly. 'Well, I suppose I'll have to. You three can give evidence against these three guys, so it's worth while for me to break my cover. I'm an undercover cop, and I've been after these men for quite a while, pretending to work in with them. When I followed you, Aine, I was working for them, so you weren't so far wrong – not that I'd have done you any harm, mind you.

But when I saw them snatch you all at the Mac, I wanted to help, especially you, Christie.' He shot a swift glance at her, pleading for understanding. 'I followed the van, and I've been watching, and wondering about my next move, since then. When I saw you breaking out, it was clear I needed to help by providing a getaway car for you. End of story.'

Christie smiled back at him. It was very much what he had hinted to her before. And now he had proved its truth by rescuing them when they were in such need.

But clearly Aine wasn't going to be so easily satisfied.

'I don't know why you ran away, then!' she said sharply. 'When I told those people you were stalking me. All you had to do was stay and tell me who you were, same as you're doing now.'

'But it's different now, Aine,' Steve said in a quiet reasonable voice. 'I didn't know then that you would be prepared to give evidence for me – in fact, I don't think you would have –'

'No way!" interjected Aine sharply.

'But now you've been kidnapped and threatened, and you've seen three of the gang and can identify then, it's a different matter. I don't mind letting you in on who I am, if I can get your evidence.'

'And who says you can?' Aine said. 'If you think I'm going to stand up in court and say that Tommy gave me a stolen necklace to pawn, you must be off your head!'

'No, no, you've got me wrong, Aine!' Steve protested. 'I just think you'd be willing to testify that these three guys kidnapped you and held you prisoner and threatened Tommy.'

'And when they ask me why? And what the threats were meant to get them?'

'Okay, I get your point. But I'm sure we could work something out.'

'And I'm not. There's no way I'm going to risk Tommy going back to prison, no matter.'

There seemed to be no way out.

'Tommy?' Steve asked. 'What about you? Would you be willing to identify the three guys, if I swore to you that there'd be no mention of the necklace of anything like that?'

'Well – maybe –' began Tommy weakly, but Aine cut in.

'No, Tommy! Don't let him persuade you. You don't know what you'd be risking.'

'But, Aine, if you don't, you'll still be at risk from the Wild West gang, don't you see? They know where you live, as the saying goes. They'll be after you both again.' Steve continued to speak quietly and calmly.

'We can move,' said Aine obstinately.

'Look, if you just hand over the necklace to me, Tommy, you'll be in the clear, right? I'll make up some story about where I got it, leaving you out, okay? Then you can testify without any risk at all.'

Tommy's face suddenly hardened. 'Like I told yer man Butch, I haven't got the necklace. It was pinched from me this afternoon. And that's all there is to it. If all you're after is to get the necklace from me, tough – you can't get it.'

Christie had kept quiet, calculating that if Steve couldn't persuade Tommy and Aine to do the sensible thing, she wasn't likely to be more successful. She didn't feel that she could give Aine away by telling Steve that she had the necklace hidden down the front of her panties. Now she spoke for the first time.

'Steve, suppose we drop these guys off somewhere – wherever they want – and find a nice restaurant for ourselves to have a drink and some food. Personally, I'm starving again by now, in spite of that Irish stew I had hours ago.'

'Sounds good to me, Christie,' Steve agreed. 'Where do you two want me to drop you?'

The immediate response from Aine was a shriek of horror. 'No, no, don't do that!' she wailed.

Tommy was equally distraught. 'The gang will catch up with us if you leave us wandering round here. We need to find somewhere to go first!'

'Why should I help you do that?' Steve asked implacably. 'You won't help me.'

'Oh, don't!' Aine wailed again. 'Maybe we could think about it, okay? Can't you help us find somewhere safe to stay?'

'Well – I suppose I could arrange for you to stay in a safe house tonight, until you can find somewhere else yourselves,' said Steve thoughtfully.

'That would be great, Steve!' babbled Aine. 'We could ring up some mates, once we were somewhere safe, and go to them tomorrow, right?'

'Okay, then.' Steve glared round at them. 'But this is on condition that you agree to testify against these guys. Only to the kidnapping, okay? I'm not asking you to bring the jewellery – and Tommy having the necklace – into it. No need for that.'

'Oh, Steve, thank you so much!' Aine said fervently. 'We'll do that, Tommy, won't we?'

Tommy didn't seem quite so keen, but a moment's thought told him that he had little option.

'Okay, man,' he said. 'But you'd better not try to drag me into this jewellery robbery, right?'

'Okay, Tommy,' Steve agreed. 'So, I'll drive you to this safe house I mentioned. You'll have to manage without night stuff. They can give you a tooth brush each, I think.'

The two of them murmured fervent thanks as Steve pulled out of the main stream of traffic back into the centre of Belfast and headed out to the suburbs.

In a quiet cul-de-sac in Glengormley, he pulled up in front of a respectable looking house and said, 'This is it. You stay here, Christie. I'll take these guys in and introduce them and get them settled. Then we can go for that meal, okay?' He gave Christie a smile which sent shivers down her spine. What was it about this guy that attracted her so much?

Ten minutes later, he was out again and slipping into the driving seat. 'Okay, here we go!' he said. 'Back into Belfast, do you think? I don't know anywhere round here except chippies. And this is too special an occasion for that sort of place, I think.'

'Is it?' Christie asked demurely.

'Oh, I think so, don't you? I've just rescued you from villains, after all. We should celebrate!'

'Well, if you put it like that.' Christie said. 'But I thought, actually, that I rescued myself?'

'And a great job you did of it, too,' Steve agreed enthusiastically. 'But once you got outside, where would you have been without my speedy chariot? You've got to agree to that!'

'Okay, I'll go with that,' Christie said demurely. 'So where do you suggest we go?'

'Well, since it isn't a Saturday, we might be able to get into Deane's Bistro, why not? Worth a try, anyway.'

And to Christie's surprise, they did.

It was a long time later, after an evening that would, she knew, live in her memory for many years, that Christie and Steve said good night with many a kiss on the doorstep of her house, and she staggered in and up to bed.

She was too excited to sleep straightaway, she knew. Rolling into bed, she took her Kindle out of her handbag, clicked on *The Pirate*, and began to read on. Prue and Jane, she remembered, had just reached the beach of Captain Hawkeye's island and had disappeared into the palm trees.

Chapter Twenty

1794

'Now what?' gasped Jane as they threw themselves panting to the ground. They had run as far as they could, if you could call their half stumbling progress – though the trees and undergrowth, hindered at every step by twining creepers – running.

Prue took a moment to get her breath back. 'Hard to say,' was the best she could come up with when at last she spoke. 'If we stay here, they'll have a pretty good idea of where to look for us, and they may well find us when they get the time for a serious hunt. On the other hand, at least here we're well hidden.' She looked at her maid quizzically. 'What do you think, Jane?'

Jane was taken aback. So far, she'd blindly followed Prue's leading. Being asked for advice, a new thing in their relationship, threw her off her stride.

'Well, Miss Prue,' she said finally, 'it's pretty dark by now. I don't think anyone is likely to find us. Why not give them time to get settled in, and then creep out and search for where they've got Captain Myles?'

'That sounds right, Jane,' Prue agreed enthusiastically. 'And by the way, don't you think you could drop the 'Miss', and start just calling me Prue? I've asked you to, before.'

'Well – maybe,' Jane said cautiously. 'Tell you what, I'll think about it.' But there was a beam over her face which Prue could just see as the faint moonlight caught her pretty white teeth shining in the darkness.

'Here's a thought, Jane,' she said. 'We should probably get dressed again, don't you think?'

'Well – er – Prue, we'll get our nightdresses wet if we do, while we're still so damp from swimming' Jane suggested cautiously. 'And it will be much harder to get away through the creepers and things, if they come after us and find and chase us. Maybe if we leave it for a while, we'll dry out soon.'

There was a lot of sense in this.

'I'm drying quite well already,' Prue said. 'The heat does it. Still, do no harm to leave it a bit longer.'

And Jane, whose underclothes were a lot thicker than Prue's, nodded agreement. She was clad in a thick warm woollen vest and woollen drawers, whereas Prue was wearing a silk camisole from Paris, and light, lacy drawers, more for appearance than warmth.

They huddled down among the creepers and hoped to get some rest. It must have been several hours later that Prue started awake. She had heard voices, and the sound of people approaching through the undergrowth.

'Jane!' she said sharply.

Jane also woke up. 'Wha'? Wha'? What is it, Miss Prue?'

Even through her alarm, Prue was reluctant to let that pass, having once got Jane to drop the 'Miss.'

'Prue!' she corrected sharply. 'Jane, someone's coming.'

'Then we should stop talking,' Jane said immediately.

They sat up and listened intently. Yes, there were definitely voices to be heard, and the sound of some people pushing their way towards them.

Saying no more, Prue gestured to Jane to follow her, and began carefully to crawl away, as soundlessly as possible, through the bushes.

Alas, it seemed that the voices were coming nearer.

Prue and Jane were unsure if they should be crawling in a different direction, or if they should stop where they were and hope that their pursuers would bypass them. It was a difficult decision.

One which was made for them.

The voices had come so close that they could make out what was being said.

The first voice which they could distinguish belonged, they were both sure, to Black Nick Hawkeye.

'Do you think they came safely ashore, Josh?' he was asking, in an unhappy, even despairing, voice. 'Did the men definitely see them get to the beach?'

'No question about it, Captain,' said Josh Tompkins's voice. 'They came safely ashore all right. But who knows what happened to them next? There are snakes about, as you well know, captain. Two young girls, on their own in this wild jungle – who knows how they've been getting on?'

Captain Hawkeye groaned. 'Who, indeed, Josh?' he said. 'Who indeed?' There was a pause, then Captain Hawkeye said, more briskly, 'Well, standing here moaning won't find them. Let's go on.'

The girls heard the sound of the two men pushing their way through the thick foliage, and were thankful to discern that they were moving further away by the minute.

It was a while before Prue or Jane felt able to speak again without the risk of being heard.

'Oh, dear!' Jane said. 'They sounded so upset and so kind. They're really worried about us, aren't they?'

'I think they must be. There'd be no need for them to put on an act for each other. Well, you already knew, Jane, that Josh Tompkins cares for you. He's made it quite clear, hasn't he?'

'And Captain Hawkeye must care a lot about you, Miss – sorry, I mean – Prue,' Jane said. 'He sounded really upset when he was asking if we'd drowned or got safely ashore.'

'And Josh sounded really worried about the snakes,' Prue added.

The thought went through both their minds at the same time. Snakes!

'Do you think there actually are snakes, Prue?' Jane whispered.

'I don't know. We haven't seen any so far.' Prue was trying to sound encouraging, but she couldn't help being aware that her voice was wobbling a bit. And when she tried to stand up, her legs were shaking.

'Anyway, no matter whether they care about us or not, these men are still pirates, carrying out a wicked trade, and we can't possibly stay with them or encourage them,' she said firmly.

'Should we try to find our way out of these trees, Prue?' Jane suggested.

'Just what I was thinking. At least we'd be away from snakes dropping on us from the branches,' shuddered Prue. They began, as silently as they could, to move in a direction which they hoped was taking them further away from Captain Hawkeye and Josh.

They had been pushing through creepers and undergrowth for what seemed like hours when they saw, just ahead of them, the glint of moonlight shining on what looked like an open space. Sure enough, as they came nearer, they saw that it was a clearing, free of palm trees, with a small stream trickling through it amid low sandy banks.

'Praise the Lord!' exclaimed Jane fervently. 'Come on, Prue, let's drink some water.'

'Yes, let's,' Prue agreed enthusiastically. 'I hadn't realised until now how thirsty I was. This is a real blessing.'

They knelt down carefully on the banks of the stream and scooped up mouthfuls of water in their hands to drink. Presently, when they had slaked their thirst, Prue said thoughtfully, 'You know, Jane, I'm not sure it's such a good idea to be out from under the trees. We'd be so very easy to find here in the open.'

'If it's a choice,' Jane said in a determined voice, 'between snakes dropping on our heads or Captain Hawkeye and Josh finding us, I know which I'd choose. No snakes for me, thank you, Prue.'

And Prue had to admit, after due consideration, that she had a point. 'But maybe we should at least get over to the edge of the clearing, where it would be easy to slip under the trees again if we hear anyone coming,' she said.

Jane agreed, and they settled themselves against a tall tree, its waving branches casting shadows before them in the moonlight, and leaned back to rest.

'I could go back to sleep very easily, Jane,' Prue sighed. 'But better not. As soon as we're sure the captain and anyone else has given up looking for us, we need to creep out as quietly as we can and see if we can find where they have Captain Myles.'

'Yes,' agreed Jane sleepily. 'But it's so pleasant and comfortable here, Prue. I'll be hard put to stay awake.' Her voice tailed off and her breathing deepened.

Chapter 20

Time passed.

Suddenly Prue, who had dozed off herself, was startled into wake-fulness by a very loud shriek just in her ears. Jane was sitting upright beside her, apparently frozen solid.

'Oh, what is it, Jane? What is it?'

Jane managed to utter the one word, 'Snake!'

Crawling over Jane's legs where she had spread them across the sandy ground for comfort was a shining length of danger.

Prue sprang to her feet.

'Don't move, Jane! It may think you're a tree stump.' She looked round her for a weapon. A large branch, stripped from a tree in some recent storm, lay close at hand. Prue seized it and struck out at the creature. It seemed to make no difference.

Just then there came a crashing sound among the trees nearby. Two large figures sprang out into the clearing.

'Mistress Prue!' cried Captain Hawkeye.

' Mistress Jane!' shouted Josh Tompkins.

As one man they drew their swords and struck the serpent where it had already crawled partly away from Jane's legs. The effect was immediate. Captain Hawkeye's sword cut the creature in two, while Josh Tompkins repeatedly pierced it in many places. A second later, they had each seized a part of the snake and hurled it into the distance.

Prue, near to fainting, dropped her useless branch and knelt to put her arms round her maidservant.

'Jane! Jane!' she cried, tears springing from her eyes. 'I thought you were dead!'

'Not with Josh and Captain Nick here to help us,' Jane said breathlessly.

Prue turned towards the two men who had been wiping their swords on the ground and were now sheathing them.

'Josh – Captain Nick –' she began, 'I don't know how to thank you –'

'No need,' Nick said crisply. 'Now, we need to get you two girls to safety. Perhaps you might like to put your clothes on before we go back to my men.'

141

Prue found herself blushing furiously. From deep gratitude her feelings for Black Nick turned to anger in a few seconds. He sounded so scathing, so superior. She had temporarily forgotten that she and Jane were wearing only their underclothes.

Trembling with fury, she untied her bundle of clothes, hastily pulled her nightdress over her head, and slipped into her dressing gown. She saw out of the corner of her eye that Jane was doing the same.

'What madness possessed you,' Nick was going on, 'To swim away from the safety of the ship and try to work through this jungle by yourselves, I can't understand.'

'Then I'll tell you!' Prue said, her words tripping over each other in rage. 'Neither Jane nor I could bear the prospect of spending the rest of our lives in the company of a bunch of cutthroat, murdering robbers and pirates, Captain!'

'There has never been any question of you and Mistress Brigham spending the rest of your lives with us,' Captain Hawkeye said coldly. 'I don't think anyone has asked you to do that. I explained to you that it would be impossible for me to sail my ship into any port without being arrested. However, we have links with a number of trading ships which call at our island home on a regular basis, and leave us necessary stores. It was my intention to arrange for your safe transport en route to America with the next ship to call. There is one due in a few weeks time. Until then, I trust you will find it bearable to remain in the company of 'a bunch of cutthroat robbers and murderers' rather than with snakes and wild animals.'

Prue could not remember when she had felt so bitterly humiliated.

'If you had explained that sooner, captain, it might have been better,' she said with equal coldness. Gathering her dressing gown around her, she said, 'Come, Jane,' and prepared to follow the two men out of the wilderness to the comparative safety of their camp.

It was when they had stumbled along for some time, each holding up the trailing skirts of their dressing gowns with one hand and using the other hand as a balance, that Jane screamed again as she tripped over a mass of tangled creepers and went head first into the undergrowth.

Chapter Twenty One

The Present

Christie resisted the urge to read on, turned out the light and lay down. But sleep did not come immediately. Instead her mind re-ran the events of the day, and in particular her evening with Steve Armstrong.

It wasn't that he had done or said anything in particular. Just that, somehow, they seemed to be on the same wavelength, to think about things in the same way, to laugh at the same silly comments – not even what most people would call jokes – to believe the same important stuff.

Christie hadn't felt so much at home with anyone outside her own family ever before.

She finally managed to get to sleep, and woke early the next morning with the happy feeling that everything in her life was wonderful.

She was putting bread in the toaster for an early breakfast when her mobile buzzed to indicate an incoming text message. Pressing the toaster down to start it, she turned to lift the mobile from the breakfast table and check if the message was important. She hoped it wasn't Aine complaining again. Her heart bounded when she saw the ID – Steve.

Eagerly she began to read the message.

'Good news,' it began. 'Got hold of the guy who stole the necklace from us, and his girl friend. Picked them up dodging out of your place. I was there on the lookout, like you asked me.'

Christie stopped reading for a moment. What was this? Why should Steve be telling her this stuff? And why did he say, 'stole the necklace from us'? Who did he mean by 'us'?

She read on.

'Tell you where I've got them tonight. Meet at the Kitchen, 8 pm, as usual.'

It was signed Jesse James.

Christie's world collapsed around her.

It was obvious that Steve had sent the message to her by mistake. She had heard of that sort of thing happening, often when a husband was cheating on his wife and sent a message to his wife intended for his girlfriend. This message must have been intended for someone Steve was working with. But not, surely, a colleague in the police? It didn't sound at all like that. Christie desperately needed to know more, to understand.

Had Steve been lying to her all along, fooling her into believing that he wasn't a crook, that he was working undercover for the police? Was he really planning to double-cross Tommy and Aine and hand them over to the Wild West gang?

Christie didn't know, but it sounded dreadfully like it.

One thing was certain, she was going to the Kitchen that night, to find out more for herself.

She didn't, however, want to go alone. She needed the company and support of a friend, preferably a man who could help her to handle Steve's crooked friends. After some thought, she decided that Maurice Thompson, the computer trouble shooter for the library, would be the best person to come with her. He was supposed to be working that morning, and he had expressed an interest in having a night out with her in Belfast. And although he was a bit of a geek, he was, as Christie knew, quite strong. He had lifted chairs and tables, when unable to duck out of it, with a careless ease which was impressive.

She approached him just before lunchtime.

'Hi, Maurice. Are you still up for that night out in Belfast you suggested?'

Maurice's eyes narrowed. 'I thought you were against the idea, babe?'

'Can't a girl change her mind?' Christie grinned at him.

'Ah, well, then, good idea. When had you thought of?'

'Oh, no time like the present. Tonight? I'd like to go to the Kitchen, if that suits you. Get there about eight? Each of us paying for themselves, of course, like you said.'

Maurice's face relaxed into approval. 'Sounds good to me, chick. I'll meet you outside it about eight, then.'

Christie repressed another grin. Typical of Maurice not to offer to pick her up by taxi or anything like that. Still, she was relieved to have set up the arrangement and to be sure of his company.

She made it to the Kitchen by five minutes to eight, but had to wait for a while longer before Maurice appeared, sauntering along casually.

'Hiya, babe! Lookin' good.' He took her hand to go into the bar, and Christie, unwilling to let that sort of thing set the tone for the evening, managed unobtrusively to get free of his grasp after a few minutes.

The place wasn't too full as yet, although no doubt it would liven up considerably, later on. Christie looked round for any sign of Steve or whichever member of the gang he was meeting.

'Better set up a kitty,' Maurice suggested. 'A tenner each, say? If you give me your contribution, I'll go and get us the first round.'

'Fair enough.' Christie produced her tenner and Maurice drifted off to the bar. 'White wine! Pinot Grigio!' Christie called after him, hoping he'd heard and wasn't going to come back with the lager which she hated. It seemed typical of Maurice, somehow, for him not to bother to ask what she wanted to drink. She continued to look all around.

Suddenly, out of the corner of her eye, she saw someone she was sure was Butch. He was sitting at a table in the far corner, obviously waiting for a friend. As Christie watched, a man sidled up to him and sat down. Christie hardly recognised Steve Armstrong. He had done something to himself that made him look different. His hair was a mess, his face looked red, and the clothes he was wearing, although not shabby, looked untidy, almost as if he had slept in them, and slept rough at that. But it was Steve, all right. Christie was sure of it.

Now what?

full pint for himself, from which he was already beginning to gulp. He had clearly drunk quite a lot of it on his way from the bar.

'Don't sit down, Maurice,' she ordered. 'I want to take you over to meet a friend of mine.'

She jumped up, ignoring the half pint of lager.

Maurice, his jaw dropping already, looked even more surprised when he saw her begin to move off without her drink.

'Hey, don't forget your lager.'

'I told you, when we had that pizza, that I hate lager,' Christie said casually. 'Come on, over here.'

Maurice took another gigantic gulp of his own drink, then poured Christie's rejected offering into his pint glass. 'Pity to waste it,' was all he said. No apologies, Christie noted. But she was too upset about Steve Armstrong to worry about Maurice just now. His job was to come with her and to help out at any threat of rough stuff from Butch – or Steve, either, of course, but she somehow couldn't believe there would be any of that, even now.

'So, Steve,' she said, as they reached the table. At the sound of her voice, Steve gave a jump and turned to face her. 'I thought my friend Maurice and I might join you. Oh, this is Maurice. And, of course, I already know Butch, don't I?' She glared at the gangster.

Maurice, demonstrating that he occasionally had some manners, pulled out a chair for her, and she sat down.

'Christie! What are you doing here?' Steve's voice was shaky.

'Oh, but you sent me a message to meet here, didn't you, Steve? Or was it meant for someone else? For Butch here, maybe? The guy who captured me and my friends and threatened us with all sorts?'

'Hey, what is all this, Christie?' Maurice interjected, with a puzzled expression on his normally self-absorbed face.

'Oh, didn't I tell you, Maurice?' Christie asked innocently. 'Butch is a gangster. He and his gang kidnapped me and two of my friends yesterday afternoon. We thought Steve had helped us to escape, but it turns out he was working for Butch all the time. He came here to hand over my friends to Butch. Over my dead body, he'll do it!' Her voice suddenly flared into violent anger.

'Christie –' Steve's voice sounded anguished, but Christie was past caring.

'So, I think my best move now is to contact the real police, don't you agree, Maurice? I can't expect Steve or Butch to agree with me, of course, but there's not much they can do about it, in a public place like this, is there?' She lifted her mobile and began to ring the local police station, whose number she'd looked up before leaving her house.

'Oh, isn't there?' roared Butch, springing to his feet. With a sudden movement he snatched the mobile from Christie's hand, dropped it in his pocket, and moved round behind her. Grabbing one arm he twisted it up her back. She could feel something sticking into her other side at the same time.

'This is a knife, see? One move from you and it goes into your ribs, straight to the heart. Maybe I'd better do it anyway, save a lot of trouble. No one would notice. I'll drop you on the table and it'll look like you passed out.'

'Maurice!' Christie shouted. 'Do something!' This, after all, was what she had brought him for.

But the only thing Maurice seemed able to do was to spill his lager. 'What? Do what?' he asked, sounding dazed.

Christie gave up. It was hopeless. Then, as if from a far distance, she heard Steve's voice.

'Butch! Let her go! She doesn't know anything. Can't you see she's just bluffing? Don't be mad enough to stab her here. You'll never get away with it.'

'Maybe not,' Butch said. 'But she really deserves it.'

'So what? Think of yourself! You can't take the risk. If anyone figures it out and they catch you before you get outta here, you've had it.'

'Okay,' Butch said suddenly. 'Let's shift it.' He threw Christie down onto the table and made for the door, closely followed by Steve Armstrong. He still had Christie's mobile, she realised.

It was several moments before Christie recovered herself enough to raise her head.

'Thanks a bunch, Maurice,' she said bitterly. 'A real help you were. Waste of time bringing you.'

'Well, what did you expect?' Maurice asked reasonably. 'I'm not Superman. As you may have noticed, I don't wear my underpants outside my jeans.' He turned away huffily, and slid on the lager he had spilt a moment earlier.

Christie couldn't help giggling as he slid wildly across the floor, grabbing at a chair which he then brought down on top of him.

Christie felt remorseful. Darting forward, she helped him to his feet. 'No, why should I have expected that you would be able to do anything against a thug armed with a knife, when I couldn't do anything myself?' she agreed. 'But come on! We need to follow them!'

'Why?' asked Maurice belligerently.

Christie wasn't sure why. But she felt that they had to. They needed to do something, and what else was there to do?

Dodging away from the approaching staff member, who was clearly on his way to complain about their behaviour, maybe even to throw them out, she dragged Maurice by his arm to the exit where Butch and Steve had just disappeared.

'Don't argue! Just come,' she said severely, and to her astonishment Maurice meekly came.

They reached the street unmolested and Christie looked round anxiously.

'Look! There they are!' she exclaimed suddenly. It was just possible to see the tail end of Butch rounding the corner not far away. Taking to her heels, Christie ran at top speed after him.

Followed, to both her surprise and his own, by Maurice. It seemed that the excitement of the chase had taken hold of him.

As they in their turn rounded the corner they saw Butch and Steve heading to a small Fiesta which Christie recognised as Steve's car, parked along a side street.

'We need to stop them before they get into that car!' she panted. But they were too late.

Chapter Twenty Two

'Well,' said Maurice, 'I don't know what you thought we could do if we had caught up with them.'

Christie didn't try to make clear that she had wanted to get an explanation out of Steve Armstrong.

'I suppose you're right,' she agreed with a sigh. 'I'm sorry I got you out tonight for nothing, Maurice.'

'Never mind,' Maurice said, unexpectedly philosophic. 'After all, it's been fun. Let's go and have that drink somewhere else, okay? Maybe not go back to the Kitchen. I'm not sure we'd be welcome.'

'I'm quite sure we wouldn't,' Christie giggled.

'But there are lots of other bars,' Maurice said. 'Let's try the Sunflower, for a start.'

So they did. And to Christie's surprise, they had a really fun evening. When at last they called it a day, she went home and up to bed determined never again to think about Steve Armstrong. The loss of her mobile was a problem, but she'd deal with that the next day.

Meanwhile, she crawled into bed and picked up her Kindle. *The Pirate* should take her mind off the bad day she had had.

1794

'Jane!' shouted Jake Tompkins, his voice sounding desperate. He sprang forward, seizing Jane in his arms, and lifted her, apparently effortlessly. 'Are you all right?'

'I'm fine,' Jane said breathlessly. 'I just tripped over a creeper trailing across the path. Oh, Josh!'

She buried her face in his shoulder.

''That settles it,' Josh said sternly. 'I'm going to carry you for the rest of the way.'

'Oh, but Josh? Can you?'

'It's not far, darling. I can't risk you hurting yourself any more.' He set off, Jane in his arms. Prue couldn't help feeling admiration for him.

'You have a good man for mate, Captain,' she volunteered, presently, as she and Captain Nick trailed after Josh and his burden.

'I know,' said Nick briefly.

Prue said no more.

After what seemed a short enough time, they came out of the trees, and Prue saw before her a wide clearing with numerous buildings, some made of bamboo with straw roofs, but many of them more imposing, higher and made from bricks, extending over a wider area, with roofs built from wood and some sort of tiles, probably fashioned from clay. The main building, the biggest of all, seemed to have been there for some time.

'Why, Captain, did you build this?' she asked in amazement.

'Why, no, Mistress Prue,' said Captain Hawkeye. 'This once belonged to the British governor of this group of islands. When he pulled out, the house was abandoned, so I took it over. As you can see, this island is still British, and flies the British flag.'

Prue, looking upwards, saw the Union flag fluttering on the mast above the roof.

'What a shame you don't fly the same flag on your ship, Captain,' she said coolly.

'Sometimes I do, Mistress Prue. It would not do to fly the British flag when I plan to attack another ship,' Captain Hawkeye said.

Prue was silenced.

Captain Nick led the way to the largest building, followed by Josh, still carrying Jane, although the necessity to protect her from snakes or trailing creepers was long past. Prue followed. She was aware of strange, confused feelings.

'Welcome to my humble abode, ladies,' said Captain Nick. Prue could not help noticing the bitterness in his voice. 'I hope you *will be comfortable here, until such time as I can arrange for your safe passage on a trading vessel to your homeland. Josh, will you direct the ladies to the rooms we have prepared for them. I think you may allow Mistress Jane to walk there by herself, now.'*

Josh and Jane matched each other with blushing faces, as Josh hurriedly set Jane on her feet.

'Thank you, Josh,' said Jane, recovering her composure. 'You have been more than kind.'

'It's been a pleasure, Mistress Jane,' Josh muttered. 'I hope you'll be comfortable in the room we've allotted to you.'

He turned and led the girls along a passageway to the area where the bedrooms were located.

They had separate rooms.

As soon as Josh had left them to settle in, however, Jane knocked hurriedly on Prue's door, and in response to her, 'Come in,' entered quietly.

'Oh, Prue, what shall we do? They are so kind. I can't think they are as bad as we've thought.'

'I know, Jane,' Prue answered worriedly. 'But what about Captain Myles and his crew? Are we to leave them captive and in despair, just because we ourselves have been well treated?'

Jane's face fell.

'No – I understand, Miss Prue,' she answered, reverting without being aware of it to her position of obedience to Prue. 'We need to think about them.'

'I suggest', Prue said firmly, 'that when we think everyone else has gone to sleep, later tonight, we should slip quietly out and search for the hut where he is being kept prisoner.'

Jane hung her head. 'You're right, Mistress Prue.'

'Jane! What's with this 'Mistress Prue' again? 'Prue' is quite sufficient!'

'Prue, then,' said Jane.

There was a knock on the door. 'Come in,' Prue called.

The door opened and Josh entered. 'Oh, you're both here. I came to tell you that Captain Hawkeye would be glad if you would both give him the pleasure of dining with him?'

'You may tell the captain that it will be a pleasure, Josh,' replied Prue formally. 'We are both ready, having nothing to change into. You may lead us to the captain's dining room.'

'The captain is expecting you in another fifteen minutes, Mistress Prue. He thought you might like to have time to wash, and tidy your hair. The warm water is on your washstand, and brushes and combs have been laid out on your dressing tables. Moreover, dresses have been provided in your wardrobes, which he hopes will be to your liking. I'll come back to take you to the dining room presently.'

Prue blushed. 'That is kind of the Captain,' she said. 'If you will come back in fifteen minutes, then, Josh, we will be ready for him.'

'You will find the same arrangements in your own room, Mistress Jane,' Josh ventured, and was rewarded with a beaming smile from Jane.

'Thank you, Josh,' she murmured, and slipped out of Prue's room.

Prue's first action was to fling open the doors of the large, impressive wardrobe which stood against one wall. There were a number of dresses, any one of which she would have been delighted to wear. Almost better, there was a shelf of fresh underclothing. Prue breathed a sigh of sheer delight.

Stripping off everything, she washed happily in the warm water and scented soap provided, then chose a pretty Parisian camisole and matching pantaloons. It was difficult to decide on a dress, but eventually, aware that time was running out, she picked a wide skirted silk in her favourite dark blue, and slipped it on. The huge mirror over the dressing table showed her a pretty blued eyed young woman, with, alas, very disheveled hair.

Hastily snatching up the brush and comb, she did what she could to remedy her appearance, ending by threading her now tidy dark hair with one of the satin ribbons set out on the dressing table, a blue one to match her dress. Finally, she pirouetted before the mirror in great satisfaction. It was a pleasure to feel that, after the last week or so, she once more looked as she should.

A knock on the door heralded the arrival of Jane. Prue gazed at her in admiration. Jane was also wearing a pretty dress of the sort she had never previously had, in a pale green in her case, and looking very different from the little maid Prue was used to seeing.

'Why, Jane, how pretty you look!' she exclaimed impulsively. 'A real young lady, my dear!'

And when Josh arrived at that moment to take them to the Captain, it was clear from his expression that he thought the same.

The dining room was large and impressive. Clearly it had been designed and furnished for the days when the Governor of the islands entertained visiting nobilities. The polished mahogany table and the elegant matching chairs were in the latest style. Prudence had only once seen such an impressive set of furniture, when she and her father had been invited to the official residence of the Governor of Jamaica, some years after her father had been appointed to control the British forces there.

It almost made it up to them for having had to leave the mainland after Britain's defeat in the American war, her father had whispered to her. Heaped dishes of fruit and a steaming tureen of delicious smelling soup covered Captain Nick's sideboard.

The table was laid with shining cutlery, and gleaming glasses reflected the light from the huge candlestick with its numerous candles, which shone on the polished table top. Prue was both dazzled and delighted. The room and especially the table impressed her beyond anything she had expected.

But to her eyes, Captain Nick Hawkeye outshone everything else in the room.

She had seen him before, clad for evening, on board his ship, but she now discovered that that had been as nothing to the splendour of his present attire. His waisted, wide skirted coat, a delicate pale blue shot with silver, showed off his magnificent figure to perfection. Across his breast was the deep blue ribbon of the Order of the Garter. Jewels gleamed in the tumble of lacy cravat which fell from his throat, a single jewel, a deep sapphire, hung from one ear, and his slim white fingers carried more jewels set in golden rings.

Prue found to her embarrassment that her eyes were fixed on him, and that he could hardly have avoided noticing this.

He came forward smoothly and took her hand in one of his and Jane's in the other.

'Ladies,' he said, in his mellifluous voice, 'may I compliment you both on your excellent choice of gowns? You could not have chosen better. Indeed, Josh,' he added, turning to the mate, who, Prue now discovered, was also dressed as she had never seen him before in a striking coat of purple, 'are we not honoured to dine with two such beautiful ladies?'

Josh murmured agreement, but his eyes were fixed on Jane, whose own eyes dropped and whose cheeks were once again red.

Prue found herself wishing that Captain Nick's eyes could be focused on her in the same way.

The Captain led them to the table, Prue on his right hand and Jane on his left. Josh sat opposite the Captain, which meant that Jane was on his right.

'Mistress Prue, will you take a glass of wine with me?' Captain Nick asked, and Prue found herself shyly agreeing.

'I must begin by apologising for the poor fare I have to offer you both tonight,' Captain Nick said. 'The next schooner will not call at the island for another week, and meanwhile our provisions are running low. But we have given you the best we have, and can only hope you will enjoy it, such as it is.'

As he spoke, a servant set a dish of the wonderful smelling soup before Prue, and swiftly moved round to serve Jane, then Josh, and finally Nick.

'You have no need to apologise for this soup, at least, Captain Hawkeye,' Prue said. 'I don't believe I've ever tasted better.'

'Thank you, Mistress Prue. It's a special island recipe which our cook invented. I believe I can say that his skill is as great as any I used to experience in London or even Paris as a youth.'

And, indeed, the rest of the meal, a delicate flavoured fish unfamiliar to Prue, a bird, also unfamiliar, in a delicious sauce, and a confection of sweet flavoured ice designed to look like a towering castle and impossible to resist, lived up to everything Nick had said about his cook. But for some reason, what it was she could not tell, Prue found herself without much appetite. And so, she noticed, did Captain Nick.

Chapter 22

However, Jane and Josh more than made up for it.

Jane, unused to such dishes, was enjoying herself to the full, and Josh was displaying his seaman's appetite for shore food with its more varied choice and abundance.

When the meal was over, Captain Nick rose to his feet and bowed ceremoniously to both girls. 'Ladies, I trust you will sleep well,' he said. 'Josh will escort you to your rooms.'

Prue felt disappointment flooding through her. But why had she hoped that Captain Nick might have suggested a walk, a chance to look up at the moon and stars together, as they had done on board ship? She had shown him all too clearly what she thought of him. Why should she expect he would want to spend time with her after that?

And, she reflected, she still knew that she must not become too close to someone who was, in spite of everything, no more than a cruel pirate. She had warned Jane against it – she must not fall into the same trap herself.

When she was alone in her cabin, she remembered the plans she had made to rescue Myles and his crew. And sure enough, it wasn't long before a knock on her door announced the arrival of Jane.

'Well, Jane,' she said briskly, 'are you ready for our voyage of exploration?'

Hel's Heroes 2: Christie & The Pirate

Chapter Twenty Three

The Present

Christie closed the Kindle with a sigh. She could not help reflecting on the similarity between her own position and Prue's. Christie, too, had apparently fallen, she thought gloomily, for a guy who was a crook, and one who had set out to deceive her badly, moreover. And that in spite of Helen McFadden's words of warning when they met at the Library book signing.

Meanwhile, it was time to stop reading and get some sleep. Morning, and the need to get up and go to work, would come only too quickly.

But it was a long time before sleep came to Christie that night. She tossed and turned restlessly for what seemed like hours, until a sound downstairs jerked her suddenly upright in bed. What was that?

It had sounded, of all things, like the flap of her letterbox when the postman put letters and small parcels through it.

Christie was in two minds. Should she put her head under the bed-clothes? Or should she ring the police on her landline? (Although they might think she was imagining things.)

But instead of either of these options, she found herself getting briskly out of bed, wrapping her warm fleecy dressing gown around her, pushing her feet into her slippers, and creeping cautiously out of her room to the head of the stairs. Then, moving as quietly as she could, she began to descend into the hall.

When she was halfway down the stairs, she suddenly let out a squeak of surprise. Lying on the hall carpet, where it had dropped from the letter box, was her mobile phone, the one which Butch had stolen!

Tumbling down the remaining stairs, she rushed to snatch it up. Underneath it was an envelope, addressed to 'Christie.' She opened it, and read the letter inside it swiftly.

It was from Steve Armstrong.

'Christie,' it began, *'I know you'll be wanting your phone, even needing it. I'm sorry Butch took it – I couldn't stop him at the time, but I sneaked it out of his jacket pocket later. I looked at the message you mentioned. It must have given you a bad shock. As you figured, it wasn't meant for you. I can only think that I put your number in because you were so much on my mind. You've got to let me explain. Please meet me for lunch at the same place tomorrow. It's really important to me to talk to you.*

Love, Steve.'

Christie moved as if in a dream into the kitchen, made herself some coffee, and sat down at her kitchen table to drink it and to read Steve's letter again. And again.

What was she to believe? And was she going to meet him at the Purple Cat or just refuse to have anything more to do with him?

First she thought she'd go, and tell him once again what she thought of him.

Then she reckoned that the best thing would be to ignore him completely. But did she have a duty to tell the police about him? To set a trap, even? She had already failed to report his involvement with the gang, the first time she saw him running away from the robbery in the Victoria Centre. Why, she was still not quite sure. Was she going to repeat her behaviour then?

A long time later, she staggered back up to bed, still clutching her letter as well as her phone, lay down, and tried once again to get to sleep. But she had heard the birds beginning to chirp in the dawn light before she at last dropped over the edge of the abyss into sleep's black depths.

It should have been a good day at the library. The sun was shining, Hazel for once wasn't talking about her latest boyfriend – something had gone wrong between her and Luke. According to Hazel he had got mean and boring, and never wanted to take her anywhere interesting. He'd actually suggested that they went for a walk in the park!

'You can't expect him to spend a fortune on you every evening, Hazel,' Christie pointed out. 'If you can't enjoy his company for something simple like a walk in Ormeau Park, then you're wasting your time going out with him.'

But Hazel, who didn't enjoy being given good advice any more than the rest of us, merely sniffed, stuck her nose in the air, and took herself off to the other side of the Library, much to Christie's relief. It wasn't Maurice's day to be in, and the few customers were all pleasant and easy to deal with. But none of this helped her to feel less miserable.

Lunch time came round all too quickly, and Christie still hadn't decided whether she would go to the Purple Cat or not. But somehow when she ran down the steps out of the library she found her feet taking her, apparently of their own accord, straight to it. She pushed open the door and walked in.

Steve Armstrong was sitting at a corner table. He stood up eagerly when Christie came in, but the beam disappeared from his face when he saw her expression.

Christie sat down in the seat opposite him and he sank back down in turn. 'I've come here for one reason only, Steve,' she told him quietly, 'and that is to make sure you know what I think of your despicable deception of me. And to warn you that I'm seriously considering reporting this whole business to the police. I don't want to listen to any more of your lying explanations. I've heard all I want to of them. Now I'm going. I hope never to see you again, unless it's to stand up in court and identify you as one of the Wild West gang.'

'But, Christie, darlin' – wait!' Steve sprang up again and took hold of her arm as she rose to go. 'You've got it all wrong. I told you I was pretending to work in with the gang – well, I didn't exactly spell it out, I'm not supposed to do that, but I thought you understood. Don't you see – that text was meant to go to Butch – I copied it to you by mistake!'

'I know you did,' Christie snapped. 'I didn't think you'd be brazen enough to send it to me deliberately.' She pulled her arm free and left the café.

'Christie, where are you going, darlin'? Slow down! Listen, things are so nearly coming to a head,' Steve said urgently, following her out and hurrying along beside her. 'If you'll only give me a few more days to finish it off! Please don't wreck everything now!'

Christie stopped and looked at him. 'What do you mean?'

Steve looked at her despairingly. 'I'm not supposed to tell anyone. But I can't help it. I can't let you go on thinking I'm a crook and a villain. Please come back in and sit down quietly and I'll try to tell you as much as I can.'

Why, she wasn't sure, but Christie allowed him to lead her back into the café. When they were seated at the same quiet corner table, Steve looked round nervously, then began to speak in a voice so soft that it was all Christie could do to hear him.

'I'm an undercover cop,' he said. 'I thought you'd sort of picked that up, without me spelling it out more than I did, especially when I told Aine and Tommy. That means that Butch and his gang think I'm one of them, and they have to go on thinking that until I've got enough evidence against them to take them to court. I'm so nearly there, Christie. I'm meeting Butch tonight in their secret hideout, and he's going to show me an outline of their plans for the next six months and the stuff they're snatched recently.

'Oh, they're very organised. Butch thinks I'd be the right person to be his second-in-command. Got more brains than the rest of them, he's kind enough to say. Not much of a compliment, really, is it? Doc's the only one with any brains at all. I think Butch might even give me the combination of his safe. That's where he still has the jewels and stuff from his last couple of heists, he's told me that much. But even if he doesn't give me the combination, once I know the sort of info he has in the safe as well as the stolen property, I can come back with a search warrant and have the safe blown open, and Butch and the gang arrested on the strength of the contents.'

He paused and looked anxiously at Christie to see how she was taking this. The waitress was leaning against the wall, wondering whether or not to interrupt them. She'd apparently decided not to come over quite yet.

'That sounds all right, Steve,' she said slowly, 'but what I can't understand is how you could have been planning to give Tommy and Aine up to Butch, telling him where they were. That's something I just can't accept. You didn't need to do that to keep up your cover.'

'But, Christie, I didn't! I never intended to! It was just a trick to make Butch certain I was on his side.'

'And when he asked you for details of where they were?'

'I planned to say they'd gone, moved on when I wasn't there.'

'Oh.'

Steve looked at her.

'Would that not have made him pretty suspicious of you?' Christie said. 'I should think you'd have been better off not mentioning that you knew where they were in the first place.'

'No, because I'd have said that they'd never trusted me, and that moving on like this proved it. I'd have given him the address of an empty house, not the one where they are, of course, if he'd wanted more. But I need to tell you, darlin', that Tommy caved in and gave me the necklace – he had given it to Aine to hide for him, and she had it on her somewhere all along.

She made me turn my back while she produced it, why I don't know.' Christie, who did know why, couldn't help grinning. 'I knew he'd pinched it from the rest of the gang, in spite of his story about someone giving it to him to pawn. I told you the gang hadn't many brains, not to search Aine after they searched him! I'll leave him and Aine out of my official report, of course. Tommy can go back to his job with no fear of bring shopped, and he and Aine can get on with their lives.'

Christie thought about it. The waitress came over with menus, and Steve ordered omelettes. 'At least – is that okay, Christie? You liked it the last time?'

'Yes, yes, anything,' she said impatiently. She waited until the waitress had moved away. 'I still don't know if I believe you, Steve,' she said. 'The thing is, I want to. So I think the only thing for you to do is to prove it. Take me along with you tonight, and let me hide round a corner or something where I can hear what the two of you say. Okay?'

'But, Christie! Suppose Butch catches on that you're there? You'll be in real trouble!'

'And so will you, I suppose.' She paused to let the waitress deposit their food on the table and go away again. 'We'll deal with that when it happens, right? Either you take me there or I go straight to the nearest police station, boyo. You want me to trust you? Right, then you have to trust me, not to mess this up. No reason why Butch should know I'm there if we find a good place for me to hide. We can go early and scoop it out. Don't tell me you don't know where the 'secret hideaway' is, because I bet you've followed him there and checked it out long ago.'

'Well, yeah, I have,' Steve admitted with a grin. 'And as a matter of fact Butch showed it to me himself recently. He's expecting me to make my own way there tonight. But Christie, this is still way too dangerous for you.'

'Shut up about that. I'm doing it, or turning you in.'

'Okay. I'll pick you up at the library when you're leaving, then. We'll need to get there well before Butch, so we can get you safely hidden.' Steve picked gloomily at his omelette. 'We'd better grab something to eat first.'

'And you'd better not waste the food you've got,' Christie told him. 'We'll both need lots of nourishment if we're going to tackle the Wild West gang tonight.'

The afternoon seemed endless. Christie found herself half looking forward to the adventurous evening she had planned for herself and half dreading it. Suppose they couldn't find a good enough hiding place for her, or supposing Butch heard her, if she sneezed or coughed or something?

And did she believe Steve Armstrong or not? The fact that he was willing to prove his story by letting her come with him and hear for herself what he said to Butch might mean that he was telling her the truth. Or it might not. She was torn between her desire to believe him and her revulsion from him if he was, in fact, a member of the gang. She found herself praying, 'Show me the truth, Lord.'

Time eventually moved on. Christie's day's work finished. She left the Library, and walked over to where Steve's car was parked across the street.

The hideout was a small farmhouse in the country many miles to the north of Belfast, in the barren hills of County Antrim. It took them well over an hour to drive there.

'I picked up some subs to eat on the way,' Steve said. 'Didn't think there was time for a sit down meal somewhere.' He handed Christie a wrapped chicken and salad sub, and she did her best to eat it without getting drips from the sweet chilli sauce all over her.

Steve seemed to have no problem with his, even though he was eating one handed while driving.

'Don't eat and drive,' Christie murmured to him, and was rewarded by a chuckle.

Some time later, he pulled up in front of the farmhouse and they got out. Steve took a thin metal instrument from his pocket and did something clever to the front door lock. Christie had never seen a picklock before, but assumed this must be one. The door opened in a remarkably short time.

Inside, the main priority was to find somewhere for Christie to hide.

"I've been thinking about this,' Steve said. 'Butch and I will probably be in what he calls his office, where the safe is. So you need to be within hearing distance of that, otherwise it's pointless you being here. Let's go and look round the ground floor.'

They moved off down the hall which led to the kitchen and put their heads round the door. One look was enough for Christie. It was a small, grubby room, too far away from the office for Christie to be able to see and hear. She walked in for a better look, but there was nothing useful to be seen. Through the dirty window she could see a number of strong looking stone outbuildings with weeds growing up round their bases.

'We're wasting our time, Steve,' she said decidedly. 'Let's go back to the hall and see if we can come up with something there.'

'Okay,' said Steve equably. 'There's only one other place I can think of – the small closet in the hall. It might do. I'll try to keep the office door open, so's you can hear better.'

He opened the door of the closet, which was small and quite stuffy looking. There were hooks for coats, and a few items hanging there as if left for emergencies or by mistake. There seemed to be enough room in it for Christie to stand. Nowhere to sit, though. Christie decided philosophically that she could manage.

'I'm going to take off in a minute,' Steve said. 'Don't want Butch to catch me here without him. I'm supposed to meet him at eight, outside. I'll re-lock the front door after me, of course.' He looked worried for a moment. 'It's only seven o'clock now, Christie. Will you be okay? If you want to change your mind, I could take you back to the nearest café and you could wait there until I can pick you up and run you home again.'

'No way!' said Christie decidedly. 'I want to see for myself.'

'Okay, darlin'. One thing, though. I don't want Butch to be able to open this door and find you. So just in case he decides to look inside, here's the key.' He was taking it out of the outside lock on the door as he spoke. 'I don't want to lock you in and keep the key myself. Too risky. Who knows what might happen? So I want you to promise me that you'll lock the door on the inside as soon as you're settled.'

'Good idea.' Christie took the key, then on an impulse, leaned up to give Steve a quick kiss on the cheek. 'Look after yourself, right?'

'Sure, it's you that needs to be told that. You're crazy, do you know that?' Steve said. 'Gotta be away, now.' He waited until Christie had gone into the closet and shut the door on herself. As she stood in the darkness, wondering how to endure the next hour, she could hear his footsteps going quickly away down the hall, and then the sound of the front door shutting.

An answer to her question came to her. Taking her Kindle out of her shoulder bag, she opened it, and saw the light from the screen giving her some relief from the darkness inside the closet. Then, with a sigh of relief, she began to read the next chapter of *The Pirate*.

Chapter Twenty Four

1794

'I'm ready to go,' said Jane. 'But I don't think you are, Prue.'

Prue looked down at her elaborate evening gown and laughed. She discovered that Jane had changed into a much simpler day dress which would be easier to move about in.

'Just give me a minute,' she said. 'And maybe you could help me get out of this?'

Jane helped her to untie the fastening of her gown, and together they searched in the wardrobe and decided on a dark green day dress with no voluminous skirt or impeding train.

When they were both ready, Prue said, 'I wonder if we should try to bring some food? We could check in the kitchen and see what there is.'

'I don't think so,' Jane said. 'There may be people still there, clearing up or preparing for tomorrow.'

Prue bowed to Jane's superior knowledge of what went on in kitchens.

'In that case, our first task is to discover where Captain Myles is being held,' she said.

'And our second is to release him,' Jane added.

'I would guess that he's not in this building. Probably in one of the huts we passed on our way in.'

Jane nodded, and the girls set themselves to slip quietly out of the nearest door.

This was harder than they had hoped. There were quite a few rooms and passages, and they were aware that if they took the wrong turning they might find themselves going into an occupied bedroom or some such place and giving their plans away.

But eventually they found their way to the massive door they had come in by. There was a huge iron key in the lock. Prue's first action was to turn it. And then all that remained was to manage the huge and unwieldy bolts. There were three of them, stiff and unhelpful. It was a lengthy struggle, but in the end they were successful in drawing them back in, for the most part, silence.

The door itself was another matter, however. As soon as Prue started to draw it cautiously open, it gave out a loud creaking noise. Prue stopped immediately.

'We'll need to take this slowly and carefully, Jane,' she said in a whisper. 'I'll try again, and as soon as there's enough of a gap, you slip through and I'll follow you. I think we'll not try to close it. It just doubles the noise, and if anyone comes looking they'll know we've got out when they see the bolts drawn, so what's the difference?'

The two girls began to pull cautiously at the heavy door again, and soon were able to slip out. The door wasn't especially wide open. In the dark, it wouldn't be immediately obvious. 'Thank goodness you and I are both slim, Jane,' Prue whispered when they were safely outside and at a reasonable distance from the house.

'Now comes the difficult part,' Jane said. 'Finding Captain Myles without blundering into the crew's sleeping quarters. And getting him out.'

Prue smiled. 'You're right, Jane. Let's just hope he's in a hut with a door which has obvious bolts on the outside to keep prisoners shut in.'

'And not one that's locked,' Jane added. 'It was as well for us that the key to the house door was in the lock. We can't hope for a repeat of that.'

'Well,' said Prue, 'someone up there was looking after us. Why not hope for a repeat?'

They moved on cautiously across the dirt road which wound through the complex. There were more huts than Prue had remembered, and some of them were quite large, although not as big as the main building. It looked as if they would have to explore the whole area, looking for a bolted door.

The worst of it was that if they went too close to any of the huts and were heard, someone might come out and catch them. And it would be goodbye to any chance of escape, let alone any hope of rescuing Captain Myles.

All they could do was move lightly, and hope for the best.

After what seemed like years, during which Prue reckoned that they had examined the doors of at least a dozen huts, they came upon one which looked as if it might possibly be what they wanted. Set apart from most of the other buildings, this one was more solid, built mostly of brick, and with a door which looked as if it was made to resist any attempts to break it down. Prue and Jane looked at it doubtfully.

It was made of a tough wood, possibly oak, although how the builders could have got hold of oak on this remote Caribbean island Prue wasn't too sure. A hardwood, at any rate.

The door was studded with iron and across the middle was a strong looking iron bolt, feeding through a huge iron keeper. Prue, examining it, was thankful to see that there was no padlock.

'I think we're there, Jane,' she said quietly. 'Now, the thing is to get this bolt moved without waking the whole camp – or any of it. Slowly does it, I suppose.'

And slowly it had to be, in any case. The bolt was slow to move, and needed all Prue's strength, combined with Jane's, to shift even a small way along. They panted and heaved, and watched the bolt move slightly, inch by inch. One thing to be grateful for was that it had been well oiled, and made little or no noise.

In the end, they succeeded. The bolt slid out of its keeper and the door was free to open. But the next question was, was it locked?

There was a knob beneath the bolt, but no sign of a keyhole. Prue breathed a quick prayer, seized the knob and turned it, and as she pushed the door carefully, felt it move.

'Done it, Jane!' she exclaimed, almost, but not quite, forgetting, in her excitement, to keep her voice low.

The next thing was to find out if Myles was actually inside. They slipped into the room as quietly as possible and allowed their eyes to adjust to the darkness. Moonlight shone through the window on the far side, enough to show them that they were in a large room with a bed over in one corner and the minimum of other furniture. Someone was sleeping in the bed, but as they watched he stirred, turned over and seemed to become aware of their presence. He sat up halfway, propped on one elbow. 'Wha'? Who is it?'

'Shush, Myles,' whispered Prue urgently. 'It's us – Prue and Jane. We've come to get you out.'

They heard him laugh. 'That's great, girls. But you may have problems.'

He held up one wrist. There was a shackle fastened to it. A chain led from it to the wall. It was quite a long chain. Myles had freedom to move about around the room. But the padlock which kept it attached to the wall looked as if it was going to be impossible to shift.

But Prue wasn't giving up now. 'Do you know who has the key to the thing on your wrist, Myles?' she asked urgently, still keeping her voice low.

'Yes – it's the second mate. A pleasant enough fellow – but tough. He won't yield an inch when I ask him to unfasten me for at least a short time, to make eating easier, for instance. Claims the chain is deliberately long enough to allow me quite enough flexibility.'

'And do you know where he keeps the key?'

'It seems to stay attached to his belt,' Myles said.

'So.' Prue's determination not to be beaten on this showed in her voice. 'We have to find out where he sleeps, and get the key from him without waking him up.'

'No chance,' Myles said.

'I don't know about that,' Prue said. 'I have a sort of idea how we might do it. Come on, Jane, let's get out of here and we'll start by exploring a bit more till we find out where he sleeps.'

The two girls retreated cautiously across the room and out through the doorway, pulling the heavy door almost shut behind them.

'I was thinking, Jane, that when we find out where the second mate sleeps, we need to cause a distraction – lure him outside. Maybe if one of us started screaming and calling for help. Not too loud, of course. We don't want to wake up the whole camp. Just outside his window would work, I hope. Then the other one slips in and takes the keys. What do you think?'

'*I'll do the calling for help, then,*' *Jane said firmly.* '*You can get the keys, Prue. But what excuse can I make?*'

'*Easy.*' *Jane could see Prue's grin even in the faint moonlight.* '*You weren't able to sleep, so you came out for a walk, and you tripped over a snake. After your experience earlier, that should be second nature to you, Jane.*'

'*Well – maybe,*' *Jane said cautiously.* '*He'll probably be pretty annoyed with me for coming out by myself alone at night. And suppose he says there are no snakes inside the camp?*'

'*Oh, it doesn't have to be a real snake. You can find something lying about to pretend to trip over. A rope, or a tree branch, or something. The point is, you thought it was a snake, after what had happened to you earlier.*'

'*Yes. All right. I suppose it might work,*' *Jane admitted.* '*At any rate it's worth trying.*'

'*He might want to escort you back to the big house,*' *Prue added.* '*All the better if he does. He won't feel any need to go in with you, I suppose. As soon as he's gone, come straight out again and meet me back at Myles' prison hut. So, now we have to find where the second mate sleeps – and hope he has a hut to himself.*'

'*Yes, suppose he shares with some of the crew?*' *Jane asked anxiously.*

'*Well, then we'll have to think again,*' *Prue said briskly.* '*But he had his own cabin on the ship. Remember, when Josh gave us his cabin, he moved in with the second mate? Josh has a room in the big house, as we know, and that means the second mate is the senior man out here. So I hope it's the same, and he has a place to himself. Come on, let's get started exploring.*'

It didn't take them too long to identify the crew quarters. It was a long single story building, whose door stood open to admit the fresh air. Mingled snorts and snores came from within. Prue and Jane slid cautiously past it, and saw a couple of smaller huts not far away. One of these must be the place they were looking for. The first one, when they glanced carefully in, smelt of spices and cooking fat, just like the ship's galley. The large figure in the bed, whose snores were almost as loud as those of the whole crew put together, could only be the cook, they agreed.

So the other single hut was probably where the second mate slept. With the keys to Myles' shackles in his belt.

Another thought occurred to Prue. Would he have taken off his belt and breeches, including the keys, to sleep? Or would he have felt they were too important not to keep close to him?

She shrugged. No way to know that in advance. If he came out in response to Jane's screams fully clothed, perhaps Prue could attack him, render him unconscious, and take the keys from his belt? She shuddered at the thought. Suppose she injured him seriously?

Well, face that if the question arose.

They peeked through the door. Someone was certainly sleeping in the wide bed against the back wall of the room. Impossible to tell if it was the second mate or not. But who else could it be?

'All right, Jane,' breathed Prue. 'Go ahead with your screaming act. The window is just off on the wall to the left of the door. Thank goodness it's the side away from the other huts. I'll stay round the other corner, ready to slip in as soon as he comes out.'

She took up her position, and Jane obediently went round to the other side. A moment later Prue heard a faint scream, and then Jane calling, 'Help! Help! Oh won't anyone help me?'

Prue admired the level at which Jane's calls were pitched. Loud enough to wake anyone just inside the window. But not, she hoped and believed, loud enough to wake anyone further away.

The door of the hut was flung open, and a figure clad in a night-shirt came bursting out. Prue recognised the small, stocky, ginger haired figure she had seen on board ship. As he disappeared round the side of the hut towards Jane, Prue darted in through the door, looked round feverishly for the man's belt and breeches, and saw them lying in a heap at the side of the bed.

She pounced on them, and began to wrestle the keys from the belt.

Just then, a woman's voice spoke in a weak, frightened tone from the bed.

'Who's that? What are you doing here?'

Prue froze.

Chapter Twenty Five

The Present

A sudden noise brought Christie back to reality.

Hastily she closed her Kindle and listened carefully. There were two voices.

'So, here I am, Butch. What was it you wanted to show me?'

That was Steve.

'Hold on, boyo. There's stuff I might tell you, and some stuff I might or might not show you. But first of all, I need some more solid info from you about those guys who have my necklace, right?'

That was Butch. Christie recognised his rough, hoarse sounding voice easily.

She felt a tremor of anxiety move through her body. She didn't really think Steve would betray Aine and Tommy. But she wanted to hear what he said, to be really sure about that.

'Sorry, Butch,' Steve said without any apparent concern. 'They ran. I put them in a safe place, but when I went back next day to check on them, no sign. Musta bolted overnight.'

Christie was pretty sure that wasn't true. But it worked with Butch.

She heard him swear. 'You mucked that up rightly, Jesse, didn't you?' he said. 'So now, what about my necklace?'

'Oh, I got the necklace from them before they ran, Butch,' Steve said. 'Here it is. Pretty thing isn't it?' Christie could see nothing, but realised that Steve must be dangling the necklace which had caused so much trouble in his fingers.

'Yeah. Gimme!'

'In a minute, Butch.' Steve's voice hardened. 'I want to see all the rest of that stuff. I want to be sure you haven't already sold it. I want my share, Butch, see?'

'Jesse, what're you doin'?'

'Threatening you, Butch.'

'Jesse, put the gun away. We're partners, mate. No need for that.'

'No?'

Christie realised with a thrill of dismay that Steve must have pulled a gun on Butch. But that was so dangerous – suppose Butch managed to get his own gun out and shoot Steve? Christie shuddered at the thought. She must care more about Steve Armstrong than she'd known, she thought wryly.

A moment later, she realised that there was no need to worry.

'Jesse, Jesse,' Butch said. 'Hey, you know I wouldn't cheat on you. The stuff's right there in my safe. When I fence it, you'll get your cut, no problem.'

'Good news, Butch.' Steve sounded implacable. 'So show me.'

Christie could hear noises which she guessed were the two men crossing the room. Then Butch's voice again.

'The combination's secret, Jesse. You need to move away where you can't see my fingers when I enter it.'

'Okay.'

She could hear Steve moving back across the room. There were more sounds, then a click as the safe opened. There was a pause.

'Okay, Jesse. This is the stuff from the last two snatches.'

Christie heard Steve move forward again to see the jewellery.

'Here, boyo,' Butch said. 'Take a dekko at this one. Stretch out your hand.'

'Wow!' Steve said. 'That's something, Butch. Diamond and emerald tiara, right?'

'Right. And just let me get something else from the safe to show you. Come a bit closer.'

She heard Steve moving even closer to the safe and to Butch.

Then she heard a loud cry and a thump, as if a heavy body had fallen.

'So maybe you won't pull a gun on me another time, Jesse boy,' Butch sneered in a self-satisfied tone. 'I keep more in there than hot ice. How d'ye like my cosh? Not diamond studded, but worth its weight in gold to me, right?'

Christie froze with horror. What had happened to Steve? Was he dead? Butch must have hit him with the cosh he'd mentioned – he must have kept it in his safe as a precaution. Steve must have been knocked out, which was bad enough – but suppose it was worse?

Before she let herself think too much about the consequences, Christie had pushed open the cupboard door and tumbled out. In a flash she was across the hall and into the room.

'Freeze! Police!' she shouted like the cops in all good crime series she had ever seen. 'Get on the floor! Now!'

She had no gun. But the Kindle made a satisfactorily solid shape in the pocket of her jacket as she held it there with one hand and pointed it at Butch.

It must have been the shock and surprise as much as anything else that made Butch, for the few brief seconds necessary, stand motionless as Christie rushed into the room and over to Steve. It was enough. Steve's gun was lying where he had dropped it as he fell. It had skittered across the room, ending up much nearer to Christie than to Butch. Christie's hand came out of her pocket and she seized the real gun. A second later she was pointing it at Butch instead of the Kindle.

She wanted very badly to look at Steve, to check if he was seriously hurt or worse, but she knew she couldn't risk it.

'Down on the floor, I said!' she barked again at Butch. To her secret surprise, the gangster obeyed her, getting down on his knees first of all and then lowering himself cautiously to spread out at full length on his front.

Christie wasn't sure what her next move should be, but she knew she had to continue to act the part of the tough cop completely in control. She risked a cautious sideways glance at Steve, and to her relief heard him start to groan. He wasn't dead, then. Overwhelming thankfulness filled her. 'Thank you, God,' she said under her breath, then began to bark at Butch again.

'Hands straight forward – that's right! Spread them. And spread your legs, too!' Kneeling down, careful not to get within range of his grasp, she patted him down for weapons. The only thing she found was already lying beside him where he'd dropped it in the first shock of her invasion of the room – the unpleasant looking cosh which he had clearly used against Steve. She slipped it into her pocket for safety – no sense in letting Butch get hold of it again, if it was left lying about. The contents of the safe must have distracted Steve and taken him off his guard for long enough for Butch to get his blow in.

Christie stepped away, holding the gun carefully aimed at the helpless man stretched on the floor. She risked another glance at Steve and was relieved to see him beginning to move. Presently he sat up and rested his head in his hands for a moment. Then slowly and carefully he began to get to his feet.

'I don't feel great right now, Christie,' he said. 'Can you go on covering this scumbag while I get myself a drink of water and try to recover?'

'No problem!' Christie assured him. She stared grimly at the gangster spread-eagled on the floor, and held the gun carefully pointed straight at him.

'Aim for the middle mass,' Steve advised her, before making his way slowly to the door. She heard his footsteps heading down the hall, presumably in search of the kitchen. All was silent in the front room. Neither Christie nor Butch had anything they wanted to say. Presently she heard Steve coming back. His footsteps sounded more confident, and when he came back into the room she saw out of the corner of her eye that he looked less pale and damaged.

'Can you keep the gun on him for a few more minutes, Christie? I want to tie him up.'

He took handcuffs from his pocket and slipped them on Butch's wrists, pushing his arms together to get at the second wrist, and being careful not to get between him and the gun. Then he pulled off the belt from Butch's waist, pushed his legs together, and twisted up and looked satisfied.

'I think it would be better now if I took over the gun, Christie,' Steve said. 'Can you back away a bit from this guy? I'll come round behind you and get it. Don't let go of it, and don't stop pointing it at him until you're sure I have it safely.'

'Okay,' Christie said faintly. She was beginning to feel the effects of the recent events, and discovered how relieved she would be to have Steve take over. Holding a gun on someone wasn't really her style, although she felt that she had made a good job of doing it. But enough was enough.

They managed the transfer of the gun successfully and Steve took a secure stance, his legs spread firmly and both hands on the gun. Butch looked up at him and sneered.

'So, you've blown your cover, boyo? Undercover cop, right? Two cops on my trail. But you still haven't won, see? The rest of the gang will be along shortly. Then you'll be the ones in trouble.'

'Bluffing, aren't you, Butch? You told me no one else would be here, just you and me, to discuss some private plans. And you've got it all wrong. Christie isn't a cop – just my girlfriend. She was waiting for me. When she heard you double crossing me she did a bit of bluffing of her own. Took you in rightly!'

'Okay, but you're one, right?'

Christie saw Steve decide to come clean. He could possibly have bluffed it out, but he had all he needed now.

'You got it, Butch,' he said. 'And I'm about to call for backup. I need witnesses besides myself to see what you have in your safe – necessary when we come to court. You're going down for a long stretch this time, Butch. And if the rest of the gang turns up, they can join you in the dock.'

He held the gun firmly and spoke to Christie. 'Should have done this before swopping over the gun. Can you take it again for a few minutes?'

They repeated the manoeuvre and Christie held the gun again. Steve took out his mobile phone and spoke into it. Then he shut it off and turned back to Christie, grinning at her.

'Okay, Christie, they'll be here in a while. Maybe you should disappear. Better if they don't know you were involved. Nip out to the car and wait for me there, right? I'll set the car keys down here on this table and you can pick them up when I've got the gun again.'

'Okay', Christie said.

'And you, Butch, do you want to say anything to help yourself before the boys get here? I'm ready to listen.'

He retrieved the gun, and Christie went quickly out of the room.

The car was standing where they had left it at the front of the house. She walked over, opened the door, and climbed in. It was good to sit down. She had felt increasingly weak and shaky for the last few minutes. Now, surely, it must be over. Christie leaned her head back against the car seat, closed her eyes for a moment and sighed with relief.

She remembered that Steve had called her his girlfriend. He must feel serious about her, then. And she became aware that she felt the same about him. Where would it lead?

Presently, she stopped dreaming, opened her eyes, and switched on her Kindle, in an effort to make the waiting time until the police arrived pass quickly. She had left Prue in the hut belonging to the second mate, hearing a woman's voice in what she had thought was an empty room.

Chapter Twenty Six

1794

The shock which had held Prudence silent and motionless only lasted for a moment. Then, clenching the keys in her fist, she darted back towards the door, pulled it open again, and ran full tilt across the enclosure and back to the distant hut where Captain Myles was imprisoned. She was glad they hadn't bolted the door again behind them. It was heavy enough to push open without the added effort of unbolting it first.

She opened it quietly and slipped inside.

'Myles!' she said softly. 'It's me, Prudence. I have the keys.'

Myles Whitehead came over to her, a dim figure in the faint moonlight filtering through the narrow window.

Heart beating fast, Prue struggled with the keys, first of all trying to identify which of the huge iron instruments opened the shackles on the captain's wrists. By trial and error she eventually found it, then inserted it in the lock and turned it, not without much panting and effort. But at last she heard a click, and Myles was able to shake the chains from his wrists and utter a brief exclamation of relief.

Taking the other keys from her, he himself leant down and undid the ball and chain and the wall fastening which had held him a helpless prisoner since their arrival on the island. He stood up, stretching his arms and stamping his feet, trying to restore full circulation to them. Then he seized Prue in his arms.

'Prue, you marvellous girl!' he exclaimed softly. 'Some day I'll thank you properly for this. We must get out of this hut straight away. But not until I kiss you at least once.'

And before Prue had quite realised what he was doing, he had tightened his arms around her and was kissing her hard on her mouth. Prue jumped back with a smothered shriek.

She freed herself from his arms with a struggle and stood glaring at him, her eyes blazing.

'Captain Whitehead, you are aware that I have no father to protect me, and it is ungentlemanly of you to take advantage of that fact! Don't ever dare to lay a finger on me again!'

Myles Whitehead looked both surprised and dismayed.

'Mistress Prudence, I can only apologise. I thought – I mean – why are you helping me like this if not because you love me?'

Prudence's anger swept over her more fiercely. 'I am helping you, sir, as I would help any human creature imprisoned by a villain! I mean nothing more than that by my actions, I assure you.'

Captain Whitehead bowed stiffly. 'I can only apologise again. Meanwhile, Mistress, it would be as well if we refrained from talking, in case we wake my jailers, and remove ourselves from this loathsome hut as quickly as possible.'

He held open the door for her, and Prudence walked out before him with as much dignity as she could.

Once outside, she said in a whisper, 'I must wait for Jane. You may go on to the boat if you wish.'

'I will wait with you, Mistress Prue. I would hesitate to leave you here on your own. There are dangers all around, from both man and beasts. Can I take it that you still intend to escape with me?'

'I have little option, sir. But I would be glad of your assurance that there will be no repeat of your recent behaviour.'

'You have my assurance, Mistress,' he said, bowing coldly. 'Where do you expect to meet Jane?'

'I had intended to wait outside this hut,' Prue told him, wrinkling her brow thoughtfully. 'But the second mate, when he comes back to his hut, will be told at once that someone has been there, and will more than probably suspect that his keys have been stolen. When he checks and finds them gone he'll come here straightaway to reassure himself that you haven't escaped, and to lie in wait for the person with the keys. I didn't tell you, sir, that there was a woman in his hut.'

'That would be his wife.'

'Wife?'

'Yes, why not? Several of the permanent crew have wives on this island, I'm told. A clergyman visits the people here regularly.'

Prue wasn't sure why she should be so surprised. Why should the men not have wives? And yet it seemed so out of keeping for the rough pirate crew she had met. Women, yes. Wives, no. She swallowed her surprise and pulled herself together. 'It seems to me, Captain, that we should make our way as quietly as possible towards the main house, where Jane and the second mate were going – oh, I forgot to explain.'

Briefly she gave him an outline of the tactics she and Jane had employed to get the second mate out of the way. 'They are probably both on their way back by now – the second mate first, and Jane creeping along quietly after him, having left him some time to get well away. If we keep to the edge of the enclosure, and don't make a noise, we should escape his attention, and then when we know he's safely past we can look out for Jane.'

Myles Whitehead agreed that that seemed like the best plan, and together they made their way cautiously over to the side of the open ground, and edged carefully along, keeping as much as possible under the overhanging trees.

After some minutes, Prue heard the sound of someone approaching, making no attempt to keep quiet. He was muttering to himself, and seemed annoyed.

'Silly wench!' they heard him mumbling. 'Why could she not keep to her bed instead of wandering around causing trouble, robbing hard working men of their sleep?'

Prue twitched the sleeve of Captain Myles' coat, but he had already heard. They both drew back as far as they could under the overhanging trees, to allow the man to pass them as far away as possible, before moving quietly on towards the big house and, they hoped, Jane.

They stood like statues, waiting for the second mate, for it was clearly him, to pass them and return to his hut. Then, moving as silently as they could, they edged forward again, keeping their ears pricked for any sound of a person approaching.

It seemed to Prue like forever before she heard cautious noises. Someone was moving towards them, stopping frequently and then coming forward again. Prue decided that it was worth taking a risk.

'Jane!' she whispered, in a voice which would only be heard by someone on the alert for any sound.

The person stopped again. Then, so quietly that Prue had to strain her ears to hear it, a voice said, 'Mistress Prue?'

'Yes, yes, it's me Jane! Oh, I'm so glad to find you!"

Prue ran forward, and embraced Jane eagerly.

'Are you all right? Did everything go as we planned?'

'I suppose so,' Jane said. 'The second mate – his name is Timothy – was quite kind at first, but after we'd gone a bit he started to feel annoyed at having been woken up and having to escort me back to the big house. I said I was sorry I don't know how many times, but he told me he felt it would be his duty to tell Captain Hawkeye tomorrow morning that I'd come out and wandered about and got into trouble. They'll be so cross with me!'

'Never mind, Jane,' Prue said bracingly. 'We won't be around here tomorrow to hear how angry they are. So, now we're all together, it's time we headed for the boat and got ourselves out to the ship Freedom.*'*

'But what about you, Prue?' asked Jane, remembering in her anxiety about her friend to drop the 'mistress.' 'Did everything go well with you?'

'Oh, yes,' Prue assured her airily. 'Except that the second mate – okay, Timothy – had a wife in his hut, and she was awake, and will have told him someone was there. He'll be bound to check and find that his keys are gone. That's why we didn't wait for you at the prison hut. And we'll need to give it a clear berth on our way to the boat.' She turned to Myles. Her anger against him was long gone, and she judged it right to show him some friendliness again, although not enough to encourage him to further attempts to kiss her.

'Myles, can we reach the boat without going near the prison hut?' she asked.

Pleased to find Prudence prepared to ask his advice, Myles brightened up.

'Oh, certainly,' he said. 'The long boats are beached not too far away. They're on the nearest stretch of beach to the enclosure. A long way from where you two came ashore, from what my jailer told me. I can lead you there easily.'

'Then let's go, Captain!' said Prue briskly, giving Jane's arm an encouraging pat. 'We've spent enough time in this horrible enclosure without spending any more.'

'Certainly, Prue,' Myles Whitehead ventured on the name again, sensing a willingness on Prue's part to be friendly again, if nothing more. 'But before we leave this place there's just one more thing I want to do.'

'Oh?' asked Prue.

'Yes, I mean to lower that damnable flag from the flag pole and destroy it. You can wait here for me if you like. The flagpole is over there, near the centre, in an exposed position. I wouldn't like to take you both into danger.'

'I don't see why it matters to lower the flag,' Prue said, 'but if you're determined to, we'll come some of the way with you. No point in all three of us going over to the flagpole. Jane and I will wait nearby, under what cover we can.'

'Yes, three people would be seen more easily than one,' Jane agreed.

They set off, making their way round the outskirts of the enclosure until they were opposite the site of the flagpole. Prue couldn't remember looking at it closely on their arrival. She supposed Myles wanted to make clear his contempt for the Jolly Rodger, the flag of piracy, and privately thought his determination to lower it and remove it silly, but maybe understandable.

She and Jane stood silently watching as Myles strode across the clearing, reached the pole, and unwound the rope which raised and lowered the flag when necessary. Then he began to haul the flag down, and Prue, looking more carefully at it, suddenly stiffened in anger.

The flag Myles Whitehead was stripping from the pole was no Jolly Rodger. Instead, as she now remembered, it was the Union Flag, the flag of Britain, Prue's own country.

She gave one horrified gasp, then darted impetuously across the open ground, reckless of anyone who might see or hear her. Followed by an equally angry Jane.

'What do you think you're doing, Myles Whitehead?' she demanded furiously. 'Leave that flag alone!'

Jane, choosing action rather than words, seized the flag from Myles Whitehead's suddenly nerveless hands, and began to raise it again.

'But, Prue!' Captain Myles was taken completely by surprise. 'But I told you what I was going to do!'

'I thought you meant the Jolly Rodger!' stormed Prue.

'So, he's tricked you, too?' Myles asked. 'Nick Hawkeye uses the cover of piracy, but beneath all that he's one of the enemies of our country. He roams the seas, capturing French and American ships, and taking prisoners of war to be sent to the nearest British possession – usually Jamaica. Because he claims to be a pirate, he can approach ships and come close before they realise he's a serious enemy. A pirate will rob you of valuables – but an enemy vessel will scuttle your ship or capture it, and throw yourself and your men in jail. And because the United States are not currently at war with Britain, since we signed the peace treaty, the British don't want official navy ships to be seen attacking ours.'

'But since America and Britain are not at war, why should they want the ships attacked at all?' Prue asked in bewilderment.

'Because we use the ships to send gold to France to aid and support them in their armed struggle for freedom against the might of the British!' Myles explained.

' Captain Whitehead, you seem to have forgotten one thing,' Prue said coldly. 'Jane and I are not American. We are British, and as much your enemy as Captain Hawkeye. Indeed, my father, until his death, led all the troops in Jamaica on behalf of the British government.'

'And proud of it!' Jane put in.

'But, Prue!' Myles Whitehead protested, 'Why, then, do you want to escape from Hawkeye and this island? He will do no harm to you, naturally.'

'I've been a fool,' admitted Prue. 'I didn't understand the true facts. And no one explained them to me!' she added indignantly.

'I thought you knew all this,' Myles said. 'And I also thought you were American. Probably Captain Hawkeye thought the same. He wouldn't have wanted to tell the enemy his secrets – that he's not really a pirate, but works for the British government.'

'Oh, if only I'd known sooner!' Prue burst out. 'I would never have –'

Suddenly she stopped. Absorbed in what they were saying, no one had noticed the growing noises around them, but now it was impossible not to hear the loud voices and footsteps, and to see the noisy crowd of people running across the ground towards them.

Hel's Heroes 2: Christie & The Pirate

Chapter Twenty Seven

The Present

Christie looked up from her Kindle at the sound of a car approaching along the lane which led to the farm house where Butch had arranged to meet Steve.

She expected to see a police car pull up, and several policemen get out. Instead, she saw, to her horror, a battered old red Audi. And the men getting out, far from being police, were Sundance, Doc, and the Kid, the members of Butch's Wild West gang. So Butch had been speaking the truth when he said that he was expecting them to arrive soon! Now what on earth was she to do?

The three men stood stretching in the sunshine, obviously glad to be out of the car after their long drive. Sundance looked as lanky and foolish as he had done at their first meeting, while the Kid, small but wiry, had a look of cunning on his face mixed with stupidity. Only Doc showed signs of intelligence on his lean sun tanned face.

Christie thought hard. Should she lie flat in Steve's car and hope they didn't notice her? But suppose they did – suppose they came over and dragged her out? She'd be helpless then, helpless to stop them going on inside. And if she did manage to hide so well that they didn't see her, they would still go on into the house, where they would take Steve by surprise. Three to one wasn't a hopeful set up for Steve. True, he had a gun, but probably so had they.

Christie thought hard. Any moment now they were bound to notice her. Better to take the initiative. Throwing open the door of Steve's car, she sprang out. 'Hi, guys!' she called over to them. 'Butch asked me to give you a message.'

'Huh?' Sundance asked. No doubt he was wondering why Butch should have asked Christie to do anything. But Christie didn't give him time to wonder.

'He wants you to come round the back,' she called out. 'He's got something to show you there.'

Turning, she moved quickly to the corner of the building and followed the path around to the back, where she had noticed earlier, looking out of the kitchen window, that there were a few outbuildings. She hoped that the men would be too bemused to refuse to follow her. Sure enough, they trooped after her, the Kid tripping clumsily over some stones lying on the rough track.

The nearest outbuilding, which might have been used for keeping farm machinery such as a tractor and an old fashioned plough, had strong looking double doors made of hardwood, with a couple of bolts on the outside, she was glad to see. Christie flung open one of the doors.

'Inside here, boys!' she said, and Sundance went past her into the building, followed by the Kid. Doc, however, hung back suspiciously. The interior was very dark, and the first two gang members stood just inside the door, peering round the inside of the building cautiously for a sight of their boss. It was hard for them to tell if he was there or not. 'Butch?' called Sundance uncertainly.

'He's down at the back,' Christie told them quickly.

Only Doc still hung back.

'What would Butch want us to go in there for?' he demanded, glaring distrustfully at her. Christie's heart sank. Doc was the brightest of the gang, as she had already noted during their previous encounter.

'He wants to explain to you himself,' she said quickly. 'Come on, don't keep him waiting.'

'Butch? Butch, are you in there?' Doc called, moving slowly towards the doorway. As he peered in, Christie darted after him, and gave one almighty shove to his back. With a roar of anger Doc went sprawling forwards into the shed, bumping into Sundance and the Kid as he did so. All three collapsed in a mixed up heap on the ground.

But as he fell, Doc thrust out one hand and grabbed Christie by the arm, yanking it hard. A moment later she was making part of the struggling group on the ground. Wriggling to free herself, she found that the gangster was a lot stronger than she was. It was impossible to escape his clutch.

'Let go of me!' she panted, uselessly.

'Oh, no, my dear,' Doc said. 'I'm not letting go of you until you tell me what's going on here.'

'I told you! Butch asked me to give you a message. I thought he'd be waiting inside the shed for you, but he doesn't seem to have got here yet,' Christie panted.

'And why was Butch giving messages to you, girl? The last I heard, he'd grabbed you and your mates and had us guarding you until he got back his necklace. Until you tricked us and escaped. This is another of your tricks, isn't it?'

'No, no,' Christie lied. As she spoke, it occurred to her that she was lying freely, and wondered if she should. But then she remem -bered Rahab, who had hidden Joshua and Caleb, and got nothing but praise for lying to their pursuers. 'Butch discovered that I wasn't on the side of the two guys who took his necklace. He trusts me now.'

'Maybe.' Doc didn't sound convinced. He struggled to his feet, still holding Christie's arm tightly. Sundance and the Kid were also managing to sort themselves out and were about to stand up.

Christie's heart sank. It seemed as if her plan had failed. Time for another trick – if only she could come up with one.

Doc was the main problem. The other two, dazed from their recent fall, seemed still puzzled as to what was going on.

'Look – I'll show you the note Butch sent me,' Christie im-provised. 'Let go my arm and I'll get it out of my pocket.'

'No need for that, babe. I'll get it out of your pocket myself.'

Doc felt in her nearest pocket, and Christie said impatiently, 'No, no, not in that one, my other pocket.'

As she had hoped and prayed, Doc stretched across her to grope in the further pocket of her jacket.

Christie, picking her moment, kicked the side of his knee, and stepped back out of the way as he shrieked and stumbled, letting go of her arm as he yet again fell to the floor of the shed.

There was no time to waste.

Christie sprang back, darted through the doorway, slammed the wide double doors shut and shot the iron bolts home. She had the gang safely bolted into the building before they could gather themselves together.

She leant against the wall on the left hand side of the doors and heaved a sigh of mingled relief and exhaustion.

'Thank goodness!' she murmured to herself. 'And you can stay there until the back up comes along!'

She wondered if she should go inside and warn Steve about what she had done. He would need to know the guys were on the premises if he wanted to arrest them as well as Butch. He had already said he didn't want her on the scene when the cops came, but this was important. He needed to be told.

Christie returned to the front of the house and went in.

Steve was still keeping his gun on Butch, although Butch's bonds, to say nothing of the handcuffs, made it pretty well unnecessary.

'Christie, what –?' he began as she came into the office.

'It's okay, Steve,' she said. 'Butch's guys turned up – he was telling the truth for once when he said they were on their way. So I shut them up in one of the outbuildings at the back of the house.'

Steve's mouth dropped open. 'Christie, you're incredible!'

'Oh, yeah, the Incredible Hulk, that's me.'

'Not a hulk, that's for sure,' murmured Steve.

'But what worries me, Steve, is that there's no sign of your back up yet.'

'Well, they've a good bit to come,' explained Steve reasonably. 'Why don't you go back to the car for a bit longer? Butch is starting to tell me some useful stuff – names of his fences, things like that. But before you go, you might help me get this guy into a chair. He can't be left lying on the floor forever.'

'Okay,' Christie agreed. 'So, what do you want me to do?'

'I think we'll need to unbuckle the belt round his legs, first,' Steve decided. "Then you can help me to get him onto his feet. I'll put that chair in position first.' He pulled over a hard backed chair from its position against the wall and set it in the middle of the room. Then he unbuckled the belt and unwound it from Butch's ankles.' 'So, Christie darlin', if you could take him under one arm while I take the other, we'll haul him up.'

Butch was naturally stiff and sore. Once on his feet, he stamped gingerly, trying to restore the circulation in his legs. Finally, with a groan, he collapsed into the chair, and Steve promptly fastened the belt round his legs again. 'We should really tie him to the chair as well, but I haven't any rope,' he said. 'Tell you what Christie, you keep the gun pointed at him while I have a look in the kitchen for something to use.'

Christie took the gun rather reluctantly and stood aiming it at Butch – at the middle mass, she remembered Steve telling her – until Steve came back quite soon with a ball of strong kitchen twine. He did an expert job of tying each of Butch's legs to one of the legs of the chair, then relieved Christie of the gun. 'So, back to square one – you go and wait in the car, okay?

'Okay,' Christie agreed. 'That is, if you don't need me to sort out any more problems for you?'

'Cheeky face!' Steve grinned at her. 'Stop distracting me from my work here, woman!'

'See you later,' Christie smiled. She went back out to the car, taking the Kindle from her pocket as she did so.

Hel's Heroes 2: Christie & The Pirate

Chapter Twenty Eight

The crowd of shouting men drew closer.

For a moment Prudence was afraid. Then she saw Captain Nick Hawkeye among the leaders, and her heart gave a bound of intense relief.

Why, she wasn't quite sure.

Captain Hawkeye came nearer, and said, 'Why, Mistress Prudence, what are you doing here, out of your bed? And why is our prisoner here also?'

'Captain, it's my fault!' Prue exclaimed impetuously. 'I didn't understand! I believed that you were a pirate, taking helpless people prisoner for reasons of greed and robbery. I didn't know you were attacking the ships of our enemies, until your prisoner explained it to me just now.'

'"Our enemies?"' Captain Nick said with a puzzled frown.

'Yes! Jane and I are British, Captain. This man tells me that you thought we were American, like him! My father served in the British army fighting against the rebels, and then held Jamaica in the later fighting there, against the combined French and American attacks. He was the administrator of the British troops in Jamaica for many years until his recent death, when I was sent home to live with my aunt in London.'

'Mistress Prudence, I ask your forgiveness for my mistake. If I had known – if I had realised! I would have taken you into my confidence at the start. But I dared not tell the truth to my country's enemies, however much my heart longed to trust you.'

He took a step nearer to Prue, then recollected himself. Swinging round, he gave out orders to the men with him.

'Take this man back to his prison. And this time make sure he's better guarded!'

'You might need these,' Prue said demurely, producing the keys which had fastened Captain Whiteside's chains and offering them to Captain Nick.

Nick gave a short laugh. 'Ha! We might, indeed!' he agreed. As he took them from her hand, a scuffle and an outcry broke out behind him. The young American, taking advantage of the Captain's pre-occupation with Prudence, had managed to trip up one of the men and to seize the pistol from his hand. Pointing it at Jane, he grabbed her by the arm and hustled her in front of him.

'Don't come near me!' he panted breathlessly. 'I haven't come so near to freedom to let it go now! I'm going back to my ship and I plan to sail it back to my home port. If anyone tries to stop me, this lady will be the first to suffer for it.'

He began to move backwards towards the edge of the enclosure, forcing Jane along with him in his strong grip. Helpless, Jane stumbled along in his grasp.

Josh Tompkins started forward impetuously, but Myles White-head thrust the pistol against Jane's head, and spoke warningly.

'Don't try to follow me! If you do, I'll shoot her and run for it! Stay here until I send her back to you – which will be when I'm safely in the boat and rowing for my ship!'

Captain Nick put a warning hand on Josh's arm, and he stood still while Myles Whitehead, holding Jane tightly against him, vanished through the opening of the enclosure into the woods. They could hear the crashing sounds as he ploughed his way on, then he must have risked turning round, for the noises grew less as he moved forward along the beaten path.

'Right, men!' said Captain Hawkeye. 'Not a sound, now! We're going to catch him when he arrives at the beach. We'll use the short-cut to his left, and come round to his rear. Three of you, besides myself and Josh. Tom, Rob, and Peter. Quietly or I'll flay you alive!'

Prue felt that she couldn't bear to be left behind. Besides, Jane would need the comfort of another woman when they rescued her, as well as the comfort of Josh.

'Nick, I'm coming too!' she said urgently. 'Jane will need me there.'

Nick hesitated, then nodded. 'Come close behind me,' was all he said. 'And no noise.'

Following the captain as closely as possible, Prue, together with the men named by Captain Hawkeye, picked her way cautiously through the thick jungle. Presently she discovered that they were now on an established path, and the little band began to move much faster. It was all Prue could do to keep up, but she was determined not to be a nuisance or to slow the rescue party down, so she put all her effort into staying close to the captain's back.

They seemed to travel on for a very long time. Surely, Prue couldn't help thinking, Myles would be long gone by now. But she remembered what a long time it had taken her and Jane to make their way through the trees when they arrived on the beach after their swim, and decided that Nick must know what he was doing. He knew this island well, which Myles didn't, so he had that advantage over him. If this was a shorter way to the ships, then that was good.

Suddenly, taking her by surprise, the trees thinned out, and she saw with delight the gleam of moonlight shining on the water. The sea was just before them.

'Now, men,' whispered Captain Nick softly, 'spread out in a line, and don't let him get through your net. I'm going to trap him, panic him, and disarm him, and I may end up sending him in your direction.'

No one asked how he was going to do this. They all seemed to have complete faith in their leader.

Nick turned to Prue. 'I'm going to ask you to stay here, now, Prue,' he said. 'I'm setting a trap for Captain Whitehead, and I want you well out of his line of sight. I don't want him to take fright and evade the trap. I think he'll have relaxed his use of Jane as a protection by now. He must reckon himself safe enough, although he'll still have hold of her, I'm sure. But he won't have managed to come through the jungle still holding his pistol to her head, if I know anything about it.'

Prue nodded agreement. 'I'll stay well back, Nick,' she said. She watched, her heart in her mouth, as Captain Hawkeye moved forward to the start of the path through the trees where they expected Myles Whitehead to appear at any moment. At first she couldn't make out what the Captain was doing as he bent over to fasten something to a tree at one side of the path, but then she understood that he was fastening a thin rope round the trunk. Moving swiftly across the path, he held the other end of the rope in his hand, letting it drop down to lie flat over the path in a way which made it very hard to notice. He jerked it upright once, to check it, Prue supposed, for height and reliability, then lowered it until it lay across the path again.

Prue stood silently, her heart in her mouth. Although she strained her ears, she could hear nothing. The men, and Captain Hawkeye himself, made no sound. Then, so faint at first that she thought she might have imagined it, she heard the noise of someone coming through the trees. Myles Whitehead and Jane! It must be.

Then, as they came closer, she heard a voice. 'I'll be letting you go very shortly, Jane,' Myles Whitehead was saying. 'Just keep on being sensible until I tell you you're free. Then you can run back to your friends. Indeed, I'm truly sorry to have used you like this. Please believe me, I never actually intended you any harm – but I knew they wouldn't risk your life by refusing to obey me. I think we must be nearly at the beach by now.'

Prue drew in her breath. Everything depended on the next few minutes. She listened as Myles moved forward. Then she heard him exclaiming, 'Look, Jane! The sea!'

All of a sudden she could tell that he was striding forward much faster, excited to discover how near he was to escape. For a moment she felt sorry for him again, as she had done when she first saw him taken prisoner. But then she told herself sternly that if he wanted anyone to sympathise with him, he shouldn't have used Jane as a hostage and shield. After that, he deserved whatever was coming to him.

She watched eagerly to see if Nick had moved into action yet, but could see nothing, and all she could hear was the noise of Myles Whitehead's footsteps as he drew nearer.

Then there was a sudden shout of alarm, a crashing sound as some-one fell, and a devastatingly loud shot breaking through the clear night air as the pistol exploded.

Prue froze with horror. Had someone been hit by the bullet? And if so, who?

Then her fears were removed by the sound of Captain Nick's voice, speaking sharply and urgently. 'Run, Jane! Prue is just over there, waiting for you!'

A moment later, a panting, sobbing figure burst through the trees and hurled herself into Prue's outstretched arms.

'Jane!' Prue cried. 'Oh, I'm so happy to see you back safe! You must have been so frightened!'

'Not any more,' sighed Jane, beaming in relief. 'Everything's all right now.'

A second later, two figures emerged onto the beach. Myles White-head came first, his hands bound behind him by the same rope which had tripped him up, propelled by Captain Nick, who to Prue's amazement looked as calm as ever.

'Take this ruffian, some of you,' he said. 'Tom. Rob. Peter. Get him back to his prison and this time look after him properly. His gun went off as no doubt you heard – it must have been on a hair trigger – but the bullet went into the sand. Take it with you. I'll make arrangements to morrow to have him and his crew taken to the official prison in Jamaica, and his ship towed there as a prize.'

Prue stopped stroking Jane's hair soothingly as she found her maid and friend abruptly snatched from her arms. Josh Tompkins spoke into her ear.

'This is my business, Mistress Prudence! I'll handle it.'

He took Jane in his arms lovingly, and began to speak to her in tender words.

'Jane, you terrified me. Don't ever run away from me like that again. I want to make you safe – to marry you, as soon as we can get the parson here. Will you, Jane? You know now that we aren't pirates, but honest British seamen. Will you, Jane?'

'Oh, yes, Josh, indeed I will,' murmured Jane, turning up her face to his for his kisses.

Prue turned away, feeling miserable. Oh, she was happy for Jane, but what about herself? Could Captain Nick ever forgive her for her lack of trust?

Hel's Heroes 2: Christie & The Pirate

Suddenly she was aware of firm steps approaching her. Captain Nick – Black Nick Hawkeye – had finished his business and dispatched his prisoner in the charge of the men he had brought with him.

Prue felt herself snatched into his arms and roughly kissed. Throwing her arms round him in turn, she kissed him passionately back.

'Prue, how I've longed to do that, from the moment I first saw you in that ridiculous dressing gown! And even more' – he laughed – 'when I saw you stripped for your swim! I love you, my darling. Tell me you love me!'

'Oh, yes, I do, Nick!' she cried. 'And from the very same first moment. But how could I let myself love a pirate?'

'Well, you know now that I'm not a pirate,' Nick said. 'I didn't think I could tell you the truth while I believed you were an enemy of our country, Prue – that I'd been requisitioned to do this by the Prime Minister himself, Mr William Pitt, to stop American gold going to our enemy, France. I'm so glad you're not American! I want you so much, Prue. You're all I've ever wanted in a woman!'

'Ah, but imagine being Mrs Black Nick Hawkeye!' Prue said mischievously. 'I'm not sure I could bear that!'

'You won't have to, my darling,' Nick said in amusement. 'Black Nick Hawkeye is my nom de guerre. My real name is Sir Nicolas Cavendish. Could you bear to be Lady Cavendish, and to help me to administer this island and develop it, as I've been promised I can do as soon as I choose to retire from piracy – which is now?'

'Indeed I can,' Prue said enthusiastically. And she reached up to kiss him again.

Chapter Twenty Nine

The Present

Christie closed her Kindle with a sigh of satisfaction. Things had worked out for Prudence. She wondered if they would work out as well for herself. There was still no sign of Steve's back up. Were they real? And were they actually coming?

Surely Steve hadn't been deceiving her all along, being a part of the Wild West gang and tricking her into thinking he was an undercover cop? Pretending to ring for backup and maybe actually phoning the rest of the gang? But Butch had hit him over the head. Or had he? Had that been a pretence, too? Steve had certainly recovered amazingly quickly. And he had been equally quick to send her to wait outside, where the gang could catch her when they arrived.

No, she wouldn't believe it! Steve was straight. He was honest. He wouldn't have deceived her like that. And why should he?

The answer loomed up in her head at once. He'd needed to stop her going to the police, as she'd threatened to do. Maybe he wanted to keep her imprisoned until he and Butch and the rest could make their getaway to some safe country without an extradition treaty.

But then she remembered the times they'd spent together, and how close they'd grown, and something in her struggled to reject these ideas and to trust Steve as her instinct told her to do. Trust was important. She remembered Niall MacBride, the young minister of St Peter's, speaking about trust on Sunday morning. 'If you know someone well, you know whether you can trust them or not,' was one of the things he'd said.

'Help me to see the truth, Lord,' Christie prayed.

Peace flooded over her. She knew Steve. She knew him well enough to know that he could be trusted. Why was she doubting, just because his backup was slow in coming?

She was going to keep on trusting him, no matter.

But maybe it would help if she went into the house to see if he was getting on okay with Butch.

No sooner had the thought crossed her mind than Christie was out of the car and hurrying across to the front door of the house.

There was nothing to be heard from the office. This was worrying. Surely she should hear Steve talking to Butch, looking for more information, as he'd said. She went over to the office door, which was slightly open, and peered in cautiously through the crack.

At first sight all was well. She could see Steve and Butch, and they were both sitting looking at each other just as she had left them. Then Christie noticed with horror that Butch was no longer tied to his chair – but that, instead, Steve was tied to his!

How on earth had Butch managed it?

Then she saw that Butch's hands were still cuffed. What was going on? Another figure loomed into sight, and a hoarse voice spoke. Sundance.

'He must have the keys on him, Boss, but I can't find them. You saw me searching him.'

'You need to get them, Sundance. I can't stay stuck in these handcuffs forever. Kid, can't you do something?'

The Kid came forward into Christie's line of sight. 'Sure, Boss,' he said soothingly, 'I can open any lock ever made, you know that. But it might take me a bit of time.'

'We can't afford time!' Butch shouted. 'This cop rang for backup. It's bound to be here soon. We need to grab everything and get out before that.'

'What about the bird, Boss?' asked Doc. He would think of that, Christie thought bitterly. He was too intelligent to be a crook. If some of them were going to come looking for her, maybe she should get back into the closet and hide. It was no wonder they'd managed to turn the tables on Steve. A couple of shots over his head from cover, and a threat that the next one would take him out if he didn't drop his gun, would have done the trick. But how had they escaped? She'd had them securely bolted in, and the door of the outbuilding was surely too strong for them to have broken it down.

Next moment her question was answered. The men must have arrived on the scene only minutes before Christie herself, for explanations hadn't yet been given, and Butch, who had heard Christie tell Steve she's shut them into the outbuilding, also wanted to know the story. 'You were bolted in, weren't you, guys?' he demanded. 'How did you get out? The Kid could have picked a lock but I never heard yet of a picklock that can draw a bolt!'

The gang laughed politely at their boss's joke, and Doc explained.

'When we knew we were securely bolted in, we had a look round. There was a window at the back. It was too small for Sundance and me, and too high up, and there was a huge pile of junk in front of it. But when we'd moved the junk – which we didn't do in a minute, I can tell you, Boss! – the Kid managed to use an old table to climb up to it, and when he'd broken the glass and knocked out the shards, he was able to wriggle through it, being as you know, just the size of sixpence. Then he got himself round to the front –'

'– getting torn to bits by thorn and stung rigid by nettles,' the Kid interpolated –'

'– and he got the bolts drawn and Sundance and me were able to get out too.'

'Then I picked the lock on the back door and we sneaked in that way, so's the cop wouldn't see us,' the Kid finished, glowing with pride in his abilities.

'Great work, guys!' Butch said, rather grudgingly, Christie felt. 'Just a pity you couldn't be a bit quicker. And a pity you can't get me out of these miserable handcuffs! Now Sundance, you and the Kid go and get that bitch. Me and Doc will keep our eye on this guy, and gather up the stuff from the safe. Oh, and I've got that necklace back, you'll be glad to know. All the more for us all when it comes to the share out.'

Time for her to move quickly, Christie knew. Swiftly she darted back and opened the closet door. A moment later she had locked herself securely inside it again.

She heard the sound of footsteps – Sundance and the Kid going out to bring her in from the car. Christie was glad she wasn't there. An idea came to her. Waiting until she heard them go out of the front door, she unlocked her closet and went after them along the hallway. Reaching the front door, she quickly pulled it shut, locked it on the inside, and for good measure thrust home the bolt at the top. The enemy numbers were cut by half at a stroke. And one of them, Butch, was still in handcuffs.

Could she get Doc to come out into the hallway? She was pretty confident she could. She looked round for something large that she could use.

A huge empty chest was placed over against the back wall, beside the kitchen door. That would be just the very thing. But before she did anything else, she needed a weapon. At first she could see nothing of any use. Then she felt the weight of something in her pocket, and remembered that she still had Butch's cosh there.

She went over to the chest, raised the lid to its full extent – not without effort, for it was as heavy as she'd hoped it would be. Then, holding the cosh in one hand to be ready for use, she let the lid fall violently back into place. The resulting din was all she had hoped for. Butch and Doc couldn't fail to hear it.

Nor did they.

'What's that? Someone in the kitchen!' she heard Butch cry out. 'Doc, go and see.'

A moment later Doc came bustling out from the office, his gun in his hand. But Christie had already positioned herself just inside the kitchen, flattening herself against the wall on the side away from the opening door, out of Doc's line of sight as he moved to the back of the hall and pushed open the kitchen door. As he came through the doorway, Christie raised the cosh, and hit him as hard as she could. Doc fell in a heap at her feet.

Christie stood back and gazed in horror at what she had done. The blood was streaming from Doc's head. That meant that at least he wasn't dead. Christie seized the gun from his flaccid hand, and turned back to the office.

'Don't move, Butch!' she ordered him sharply, in the same voice that she had used on him what seemed like an eternity ago.

Butch sat like a statue, staring at the gun.

Coming into the room, Christie began with some difficulty to release Steve from the cord twisted round his arms, which fastened him to the chair. It was the twine Steve himself had used on Butch.

She needed to keep the gun on Butch while she did it, which meant that it wasn't the easiest of tasks, but at last she got the final knot undone, and Steve was free.

'Steve, I don't want to be critical, but don't you think you should phone your backup again and tell them to for goodness sake get a move on?' she suggested, grinning.

'No need!' Steve said, grinning back. 'If you listen you'll hear the cars arriving as we speak.'

'Oh, I'd better go and unlock and unbolt the door!' Christie said. 'As long as Sundance and the Kid don't come in first!'

'No worries,' Steve said, 'the first thing my backup will do is to arrest them, and ask questions later.'

'Good!' said Christie fervently. She handed the gun to Steve, glad as ever to be rid of it, and hurried out to unfasten the door for the arriving cops.

'What did you do with Doc?' asked Steve as she came back into the office.

'Oh, easy-peasy. I hit him with Butch's cosh.'

Steve's face brightened appreciatively. 'Good! I hope he enjoyed it as much as I did.'

Then the cops burst through the office door, yelling, 'Freeze! Police!' just as Christie had anticipated, and the situation was suddenly under control.

Steve identified himself and vouched for Christie. The gang were rounded up and herded into the waiting cars, including Doc, who came staggering, a bloodstained wreck, into the office, just in time to be arrested too.

And at last Steve and Christie were free to go back to Steve's car and to drive away.

'So, do you trust me now, Christie darlin,?' Steve asked, as the car would its way along the twisty mountain road.

'Forever, Steve. But you must admit that you made it hard for me to trust you at first, and in fact for quite a long time.'

'Forever?'

Christie blushed. She hadn't quite meant to imply what Steve seemed to think she was implying.

'Well – yes.'

'Wow! Here, I've got to stop this car!'

Steve pulled the car onto the grass at the roadside, and parked as far off the road as possible. Then he put his arms around Christie and drew her towards him. Then he kissed her.

It was a kiss like none of the other gentle kisses they had exchanged. It was a kiss to rock the world.

Coming up for air some minutes later, Christie heard herself sighing, 'Oh, darlin' Steve, I love you!'

'And I love you, angel! We'll get married straightaway, and go to Paris for our honeymoon, will we? I've always thought that sounded like the right thing to do. I'm owed a heap of leave, and I should have a promotion coming when the dust settles.'

'I thought you would have wanted to go on a fly fishing trip,' Christie teased him. 'I've been looking forward to it, you know!'

'Some other time, definitely! But not on our honeymoon!'

'Well, I expect I can get extra leave when it's for such a special occasion,' Christie said. 'But don't we have to hang around to make statements and act as witnesses at the trial?' she added in a bemused way.

'We can make the statements tomorrow, but the trial won't be for ages yet – they never happen quickly. So, Paris, here we come! Now, let's stop talking. I want to kiss you again.'

So Christie stopped talking. And he did.

About the author

Gerry McCullough has been writing poems and stories since childhood. Brought up in north Belfast, she graduated in English and Philosophy from Queen's University, Belfast, then went on to gain an MA in English.

She lives just outside Belfast, in Northern Ireland, has four grown up children and is married to author, media producer and broadcaster, Raymond McCullough, with whom she co-edited the Irish maga-zine, *Bread*, (published by *Kingdom Come Trust*), from 1990-96. In 1995 they published a non-fiction book, *Ireland – now the good news!*

Over the past few years Gerry has had more than ninety short stories published in UK, Irish and American magazines, anthologies and annuals – as well as broadcast on *BBC Radio Ulster* – plus poems and articles published in several Irish and UK magazines. She has read from her novels, poems and short stories at many Irish literary events.

Gerry won the *Cúirt International Literary Award* for 2005 (Galway); was shortlisted for the 2008 *Brian Moore Award* (Belfast); shortlisted for the 2009 *Cúirt Award*; commended in the 2009 *Seán O'Faolain Short Story Competition*, (Cork) and commended in the 2015 *Harmony House Poetry Award* (Downpatrick). She was the winner of the *Bangor Poetry Competition* (Northern Ireland) in 2016.

Belfast Girls, her first full-length Irish novel, was originally published (*Night Publishing*, UK) in November 2010 (re-issued July 2012 by *Precious Oil*). *Danger Danger* was published by *Precious Oil Publications* in October 2011; followed by *The Seanachie: Tales of Old Seamus* in January 2012 (a first collection of humorous Irish short stories, previously published in a weekly Irish magazine); *Angel in Flight* (the first Angel Murphy thriller) in June 2012;

Hel's Heroes 2: Christie & The Pirate

Lady Molly and the Snapper – a young adult novel time travel adventure set in Dublin (August 2012); *Angel in Belfast* (the 2nd Angel Murphy thriller) in June 2013; *Johnny McClintock's War* in August 2014, *The Seanachie 2: Norah on the Beach* in September 2014, *Hel's Heroes* in March 2015, *Dreams, Visions, Nightmares* (a collection of award-winning Irish short stories) in January 2016, *Not the End of the World* (a futuristic, humorous fantasy novel) in 2016, *The Seanachie 3* in August 2016 and *Angel in Paradise* in January 2017. *Hel's Heroes 2: Christie & The Pirate* is her fourteenth book.

Look out for more books coming from Gerry in the near future:

http://www.gerrymccullough.com

Belfast Girls

The story of three girls – Sheila, Phil and Mary – growing up into the new emerging post-conflict Belfast of money, drugs, high fashion and crime; and of their lives and loves.

Sheila, a supermodel, is kidnapped.

Phil is sent to prison.

Mary, surviving a drug overdose, has a spiritual awakening.

It is also the story of the men who matter to them –

John Branagh, former candidate for the priesthood, a modern Darcy, someone to love or hate. Will he and Sheila ever get together?

Davy Hagan, drug dealer, 'mad, bad and dangerous to know'. Is Phil also mad to have anything to do with him?

Although from different religious backgrounds, starting off as childhood friends, the girls manage to hold on to that friend-ship in spite of everything.

A book about contemporary Ireland and modern life. A book which both men and women can enjoy – thriller, romance, comedy, drama – and much more ...

"fascinating ... original ... multilayered ... expertly travels from one genre to the next"
Kellie Chambers, *Ulster Tatler* (*Book of the Month*)

"romance at the core ... enriched with breathtaking action, mystery, suspense and some tear-jerking moments of tragedy.
Sheila M. Belshaw, author

"What starts out as a crime thriller quickly evolves into a literary festival beyond the boundary of genres"
PD Allen, author

"a masterclass, and a vivid dissection of the human condition in all of its inglorious foibles"
WeeScottishLassie, UK

Danger Danger

Two lives in parallel – twin sisters separated at birth, but their lives take strangely similar and dangerous roads until the final collision which hurls each of them to the edge of disaster.

Katie and her gambling boyfriend Dec find themselves threatened with peril from the people Dec has cheated.

Jo-Anne (Annie), through her boyfriend Steven, finds herself in the hands of much more dangerous crooks.

Can they survive and achieve safety and happiness?

"starts with a bang and never quite lets up on the tension ... it will hook you from the beginning and keep you spell bound until the very last sentence."

Ellen Fritz, Books 4 Tomorrow

"The emotional intensity of the characters is beautifully drawn ... You care for these people."
Stacey Danson, author

an amazing, page turning, stunning novel ... equal to Belfast Girls *in every respect. I can't wait for her next novel to be published.*

Teresa Geering, author

an attention-grabbing plot, strong writing, and vivid characterization, ... fast-paced and highly addictive

L. Anne Carrington, author

Angel in Flight:

the first Angel Murphy thriller

Is it a bird? Is it a plane? No, it's a low-flying Angel!

You've heard of Lara Croft. You've heard of Modesty Blaise. Well, here comes Angel Murphy!

Angel, a 'feisty wee Belfast girl' on holiday in Greece, sorts out a villain who wants to make millions for his pharmaceutical company by preventing the use of a newly discovered malaria vaccine.

Angel has a broken marriage behind her and is wary of men, but perhaps her meeting with Josh Smith, who tells her he's with Interpol, may change her mind?

Fun, action, thrills, romance in a beautiful setting – so much to enjoy!

"it's a fast-paced read, ... exciting, and you can not put this book down"
Thomas Baker, Santiago, Chile

"I could not stop reading! ... a gripping thriller from beginning to the end"
SanMarie Lamprecht

*"a fast-paced, exciting read.
From the moment I read the first line, I was hooked"*
Cheryl Bradshaw, author, Wyoming, USA

*"a sassy bigger then life heroine in
an action packed adventure thriller in Greece"*
Book Review Buzz

Read the first two chapters of **Angel in Flight** **>>**

Angel in Belfast:

the 2nd Angel Murphy thriller

Angel Murphy is back, in true kick boxing form!

Alone in his cottage near a remote Irish village, Fitz, lead singer of the popular band Raving, hears the cries of the paparazzi outside and likens them in his own mind to wolves in a feeding frenzy.

Next morning Fitz is found unconscious, seeming unlikely to survive, and is rushed to hospital. Has he been driven to OD? Or is someone else behind this?

His friends call in Angeline Murphy, 'Angel to her friends, devil to her enemies,' to find out the truth. But it takes all Angel's courage and skills to survive the many dangers she faces and to discover the real villain and deal with him.

Angel in Paradise:

the 3rd Angel Murphy thriller

Angeline Murphy, 'Angel to her friends, devil to her enemies,' is on holiday in Corfu with her friend Josh Smith, hoping to relax and recharge her batteries, and perhaps develop her relationship with Josh. But Angel finds it impossible to sit back and do nothing when she learns of the assault and robbery carried out on her parents' old friend Sophie.

Before long Angel is fully involved in tracking down the brutal gang of jewel thieves who are terrorising many of the island's elderly but wealthy inhabitants. Her plan is, with Josh's help, to identify and arrest the gang's leader.

But soon Angel is in serious danger herself, from men who don't hesitate to kill to cover their tracks.

And meanwhile, the growing trust she has been feeling for Josh, as they build their relationship carefully after the disaster of Angel's first marriage, is threatened. When Angel finds Josh left for dead in an olive grove at midnight, it seems that this might be the end for them both …

Thrills, hairsbreadth escape after escape, danger, and a full helping of romance, all in the beautiful setting of Corfu, the Paradise island.

Not the End of the World

A Terry Pratchett tribute novel – a comic fantasy, set in the not too distant future

Merc Swingly – a young, naive employee of one of the seven multi-national companies, which control the world through figurehead politicians – dreams that the world has come to an end.

He is instructed by a weird creature, who calls himself a "Third Degree Representative', to go back and prevent this happening.

Sometime in the future, who knows how far away, all the things which people have been dreading and issuing warnings about for years are beginning to happen.

The planet earth has finally become one political unit. Its capital city is now called Nexus Luxuria. Luxury, after all, is clearly the thing most people have been aiming for all their lives.

Life has developed in an almost exactly similar fashion to the threatened forecasts. The world has at last achieved all those marvellous things we've at present only started to acquire for ourselves – global warming; over-use and exhaustion of fossil fuels; a third world with slave labour factories; globalisation of commerce until just seven multi-national companies are running the entire planet (under a titular World President with seven Vice Presidents – a Govern-ment with no real power, but considerable wealth and status); and a population kept happy by recreational drugs, which are no longer frowned on but instead encouraged. In fact, an other-earthly paradise – not!

Oh, and at a guess the future time when all this is happening is about a hundred years ahead of ours.

Or is it only fifty?

"I found myself enthralled by the writing, and couldn't put it down"
Thea, USA

The Seanachie: *Tales of Old Seamus*

Three collections of Irish stories, set in the fictional Donegal village of Ardnakil and featuring that lovable rogue, *'Old Seamus'* – the Séanachie. All of these stories have previously been published in the popular Irish weekly magazine, *Ireland's Own*, based in Wexford, Ireland.

"heart warming tales ... beautifully told with subtle Irish humour"
Babs Morton (author)

"an irresistible old rogue, but he's the kind people love to sit and listen to for hours on end whenever the opportunity presents itself"
G. Polley (author and blogger, Sapporo, Japan)

"This magnificent storyteller has done it again. Each individual story has it's own Gaelic charm"
Teresa Geering (author, UK)

"evocative characterisation brings these stories to life in a delightful, absorbing way"
Elinor Carlisle (author, UK)

"Like the first collection ... very well written and an effortless read"
Bookworm

"so well written that you find yourself flying through the stories"
Tom Elder

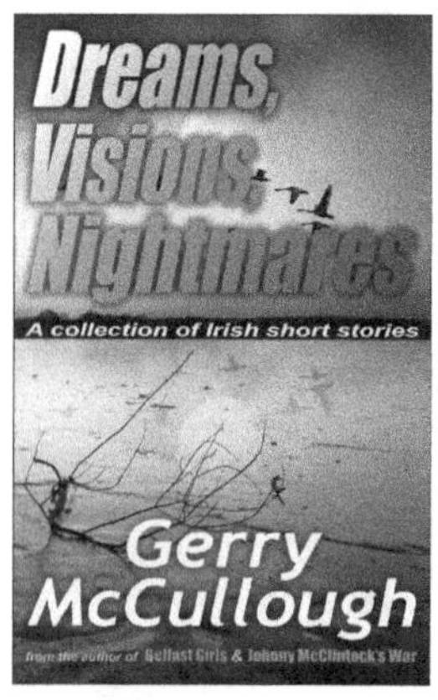

Dreams, Visions, Nightmares

A collection of eight literary and award-winning Irish short stories (newly expanded and edited)

Primroses (winner of *Cuirt international Literary Award*, Galway 2005, published in *West 47* magazine and *Cuirt Annual* 2005)

Pink Silk (published in *Verbal* magazine, Derry, 2008)

Shadows (published in *Brazen City*, Belfast 2008)

Giving Up (commended in *Seán O'Faolain Short Story Competition*, Cork 2009; published in *Sharp Sticks, Driven Nails*, Dublin 2010)

Slipping (published in *Ulla's Nib* magazine, Belfast 2009, winning Star Prize)

Ballystravey, 1988 (published by *Luciole Press*, California 2009; shortlisted for *Cuirt Award*, Galway 2010; published in *Crime after Crime* anthology, USA)

Stevie's Luck (shortlisted for the *Brian Moore Award*, Belfast, 2008)

Dark Night (Extended into full length novel, *Johnny McClintock's War* – published in 2014)

Lady Molly & The Snapper

A young adult time travel adventure, set in Ireland and on the high seas
Gerry McCullough

Brother and sister Jik and Nora are bored and angry. Why does their Dad spend so much time since their mother's death drinking and ignoring them? Why must he come home at all hours and fall downstairs like a fool?

Nora goes to church and lights a candle. The cross-looking sailor saint she particularly likes seems to grow enormous and come to life. Nora is too frightened to stay.

Nora and Jik go down secretly to their father's boat, the *Lady Molly*, at Howth Marina. There they meet The Snapper, the same cross-looking saint in a sailor's cap, who takes them back in time on the yacht, *Lady Molly,* to meet Cuchulain, the legendary Irish warrior, and others.

Jik and Nora plan to use their travels to find some way of stopping their father from drinking – but it's fun, too! Or is it? When they meet the Druid priest who follows them into modern times, teams up with school bully Marty Flanagan, and threatens them, things start getting out of hand.

Meanwhile, Nora is more than interested in Sean, the boy they keep bumping into in the past ...

"the story ... flows in authentic Irish lilt and dialogue, captures the imagination"

Book Review Buzz, USA

"excellent prose to suit the intended audience and has enough antics to keep any young mind turning the page"
J.D., USA

<u>Apocalyptic fiction by *Raymond McCullough*</u>:

In Six Hours
... the world changed:
In just six hours the Middle East – and the world – will change forever

As bitter enemies race towards nuclear conflict, only a miracle can save Israel from the hostile Islamic forces surrounding her. USA, Russia and the western world play with fire in the Middle East, as Iran rushes towards a nuclear climax.

While fighting the Taliban with the ISAF forces in 2012, four young men from very different backgrounds meet in Kabul, Afghanistan:

Shaul *'Solly'* Levine, an Orthodox Jew from New York City;
Micky *'Dev'* Devlin, an Irish Catholic from Boston;
Brandon *'Doubtin'* Thomas, a black Pentecostal from N. Carolina;
Khan Ali *'Zai'* Yusufzai, a Muslim Pashtun from Afghanistan.

They discover that they have more in common than they first thought and make a pact that one day they'll meet up again in Jerusalem after the prophesied Six Hour War in the Middle East, taking separate ways to a common destiny.

Meanwhile, they will keep in touch with one another as much as possible and work towards making that meeting a possibility. Will these prophecies come to pass? Will Israel itself survive the coming nuclear holocaust?

This apocalyptic thriller moves from war, to a couple of budding romances in very different locations, to more war and then the ultimate Middle East war. But even in the midst of conflict, new relationships are being formed. Action, friendship, romance ...

"writes with conviction and clearly knows his subject well ... [his] fluid prose draws you in and his logic and characterisation make for a believable compelling drama. Highly recommended!!!"

Juliet B Madison, Amazon, UK

"So well written and very descriptive, you actually think you're there. Raymond has obvious knowledge of the areas he has written about as that and his passionate way of writing shine throughout. Must read book"

Tom Elder, Amazon, USA

In One Hour

... Babylon will fall

Book #2 of the Six Hours thriller series

The debt will be called in and in one hour her destruction will come!

After a short, but devastating, nuclear war the face of the Middle East has changed forever! The 'Ingathering' – the world's greatest population transfer, involving tens of millions – has begun. Huge people groups – from India and Myanmar, Pakistan and Afghanistan; from Nigeria, Zimbabwe and South Africa, and many other parts of the world – are on the move, all travelling towards one destination.

Four young men, who met first in Afghanistan, are re-united in the heat of the impossible logistics of such a mammoth operation:

Shaul 'Solly' Levine , an Orthodox Jew from New York;

Micky 'Dev' Devlin, an Irish Catholic from Boston;

Brandon 'Doubtin'' Thomas, a black Pentecostal from North Carolina;

Khan Ali 'Zai' Yousefzai, a Muslim Pashtun from Kabul, Afghanistan.

Can a small nation survive a nuclear war and immediately after absorb an influx of ten times its population? across thousands of miles of nuclear war-devastated desert? Can Shaul and his comrades overcome such odds?

Meanwhile, America is no longer a safe haven – for Jews or for others there. Persecution is mounting and desperate measures are needed in order to avoid the coming destruction. Will Shaul's friends and family be able to reach safety before Babylon falls?

"chilling and timely ... reads like a peek into man's future. And now that future is upon us ... highly recommended"

Barbara Silkstone, Amazon, USA

"A futuristic adventure of biblical proportions.

Peter G., Amazon, UK

The Whore and her Mother:

9/11, Babylon and the Return of the King

Raymond McCullough

Could the writings of the ancient Hebrew prophets be relevant to events taking place in the world today?

These Hebrew prophets – Isaiah, Jeremiah, Habbakuk and the apostle John, in The Revelation – wrote extensively about a latter day city and empire which would dominate, exploit and corrupt all the nations of the world. They referred to it as Babylon the Great, or Mega-Babylon, and they foretold that its fall – 'in one day' – would devastate the economies of the whole world. Have these prophecies been fulfilled already?

"AMAZED when I read this book ... in awe of your extensive knowledge on so many levels: Christian, Jewish, and Muslim culture; the Jewish diaspora ... Greek & Hebrew; ... thought-provoking and troublesome ... many will be offended, but you consistently build your case instead of being sensationalistic."

James Revoir, author of *Priceless Stones*

Oh What Rapture!

Is a *'Secret Rapture'* going to spare believers from the tribulation to come?

Raymond McCullough

Many are convinced that very soon an event referred to as *'The Rapture'* will take place, where bible believers all over the world will suddenly disappear, leaving society at a loss to explain the disappearance of so many. Many non-fiction books, fiction thrillers and movies have capitalised on this theme, earning fat revenue for their producers.

But is this really what the bible teaches?
Is *'The Rapture'* genuine, or a deceptive false hope?

Angel in Flight

Gerry McCullough

Chapter One

Sounds and movements from the outer door. A voice speaking Greek. A key rattling in the lock.

Angel glanced quickly over to the foot of the stairs. No good. She couldn't get up there in time. Useless, anyway. It was a dead end.

She ran down the passage. There was a recess to one side. Her outstretched hands clutched the handle of the door and she tugged it open.

She was in, the door pulled shut behind her, her breath coming in ragged gasps.

The outer door opened.

People coming in, footsteps and voices. Louder. Coming in her direction.

She crouched down motionless.

Footsteps growing still louder. Voices almost in her ear.

The steps went past, the voices were no longer close beside her.

The men opened the door of a room at the other end of the passage. In another moment they had gone in.

* * *

Angel pressed further back into the closet. It was deep, a small room. Only one door. No windows. A collection of junk filling up the space, pieces of household equipment. Brushes, a mop-bucket which cut her shin.

She tried to flatten herself against the rear wall. There was something in her way. She found herself backing into it.

Old clothes. A pile of them, propped against the back wall. She turned round, feeling cautiously with one hand.

Angel in Flight – *Gerry McCullough*

She didn't want to believe it.

Up from the depths, in spite of her efforts to push it down, came realisation.

She moved her hand carefully round. Something very cold.

She knew then.

Outside the closet, all was quiet.

Her exploring hands must have unbalanced it.

The dreadful bundle fell forward, the cold face kissing hers, the dead arms embracing her.

How did she manage not to scream?

The two men had closed their door. When she looked out of the closet there was no light from that direction, only a few faint beams from the moon shining through a nearby window. She thrust the closet door open. Half lifted, half dragged the body forward until the faint moonlight fell directly on the white face.

She recognised him immediately.

There was no doubt that he was dead.

Chapter Two

When Angeline Murphy, Angel for short, walked away from Mickey Murphy, the violent man she had been fool enough to marry a year before, the first thing she did was to enrol in an unarmed combat course.

Never again did she intend to be a helpless victim of anger and aggression.

The second thing she did was get a licence and buy a gun. A small convenient .22. She thought she would be ready to use it if necessary. The gun laws in her native Belfast were stringent enough, but Angel managed to get around all the obstacles.

Never again.

Six months later, feeling a lot calmer, Angel booked a holiday to Greece and flew to Athens on a foggy day, which turned into bright sunshine halfway over. They wouldn't let her bring the gun, of course. By that time she'd learnt how to use it. But she'd no expectation of needing it on her holiday.

Angel booked into the Alexandria, on the Venizelou Panepistimiou, a pleasant hotel, well-appointed without being overly expensive. She was reluctant to venture out to explore on her first night. However, a good night's sleep in her luxurious hotel room did wonders for her morale. Breakfast in the sunny restaurant downstairs helped even more. A young, attractive looking Greek waiter took her order.

'Ach, isn't it a beautiful day?' Angel said to him.

His name, pinned to his collar, was Zervas. 'All days in Athens are beautiful, miss.'

'So far, certainly. But don't be calling me miss, Zervas. My name's Angel.'

'Angel.'

They chatted for a few more minutes about the best places for Angel to see, and then, breakfast over, she set out, relaxed and light-hearted, to begin her holiday with a little sight-seeing in the city centre.

She turned down the Korai and strolled along the Churchill Stadiou, one of the main shopping streets of Athens. A delicate breeze lifted her long fair hair and floated it out gently around her shoulders. She wandered along, delighted with everything she saw, past shops, pavement cafes, little open-air stalls and kiosks. Her huge dark eyes were constantly attracted by windows full of brightly embroidered clothes, expensive jewellery, or cheap gifts for tourists.

Presently, Angel stopped to buy a cup of coffee at one of the little cafes, and a paperback book at one of the dozens of kiosks scattered along the edge of the pavement. They seemed to have anything from Greek vases to paperback Agatha Christies, or freshly squeezed orange juice.

She sat listening with amusement to the chatter of the Athenian crowd, and the strident noise of the traffic. The sun, the noise and the colour had lifted her to a pitch of happiness she couldn't remember having felt for over a year. Since the early days of her marriage to Mickey.

Angel finished her coffee and stood up. She walked up Churchill Stadiou into Omonia Square – Harmony Square – feeling ready to burst into song. The sunlight sparkled on the fountains, the heat rose from the ground – and there he was, like the demon king in pantomime – suddenly, out of nowhere.

She was crossing Omonia Square when she saw him.

Mickey.

Walking across in front of her, not a hundred yards away.

Angel stood stock-still.

Then she began to back away, treading on the toes of an old man selling roasted almonds, bumping into a fat woman heavily laden with shopping. A watermelon bounced across the pavement.

'Sorry,' Angel muttered, and looked hurriedly round for somewhere to retreat.

The sun still sparkled on the fountain. Heat still rose from the ground. The noise of the traffic and the busy Athenian crowd filled her ears.

This couldn't be real.

This must be some kind of nightmare.

The last night she had seen Mickey, his hands had been round the throat of the girl he had called Sylvie. Squeezing. Squeezing.

Angel should have tried to help her. She should have attacked him.

But she had failed in her efforts to fight back against Mickey's strength too often.

Until later that night when she turned her life around. When she left.

She need never see Mickey again. Or so she'd thought.

Someone picked up the fat woman's watermelon. Angel slipped in behind the roasted almond stand, and peered out.

Mickey was still there, gazing into a shop window, exchanging some remark with his companion. Above the noise of the crowd, his laugh, unmistakable, floated over to her.

'No, no, Theo – d'ye think it's Onassis you're talking to?'

The other man's reply was lost in the screech of a red car – a taxi? – skidding past, its horn blaring angrily. Mickey was coming on, moving in her direction.

In the six months since she left Mickey, so much had happened.

She had become more than expert in the art of Judo and other self-defence tactics.

She had learned to use her gun.

She had a temporary job with the BBC in Belfast, which might lead to something permanent if she made a good impression. Working on the local news programme, mainly as a runner so far.

But none of that made any difference.

The sight of Mickey had the same effect on her as it used to do six months ago, while she was still stubbornly struggling to make her marriage work, still believing that Mickey would change back into the charming, loving man who had swept her off her feet such a short time before.

She didn't want to meet him.

Angel in Flight – *Gerry McCullough*

The red car pulled up level with her. A business man, tall, elegant, grey-haired and with an impressive moustache, got out and went on his way. She stepped out, raised her hand. Darted to the front passenger door. Opened it. Scrambled into the seat. Said the first thing that came into her head.

'The Herodes Atticus theatre, please. And hurry.'

www.ingramcontent.com/pod-product-compliance
Lightning Source LLC
Chambersburg PA
CBHW051508030726
47592CB00006B/2162